A ROARING MURDER

LADY MARIGOLD'S 1920S MURDER MYSTERIES
BOOK ONE

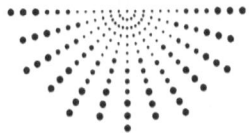

AVA NESS

ROARING PRESS

A ROARING MURDER

A Lady Marigold's 1920s Murder Mystery

Book 1

Published by Roaring Press

Copyright © 2022 by Ava Ness

Cover design by delaneyisabel.com

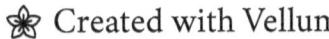 Created with Vellum

CONTENTS

CHAPTER ONE

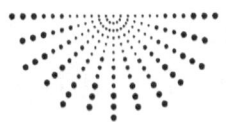

The last person Marigold expected to see in Istanbul was her uncle's butler. Yet there he stood on the mosaic tiled floor of the crowded police station—like a statue come to life.

His first name was Charles, but she'd only ever known him by his surname—Bentley. He was a tall, heavy-set man with a craggy face and uncommonly bushy eyebrows.

This wasn't the first time he'd bailed her out of trouble but travelling to Istanbul seemed above and beyond the call of duty. Perhaps she shouldn't have been surprised. Since childhood, he'd always been in her corner.

She stood beside him at the front desk, breathing in the peppery, minty freshness of his pine aftershave. Unbidden, a lump rose in her throat. She dug her dirty, broken fingernails into her palms, determined to master the long-forgotten emotion spreading through her chest. She hadn't cried since she was eight years old—she wasn't about to start now.

Another plausible reason for his presence in the Turkish city niggled at the edges of her mind, but she forced the thought away.

Once the guard had unlocked her handcuffs and departed, she massaged her wrists and gave Bentley a wry smile. 'I'm not sure how you found me, but I'm very glad you did.'

'It's good to see you too, my lady.' His stentorian voice cut across the low hum of conversation in the cavernous entrance hall. 'Although I imagined our reunion in more pleasant surroundings.'

For the first time since her untimely arrest, laughter bubbled on her lips. 'You could teach the guards here a thing or two about hospitality, but otherwise, I have no complaints.'

He tapped his highly polished shoe on the smooth, well-worn floor. 'Forgive me for saying so, my lady, but from your appearance, it appears I found you not a moment too soon. Someone appears to have attacked your hair with scissors.'

Her lips twitched as she patted her unkempt,

dark brown bob. 'It's modern, Bentley. All the ladies are wearing this style now.'

He peered down his bulbous nose at her stained and torn knickerbockers. 'Are they also wearing trousers?'

She rolled her eyes. 'Bentley, it's 1922. Trousers aren't scandalous for a woman these days.'

He opened his mouth but paused as they were joined by a police officer with dark hair slicked behind his prominent ears. He cowered as he squinted up at Bentley—like a student fearing the wrath of a headmaster.

'Excuse me, sir, but before we can release the young lady and return her possessions, you are required to complete some paperwork,' he stuttered in halting English.

Bentley gave him a perfunctory nod and turned to Marigold. 'I'll endeavour to complete the forms as soon as possible, my lady.' He turned and followed the young police officer over to an untidy desk on the other side of the room.

Left alone, Marigold peered up at the domed ceiling. A pair of sparrows were flittering through the rays of mid-afternoon sunlight. The hum of conversation ebbed and flowed as some prisoners were reunited with friends and relatives, while others said tearful farewells.

A disturbance near the entrance drew her attention to a dishevelled man in his fifties. He stumbled through the front doors, his arms flapping like propellers. After a failed attempt to regain his balance, he fell forward and skidded along the floor on his well-padded belly. Lying on the cold, hard tiles, he resembled a crumpled brown paper bag in his wrinkled overcoat and threadbare trousers.

Close on his heels was a tall man in his early thirties wearing a perfectly pressed grey pinstripe suit. He had thick, wavy brown hair, steely eyes, and a rugged jawline. He would have been handsome except for the deep scowl on his face.

The clunk of his hard-soled leather shoes echoed around the room as he strode across the hall and hauled the older man to his feet. There was a military precision to the way he moved and scoped out the room while effortlessly restraining his prisoner. His eyes briefly met hers and the corners of his lips twitched as she tucked a stray dark curl behind her left ear.

In a last-ditch effort to escape, the older man sank his teeth into his captor's hand. Marigold had been abroad long enough to recognise a foreigner. Her suspicions were confirmed when she heard the taller man curse in English.

A pair of uniformed police officers hurried to

restrain the assailant, who renewed his shouts of innocence and protests at his treatment.

The Englishman examined his injured hand impassively, then addressed the police officer at the front desk in a mix of upper-class English and beginner-level Turkish.

The desk clerk peered at him with a puzzled expression and shook his head. After a few more failed attempts at communication, Marigold cleared her throat and craned her neck to meet the Englishman's enquiring gaze. 'Perhaps I can translate?'

He gave her a close-lipped smile. 'What makes you think I need a translator?'

She inclined her head slowly towards the bewildered police officer behind the desk and raised her eyebrows.

A muscle in the Englishman's left cheek twitched, and he clenched his jaw. 'Thank you, but I can manage.'

He addressed the blank-faced police officer again, speaking slowly and clearly in English, albeit with a hint of a Turkish accent.

Marigold bit the inside of her cheek to stop herself from laughing at his stubbornness. The Englishman's scowl deepened.

She turned to the police officer and spoke in fluent Turkish. 'This man is from Scotland Yard.

His name is Inspector Gideon Loxley. He believes the man he brought in is someone you have been searching for. A man named Kazim.'

The police officer's expression instantly changed from confusion to elation, and he called across the room to his colleagues, who were still struggling to restrain the man named Kazim. A chorus of excited chatter broke out between the three of them, drowning out the complaints of the detainee.

'It seems they have been seeking this gentleman for a long time,' she mused.

'Trust me. He's no gentleman,' Loxley grunted as the officers led Kazim away.

Bentley returned carrying her possessions. He placed them on the reception desk while shooting suspicious glances at Loxley. 'Is everything alright, my lady?'

She smiled at his concerned expression. 'This is Inspector Loxley from Scotland Yard. He asked me to help him hand that fellow over to the police.'

Loxley muttered something under his breath and pulled a black leather notebook and a fountain pen from the inside pocket of his coat. 'I didn't ask, and there was no need for you to involve yourself, Miss...?' His dark eyes met hers, unblinking and interrogating.

She fought the urge to laugh. 'Grey,' she said at the same time Bentley intoned, 'Lady Marigold Grey.' His voice was full of pride but had a hint of indignation. She appreciated his protectiveness, but it seemed a little unreasonable. How was the Inspector to know who she was?

Truth to be told, she would have preferred he didn't.

In the years since she'd left England, she'd learned life was much simpler, and a lot more enjoyable, when she was Miss Marigold Grey.

Loxley turned his attention to Bentley. He took a step towards the butler and lifted his chin. 'And you are?'

Bentley held his ground and gave his name. Loxley wrote something in his notebook and asked, 'What brings you to Istanbul?'

'I'm here to be of service to Lady Marigold,' Bentley declared.

Loxley made another note and returned his attention to her. 'May I ask what you're doing in an Istanbul police station?'

Marigold poured herself a cup of water from the brass jug on the front desk. She sipped it to buy some time, weighing up how much of her current situation she should reveal or conceal.

He tucked his notepad and pen into his breast

pocket and drummed his fingertips on the reception desk while she finished her drink.

'I believe you're being hailed.' she said, pointing over his shoulder. The young police officer was waving his hand, trying to get Loxley's attention.

Bentley cleared his throat. 'We should be on our way, my lady.'

'Yes, we really should. It was nice to meet you, Inspector.'

He glanced at the Turkish policeman and then back to her, his scowl intensifying.

Laughter bubbled in her throat as she rummaged through her belongings. She picked up a Turkish dictionary and handed it to him. 'This may come in useful.'

He turned the tatty book over in his hands and scowled as he read the title on the front cover.

Before he could respond, she turned on her heel and walked towards the front doors where Bentley was waiting.

She gave him a sheepish smile. 'I suppose I have some explaining to do.'

To her alarm, his face sagged. 'As do I, my lady.'

CHAPTER TWO

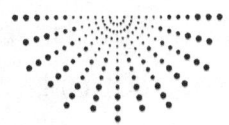

The smell of the Bosporus strait, sesame sprinkled simit, roasted coffee and smoke greeted her as she stepped onto the bustling street outside the police station.

The cobblestone alleyway was a long open market. It buzzed with locals greeting each other with warm hellos, bewildered tourists asking for directions, and sellers calling out discounted prices for shoes, clothes, and food. Waiters stood in front of restaurants reciting the specials of the day—fish, kebab, doner. Handheld bells jangled as ice cream vendors in traditional clothing tried to entice passers-by to sample the best ice cream in town.

She heard a familiar bark, and a small white dog weaved its way through a maze of trouser legs towards her. Crouching, she ruffled the dog's soft, fluffy topknot as he jumped up on her knees and barked excitedly.

She scooped him into her arms and straightened up. 'Bentley, meet Pepper.'

Bentley rubbed his chin. 'A Dandie Dinmont terrier? I've heard of the breed, but never seen one. Its legs seem disproportionately short to the length of its body.'

'And yet long enough to run away,' grumbled a short, stout, middle-aged woman as she elbowed her way through the crowd to join them. She had a round face, chin length silver hair and spoke in a thick German accent.

She tut-tutted and wagged her index finger at the little dog like a teacher scolding a student.

Marigold patted her arm. 'Miss Elke Müller, may I introduce Mr Charles Bentley, my Uncle Thomas' butler and an old friend.'

Bentley bowed, and Elke gave him a perfunctory nod.

'Miss Müller is my assistant, long-time friend, and reluctant dog wrangler.'

She paused for a moment, watching as two of the people who meant the most to her in the world exchanged formal greetings.

Elke removed her cloak and attempted to

wrap it around Marigold's shoulders. 'I feared the worst when I heard you were arrested.'

Marigold tried to hand the cloak back to her. 'Thank you, but I'm not cold.'

'I do not care about your temperature. I am concerned someone will see you in this state?' Elke pointed at Marigold's dirty, torn clothes.

Bentley cleared his throat. 'I'm afraid I must agree with Miss Müller, my lady.'

She scowled at them, but took the cloak and put it on, wriggling as the itchy wool rubbed against the back of her neck. 'Shall we go? There's a park nearby. We can talk properly there.'

They set off down the street with Pepper in the lead. The sun had lost its warmth, and the shadows were lengthening. Marigold breathed in the scent of freshly brewed apple tea and jelly rose sweets as they walked through a small bazaar in an alleyway.

Market traders sang, shouted, and cajoled them, extolling the virtues of their perfectly stacked pyramids of tomatoes and spices. Clothes, hats, and rugs in autumnal colours swung gently in the cool breeze. Warm orange lamps glowed in shop windows as the sun sank lower in the blue-grey sky.

As Marigold reached the street corner, she collided with a woman wrapped in a floor-length crimson wool shawl. A silk headscarf hid her face, and she kept her head bowed as she raised a hand as though to apologise. Marigold admired the gold ruby solitaire ring on her left hand before the woman hurried away.

'She could have at least checked to make sure you were alright,' Bentley harrumphed.

Marigold shrugged. 'Perhaps she was running late?'

They entered a park with a canopy of ash trees, an expanse of lush green lawn, and a small hill with panoramic views of the Bosporus strait. Seagulls shrieked as they soared in the sky and dived into the sea. Steamboats and ferries honked as they approached one another. Waves lapped the rocks near the shoreline.

Marigold's spirits rose as she pointed out a few hedgehogs crawling in bushes near an aromatic lime tree while Elke shooed away a group of tabby cats lurking near a pond full of colourful fish. The splash and babble of water in a nearby fountain added to the serenity of the scene, but the things left unsaid weighed heavily upon her shoulders.

'I sense your Mr Bentley has something on his mind,' Elke said as she grabbed Pepper around his middle to stop him from leaping into the pond. 'I will take this one back to the hotel before he gets into more trouble. I leave you to talk.'

Left alone, Bentley pinched the fabric of his trousers above his knees and took a seat on a wooden bench under an ash tree. He cleared his throat.

'Forgive me for saying so, my lady, but is it wise to be associating with someone such as Miss Müller?'

She raised a perfectly shaped brow, knowing full well what Bentley was implying. 'Wise?'

He shifted his weight from one foot to the other. 'What I mean to say is, is it wise to be associated with someone *German*?'

'Elke was a spy for the British during the war, Bentley.' She softened her sharp tone. 'That's how we met.'

'If you believe she's of good character, my lady, that's good enough for me.'

Marigold tucked a stray curl behind her ear. 'I'm glad to hear it. Now, where shall we start?'

'Perhaps with how you found yourself under arrest?'

She sat beside him, crossed her ankles, and waved her hand dismissively. 'It's a good story, but not for today. It was a simple misunderstanding and would have been resolved in the goodness of time, but I'm grateful for your help in securing my release. No jail cell is ever pleasant.'

'It was certainly no place for a lady,' he declared, a flush creeping up his neck.

She ran her tongue over her teeth, trying to ease the dryness of her mouth. The moment had come. 'You haven't told me why you're here.'

His Adam's apple bobbed, and a sheen of sweat appeared on his forehead. 'I suspect you know, my lady.'

A tingling sensation spread across her shoulders and down her arms to her fingertips. She scrunched her hands into fists and kept her eyes fixed on the tabby cats. They had returned to the pond and were striking out at the fish with their paws. After a long pause, she finally summonsed the courage to ask, 'Uncle Thomas?'

Bentley examined his hands. 'If it's any consolation, my lady, it was a peaceful end.'

She hugged herself and blinked back tears. 'I suppose he told you not to tell me until he was gone?'

'You had already said goodbye in Paris last year. He wished to remember you in happier times.'

She sniffed, and Bentley procured a crisp, white handkerchief from his coat pocket and handed it to her.

After blowing her nose in a very unladylike fashion, she dabbed at the corners of her eyes. She noticed he was drumming the fingers of his left hand on the bench seat. She sat up straighter and frowned. Bentley didn't fidget.

She narrowed her eyes. 'Why do I get the impression there's more to your visit than to relay the bad news of Uncle Thomas's passing? And how on earth did you find me?'

He shifted in his seat and gave her a wry smile. 'You aren't the only member of your family who has worked for British Intelligence. Your uncle made a point of keeping track of your locations.'

Despite her sadness, her lips twitched a little at the thought of her elderly uncle plotting her whereabouts on the map of the world in his study at Mayfair Manor. She had inherited her love of travel from their adventures during her breaks from school. Despite many invitations, Bentley never accompanied them. He had always declared he was happiest at home, which made his presence in Istanbul even more surprising.

She turned to him. 'I'm very pleased to see you, of course, Bentley, but surely a telegram would have been easier than coming all this way?'

He dry-washed his hands. 'The truth is, my lady, I was going to send a telegram, but then I discovered something I couldn't risk relaying in any way other than in person.'

She gulped. 'Goodness, what could be so secretive?'

He lifted his head, pulled his shoulders back, and took a deep breath. 'I'm afraid I discovered a skeleton in a wardrobe.'

She bit back a laugh. All she could think to say was, 'Literally or figuratively?'

'I'm afraid it's the former,' he confessed.

A sliver of unease crept up the back of her neck. 'You're not serious?'

'I'm afraid I'm, my lady. After Lord Harrington died, I cleaned his rooms, and just as well. When I went to transfer his belongings to an empty room in the East Wing…'

Marigold got to her feet and began to pace in front of the bench. 'That wing's been closed for at least ten years, hasn't it? Do you think there's been a skeleton there all this time?'

He nodded. 'It appears so, my lady. Judging from the clothing, it was a female guest at the last ball Lord Harrington held before the war.'

She cast her mind back. 'His birthday Ball?'

'Yes, I believe so.'

Her eyes roamed across the manicured green lawn, and she watched the rise and fall of the blue-tinged water in the fountain. 'Who on earth could it be? Was anyone reported missing at the time?'

Bentley furrowed his brow. 'Not to my knowledge, my lady, but I didn't think it wise to make further enquiries until I had spoken to you.'

'The skeleton is still there? Have you told the police?'

His silence and grim expression provided the answers.

She stared at him, fighting a bout of nausea at the thought of a woman being murdered and stuffed in a wardrobe in her uncle's home. 'How is this possible? How could she be there all this time?' Her legs felt numb as she walked towards the fountain.

Bentley fell into step with her. 'Indeed, my lady. I wanted to consult with you before I reported it. After all, you are the mistress of the house now.'

She recoiled as his words hit her. 'I'm what?'

'Oh dear. I see from your reaction you weren't aware your uncle had left you, his estate.'

Her lungs seemed to have forgotten how to work. There was a pain in her chest, and she was lightheaded. After a few seconds, she said, 'No, I certainly wasn't. What about Richard? He isn't dead, is he?'

Bentley shook his head. 'No, my lady, your

cousin is very much alive. There has been a scandal recently, and he broke off his engagement, but he has inherited the title of Lord Harrington, whilst you have inherited the manor.'

She took a few deep breaths, hoping to clear her head. 'But it's impossible, Bentley.'

He gave her a stern look. 'I assure you, my lady, it's not. Your uncle invested a great deal of time and money to ensure his will couldn't be challenged. I believe your cousin will not contest it.'

She perched on the edge of the fountain. 'What's all this about Richard and a scandal? He's been engaged forever. What on earth could have happened to make him end it?'

Bentley put his hands in his pockets and rocked gently on his heels. 'I understand he broke off his engagement after the young lady's father became involved in an unsavoury business scheme. Unfortunately, it cost many people a great deal of money.'

Despite her conflicted emotions, her interest was piqued. Her great aunt Edwina had written to her many times about Richard and his '*wealthy, but unfortunately red-headed*' fiancé and to berate Marigold for remaining '*stubbornly unmarried*'.

She extended her hand and let the water from the fountain run over her fingertips. It was ice-cold and smelled as fresh as new snow. 'Her father was a London apothecary, wasn't he?'

Bentley nodded. 'Yes, my lady. Sadly, he took his own life once details of the scheme were published in the newspapers.'

'And Richard broke off his engagement to avoid the family being drawn into the scandal? That poor girl, I've never met her, but really, she's better off without him. He's always been a cold fish—just like the rest of them—except Uncle Thomas, of course.'

Silence fell between them again, and she glanced at him. 'Are you here to take me back to England?'

He adjusted his hat and tugged on the sleeves of his coat as if to smooth out invisible creases. 'Not take, my lady, to accompany you. If you agree, I'll arrange a passage by rail for the journey home.'

Home. That was a word she'd never used in relation to herself.

She'd been orphaned when she was eight years old and had spent her childhood at boarding schools or being shunted from one disapproving relative to another. The only happy memories she had were from the summers she'd spent with Uncle Thomas and Bentley.

She pictured the towering sandstone structure

with its turrets and towers and couldn't summon any sentimentality for it.

Then she looked at Bentley—a man who had spent his adult life in service to her uncle. He'd gone to war with him and cared for him, until the very end.

Mayfair Manor might not be her home, but it was Bentley's—and while she wanted to wash her hands of it, she knew she couldn't.

The last thing she wanted was to return to England, but she'd have to go back to deal with the police investigation into the skeleton and to decide what to do with the house.

It wouldn't be all bad, she told herself, and after the excitement of the past few days, a nice, quiet train journey would probably do her good.

CHAPTER THREE

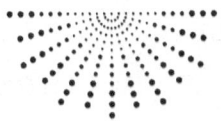

It was just after two o'clock and after an excellent lunch at the Pera Palas Hotel, Marigold, Bentley, Elke, and Pepper made their way across the street to Sirkeci station.

It was an imposing building with an Oriental-Gothic aesthetic and vaulted ceilings with chandeliers hanging elegantly from the centre and soot-stained marble columns. A rainbow of colours was projected on the brickwork from the stained-glass windows around the walls and roof.

Marigold caught her first glimpse of the Lunar Express— a gleaming midnight-blue locomotive as she emerged from the chaos of the terminus and out onto covered outdoor platform with Bentley and Elke.

The idling locomotive engine issued bursts of steam at regular intervals as engineers in grease covered uniforms made their final preparatory checks.

An odd, burnt odour wafted up from the tracks. Marigold covered her mouth and nose with her gloved hand as the lingering vapours of coal and steam tickled her throat.

There was a theatrical air about the place, as though the swarm of passengers and railway employees making their way along the platform were actors on a giant stage.

Porters in blue jackets with shiny gold buttons and matching caps pushed luggage trolleys laden with suitcases, trunks, and hatboxes.

Men in striped or herringbone suits accompanied finely dressed women wrapped in furs.

Passengers with tickets in second or third class breathlessly carried their suitcases while clutching brown paper bags full of sandwiches for the journey.

A whistle blew, and an immaculately dressed conductor clicked the heels of his shiny black boots before projecting his voice above the chatter, directions, and instructions on the concourse.

'The Lunar Express… with stops in Sofia, Nis, Belgrade, Vinkovci, Brod—with transfers to Bucharest, Zagreb, Trieste, Venezia, Milan, Lau-

sanne, Dijon, Paris, Boulogne, Calais—and connection to Dover and London leaves in thirty
minutes.'

'Perfect timing, as always, Bentley.' Marigold
quickened her step as Pepper strained against his
leash. His little black nose was working overtime
as he explored the wealth of unfamiliar smells as
they crossed the platform.

Bentley strode beside the luggage trolley,
keeping a stern eye on the porter. He glanced at
his pocket watch. 'Hopefully the train leaves on
schedule.'

They paused on the edge of the red carpet signalled the first-class section of the train. A stern-
faced conductor wearing a smart cap with gold
braid trim was trying to placate a heavy-set man
wearing a bowler hat. He had a bulldog like face
with heavy jowls and puffy bags under his eyes.
His voice rose as he waved several tickets under
the conductor's nose and gestured to two men in
overcoats and a short woman with curly blonde
hair wearing a long fur coat and matching hat.
Marigold deduced one or all three were his
employer.

Pepper, annoyed at being denied an opportunity to find new things to sniff, let out a series of
unimpressed barks were amplified by the echo
chamber on the platform. The woman in the fur

coat turned, her eyes narrowing as she searched for the source of the noise. Marigold let out a gasp as she recognised her, and she momentarily lost her grip on Pepper.

Elke stomped on his leash before Pepper could make a break for freedom. 'Who is that?' she said out of the corner of her mouth, inclining her head to the woman in the fur coat.

'It's Clara Bligh,' Marigold replied through gritted teeth.

Bentley stepped closer to Marigold and lowered his voice—it rumbled like a quiet motor. 'Now that I think of it, my lady, I did read in the newspaper Miss Bligh has been working on a film in Istanbul.'

'And you only thought to tell me now?' She struggled to control her emotions as Clara's eyes met hers.

'An unfortunate oversight,' Bentley said with a deep sigh.

Elke wrapped Pepper's leash around her wrist. 'Who is Clara Bligh?'

Bentley brushed lint from his coat sleeve. 'Miss Bligh is an English actress who at one time attended boarding school with Lady Marigold.'

'Until we were both expelled.' Marigold scowled at the memory.

'When you said you made enemies, I did not think you meant as a child,' Elke muttered.

Marigold stepped behind Bentley. 'Perhaps she hasn't seen me.'

'Alas, Miss Bligh has recognised you and is making her way towards us,' Bentley said.

'Well, well. If it isn't Marigold Grey.' Clara's voice had a nasal tone and her mouth twisted as if she'd tasted something sour. 'It's been a long time.'

Marigold crossed her arms over her chest and gave her a cold, closed lipped smile. 'Not long enough.'

The younger of the two men beside Clara threw back his head and laughed. He appeared to be just out of his teens and had a chiselled jaw, slim frame, and boyish good looks.

Ignoring Clara's attempt to stop him, he stepped forward and ran a hand through his tousled blond hair. 'I say, are you the famous Lady Marigold Grey?'

'The answer depends on who you are and what you mean by famous,' Marigold quipped.

Clara tossed her blonde curls and marched to his side. 'Perry!' Her voice was sharp and held a note of warning, but he ignored her and held his hand out to Marigold.

'Forgive my sister. She hates being one-upped.

I'm Perry—officially Peregrine—but only granny calls me that.'

Clara began to berate him, but her words were drowned out by the whistle of the train. She threw Marigold and all too familiar look of loathing, then turned on her heel and marched back to the other man, who was smoking a cigarette and watching the scene with a bored expression.

'That's Osbert, Clara's new husband. I'm afraid I'm gate-crashing their honeymoon,' Perry said.

The train whistle blew again, and Bentley gestured for them to follow the porter as he moved forward with the luggage.

'Why are you on your sister's honeymoon?' Marigold asked as Perry fell into step with her.

He tapped the side of his nose. 'That's a story for another time, but let's just say it involves a boat, a goat and a Greek heiress.'

Marigold peered up at him. 'You don't look old enough to be telling such a tale.'

'I'm nineteen and have a preference for older women.' He waggled his eyebrows at her.

She laughed 'And I have a preference for men my own age.'

Perry put a hand to his heart. 'Then I guess I have three days on the train to convince you otherwise.' He tipped his hat and gave her a jaunty smile as he re-joined Clara and her husband.

'Well, I never.' Bentley said, glaring at Perry as he boarded the train. 'The disrespect! However, I suppose I should expect nothing less from someone who is clearly one of those bright young people who have been terrorising London,' he huffed.

Marigold smothered a laugh. 'Really? Do tell.'

'Board train now, talk later,' Elke tsked as she picked up Pepper and tucked him firmly under her arm.

Marigold exchanged a quick smile with Bentley and stepped onto the red carpet. The conductor hurried out from behind the podium, tipped his hat, and bowed to her. 'Welcome Mademoiselle.'

She bid him good afternoon and waited as Bentley produced their passports and tickets. The conductor promptly stamped the documents and returned them just as the whistle blew again. He tipped his cap and bowed. 'Thank you. Everything is in order. Please enjoy your journey.'

∼

TO MARIGOLD'S RELIEF, the first few hours on the train passed without any sign of Clara. Elke had been eager to hear more, but Marigold wasn't ready to revisit the feud with her childhood nemesis. As a result, Elke had turned her attention to Marigold's wardrobe.

In the days since Bentley had arrived in Istanbul, he and Elke had clashed on many things, but on Marigold's appearance, they were as one.

While Marigold had no interest in fashion, the German woman and British butler were determined she would dress the part of an English lady.

That was why, on the first night on the train, she sat at her dressing table wearing a semi-sheer black and silver striped shift dress with sequins and a tiered fringe overskirt. She'd agreed to wear a jewelled headdress only to keep her bobbed hair out of her face but had drawn the line at Elke adding glitter to her eyelids.

She frowned at her reflection in the mirror. 'I appreciate your efforts, but I'm not sure I can play the part of this glamourous creature you've created.'

Elke didn't look up from the book she was reading. She was sitting in a velvet covered armchair by the window with her feet resting on a footstool. 'Are you fishing for the compliment?'

'Fishing for a compliment? Definitely not.' Marigold turned, knocking over a cut glass perfume bottle with her elbow. It rolled over the edge of the table and landed with a thud on the thick, navy-blue carpet. She bent to retrieve the bottle, wrinkling her nose at the pungent scent of gardenias on her fingertips. 'It's just I'd much rather spend the evening here, curled up in a robe, reading.'

Elke snorted as she turned the page. 'You cannot refuse to dine with director of the train. He is connected to your family.'

'It's not a connection, more a passing acquaintance. Before he became ill, Uncle Thomas travelled a great deal. I believe that's how he met Mr Olivier.'

Marigold walked over to the bed, where Pepper was curled up on her pillow. She scratched him behind the ears and searched the blackened window for any sign of the outside world. A transparent version of an elegantly dressed woman stared back at her.

Elke lay the book in her lap. 'He reserved this suite for you. Dining with him seems a small price to pay.'

'Don't worry, I'm going, but I don't expect to enjoy it.' She pouted and got to her feet, smoothing the creases out of her dress. Pepper opened his eyes. He gazed up at her hopefully.

She ruffled his silky topknot. 'Sorry, old boy,

you'll have to turn those big brown eyes on Elke if you want a walk.'

Pepper's eyes travelled from Marigold to Elke, as though weighing up his options, then he turned in a circle, resettled himself on the pillow, and went back to sleep.

A knock at the door was almost drowned out by a roar as the train entered a tunnel. Marigold reached for the wood panelled wall to steady herself as the carriage rocked and shuddered. The lamps flickered and Elke gripped the arms of her chair until the howl of the wind in the tunnel eased when the train emerged.

She opened the door to find Bentley standing in the corridor, his hands clasped behind his back. He wore black trousers, a starched white shirt, black tie, and coattails.

'Good evening, my lady. You look very regal.'

She tilted her head to one side. 'Thank you, but Bentley, you don't have to dress for dinner. Unlike me, you can stay in your compartment this evening and relax.'

He lifted his chin and pulled his shoulders back. 'I'm working this evening, my lady. Mr Olivier has asked for my help, as his concierge has fallen ill.'

'That doesn't sound fair. You're a guest on the train. I'll speak to Mr Olivier. I'm sure he can manage without you.' She pursed her lips; annoyed Bentley's good nature was being taken advantage of.

He gave a quick shake of his head. 'Thank you, but there is no need. I'm happy to help, and truth to be told, I'm looking forward to it. I don't enjoy being idle.'

Marigold let the subject slide and collected a silk shawl and a beaded evening bag from the dressing table. With a last, longing glance at the suite, she bade Elke farewell.

A bell rang as she stepped into the corridor. The attendant rose from his task chair and excused himself as he passed her on his way to respond to the passenger who, not satisfied with ringing once, continued to press the call button.

The corridor had a faint smell of smoke and the powerful scent of wood polish. Golden light bounced off the compartment doors and blackened windows. The train rocked from side to side, and Bentley held out his arm for her to maintain her footing. She wobbled on her black sequined t-strap heels and gripped his elbow tightly as they made their way through the first-class sleeper car.

In the space between the carriages, she paused, enjoying the sudden drop in temperature from the overheated sleeper car. 'I'd forgotten how much I love to travel by rail. There's something exciting and invigorating about being on a train. Of course, it helps to be travelling on one as luxurious as this.'

Bentley led her into the entrance of the lounge car. Through the bevelled glass doors, she could see a vase full of white roses resting on top of a baby grand piano. A woman in a black dress with her hair scraped into a bun was playing Chopin's Nocturnes.

Behind the highly polished bar, attendants in black ties and bright white shirts and jackets were tearing golden wrappers off bottles and popping champagne corks. Waiters with gleaming buttons down the front of their uniforms balanced silver trays on their white gloved fingertips as they delivered martinis to guests.

Small groups of elegantly dressed men and women sat in the curved armchairs and settees running along each wall of the carriage or stood leaning against the bar smoking cigars. The room smelled of smoke and brandy. Laughter tinkled over the clink of ice in glasses and the hum of polite conversation.

The back of Marigold's neck tingled, and a shiver ran up her spine as Bentley took a step back and gestured for her to enter the lounge car.

She screwed up her face. 'I don't suppose

there's any chance you'll accompany me inside, Bentley. I'm still dreadfully awkward in these situations you know.'

His bushy eyebrows knitted into a solid line, and the crease above his nose deepened. 'It wouldn't be fitting for a lady to enter with a servant.'

She snorted. 'You're hardly a servant, Bentley. Despite your role here tonight, I know Uncle Thomas considered you his right-hand man, and so do I.'

The butler's florid cheeks grew rosier. 'I appreciate your kind words, my lady, but all the same, I'm afraid it wouldn't be proper for us to enter the lounge car together.'

She laced her fingers together to stop her hands from shaking. 'I can see I won't change your mind, but stay close, please. I may need an escape plan.'

'If you're concerned about Miss Bligh, let me reassure you her party are currently in the south dining car, so it's unlikely you will encounter them this evening.' He gave her a reassuring nod and departed.

She watched him go, then forced her feet to move forward. There was no getting out of it. A long, desperately dull evening awaited.

Standing in the doorway, fighting the urge to

run. Her eyes roamed around the carriage, hoping to spot a friendly face. Instead, she locked eyes with a young woman with a pale face who was wearing a drop-waisted black beaded gown. The look on her face was murderous.

CHAPTER FOUR

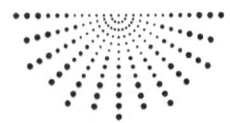

Apart from her expression, the only striking thing about the woman was the sage-green silk turban she wore over her frizzy red curls. Unnerved by the scrutiny, Marigold glanced away and moved to stand beside a potted palm in a dimly lit corner of the crowded lounge car.

As a rule, she didn't drink alcohol. She preferred to keep a clear head, but social situations such as this required an exception. She hailed a passing waiter and requested a glass of champagne, resisting the urge to check if the woman was still glaring at her.

The piano player finished her piece, shuffled the yellowing sheets of music propped on the music stand, flexed her fingers, and launched into a variation of Bach.

Around the lounge car, connections were being made, and mutual friends identified. Cries of delight and bursts of laughter rang out as guests shared stories and gossip. Unable to help herself, Marigold glanced at the woman in the turban out of the corner of her eye. Her temper flared as she realised, she was still the subject of the woman's judgemental stare.

She thanked the waiter who had delivered her glass of champagne, took a sip of the light, citrusy bubbles, set her jaw, and walked to the corner of the bar. 'Good evening. Have we met?'

The woman took a step back, and her expression became wary. She reminded Marigold of a rabbit facing a hunter. 'I say, I don't believe we have,' she squeaked.

Marigold frowned, confused at the sudden change in the woman's demeanour. 'My apologies, it's just you were looking at me as though we had—and not in a good way.'

The woman flushed and put a hand to her lips. 'Oh dear. My apologies. I have a dreadful habit of doing that. I get lost in my thoughts and as nanny used to say, the set of my face at rest can be ferocious.' She held out a gloved hand and smiled nervously. 'Hermione Carey.'

Marigold, who prided herself on a firm hand-shake, was surprised at Hermione's strong grip. When she introduced herself, Hermione's dark eyes widened. 'Marigold Grey? As in Lady Marigold Grey?'

'Yes, although I'm not overly fond of my title and given the choice, I don't use it.' She tipped her head to the side and frowned at Hermione. 'So, we're acquainted, then?'

Hermione took a gulp of her martini. 'Not exactly, but my grandmother grew up with your uncle. She always spoke highly of him.' Her hand fluttered to her turban, and she tugged it down over the tips of her ears.

'That's very kind of you to say.' To Marigold's horror, hot tears prickled at the corner of her eyes. She blinked several times and cleared her throat. 'What brings you to the Lunar Express?'

Hermione flushed and twisted her martini glass between her fingers. 'I've been visiting a friend.'

There was an awkward pause while Marigold struggled to think of an appropriate response. Small talk had never been her forte. Finally, she blurted out, 'How lovely!'

Hermione tugged at the front of her turban. 'Not really. The poor thing had her engagement called off just before the wedding. Her fiancé lost his inheritance.'

'Oh dear. Hopefully, he'll come to his senses.' Marigold drained the last of her champagne. The muscles in her neck and shoulders had relaxed, but she accepted a fresh glass from a passing waiter as insurance.

Hermione pursed her lips. 'I don't think so. He says he doesn't feel worthy of her without his fortune'.

'Then she's probably better off without him.' Marigold shook her head, thinking of her cousin Richard and his jilted fiancé.

Hermione nodded, then pointed over her shoulder. 'I say, I think Mrs Olivier is trying to get your attention.'

Marigold turned and caught the eye of an elegantly dressed woman with a long, beaky nose wearing a peacock inspired dress. She elbowed the tall man with film start good looks standing next to her in his ribs. He had suntanned face, slicked back dark hair and a pencil moustache.

The woman scowled and whispered something in his ear. He locked eyes with Marigold and smiled, revealing large white teeth.

She glanced over her shoulder to make sure the couple were trying to get her attention. Assured it was the case, she turned to Hermione. 'Is that the director of the train?'

Hermione leaned towards her, a glint in her eyes. 'And his wife. He's French, but she's English. Her father is an American businessman who married Lord Fenworth's eldest daughter.' She clapped a hand over her mouth and two red spots blossomed on her cheeks. 'Oh dear, I don't know why I shared it. I'm not usually indiscreet. Forgive me.'

Marigold touched her arm lightly. 'Please don't apologise. You've been very helpful. My uncle was acquainted with Mr Olivier, and I'm curious to learn more about him as he's invited me to dine with him.'

The fire in Hermione's cheeks became a rosy glow. 'I'm sure you'll be in great demand this evening. I won't keep you.'

The muscles in Marigold's neck began to spasm. 'You're welcome to join me. I confess I'm ill at ease in social situations such as this and would appreciate a companion.'

Hermione glanced in the direction of the Oliviers and rubbed her temples. 'How kind of you, but alas, I feel a migraine coming on and must return to my compartment. It was lovely to meet you.'

Likewise.' She turned on her heel and forced a

smile as the craggy-faced man walked towards her with his arms outstretched.

'Lady Marigold?' he inquired in French accented English. She nodded, and he reached for her hands. She fought the urge to back away as his sour breath hit her in the face.

'It's an honour to have you onboard. I'm Rueben Olivier, Director of the Lunar Express. My father was a friend of your uncle's, and I have been fortunate to visit Mayfair Manor, but never lucky enough to meet you.' His voice was a little too loud, as though he wanted the entire carriage to hear him. 'My condolences on the death of Lord Harrington. He was a great man." Mr Olivier bent at the waist in an awkward attempt at a bow and almost toppled over.

Heads turned in their direction, and Mr Olivier's hands continued to caress her wrists through her gloves. She only just controlled the urge to kick him in the shins.

'How do you do, Mr Olivier.' She wrenched her hands free with such force, her gloves slid off.

Mr Olivier's expression flickered for a moment. A hint of anger appeared in his dark eyes, then his congenial mask slid back into place. His smile widened as he moved to stand beside her.

A warm hand slithered down her back. She

stepped out of his reach, crushing his foot with the heel of her t-strap shoe as she did so.

Mr Olivier gave an undignified yelp.

'My apologies, Mr Olivier. Sometimes I can be so clumsy.' She gave him a smile, but it didn't come close to reaching her eyes.

'Not at all, Lady Marigold. I shouldn't have placed my foot in your way.' He raised his voice again and several ladies nearby paused their conversation to watch them.

'Perhaps you could introduce Lady Marigold,' his wife said as she joined them. She glared at Mr Olivier with such malice, Marigold suspected she knew exactly what had just transpired.

He clasped his hands so tightly his knuckles turned white. When he spoke, it was through gritted teeth. 'I was just getting to it, my dear. Lady Marigold, may I introduce my wife, Unity?'

Before she or Mrs Olivier could do more than nod to acknowledge one another, he continued, 'And you must meet the rest of our dining companions.'

Unity Olivier's eyes bulged, and her nostrils flared. Her husband seemed oblivious to her fury. He gestured to a glamorous young woman in her twenties who was sitting on a settee. Her eyes were fixed on a small, gold, hand mirror she was holding as she applied red lipstick to her bow shaped mouth. She had wavy blonde hair pinned up in a faux bob and wore a white silk dress with tiers of fringe that showed off her slim legs. The sapphires dangling from her ears matched the colour of her almond-shaped eyes.

Mr Olivier cleared his throat. He stuttered and stumbled over his words. 'Lady Marigold Grey, may I present Miss Vivienne Cosette?'

Marigold's jaw dropped. She placed a hand over the centre of her chest. 'Miss Cosette, I saw you dance in London. I have long admired your talent.'

Vivienne Cosette continued applying her lipstick but murmured. 'Thank you,' in a thick French accent

Mr Olivier kept his eyes on Vivienne as he vaguely gestured to the man and woman sitting beside the ballerina. 'And this is Vivienne's sister, Aline Martin, and her brother, Dennis Cosette.'

Aline was a middle-aged woman with a sallow complexion and thinning, brassy-blonde hair. Marigold searched her face for a resemblance to Vivienne but found none.

Dennis was a surly man in his early thirties. Dressed in black from head to toe, he wore his dark hair slicked back, giving him an air of menace.

Aline gave her a closed lipped smile. Dennis met her eyes with an intense, unblinking stare.

Marigold deduced good humour didn't run in the family.

She returned her attention to Vivienne, intending to compliment her on her performance in Swan Lake, but as she stepped forward, her heel caught on the carpet, and she stumbled. It only took a few seconds to regain her balance, but in time, the contents of her glass spilled on the floor near Vivienne's satin-covered toes.

The ballerina let out a shriek that suggested she'd been stabbed, rather than sprinkled with champagne.

'Clumsy fool.' Vivienne turned to her siblings and began insulting Marigold in rapid French.

She squinted at the tiny spots on Vivienne's shoes, and an apology died on her lips. 'It was an accident, and fortunately the damage appears to be minor,' she said in fluent French.

Aline clapped a hand over her mouth, and Vivienne's beautiful face twisted into ugly lines. 'Minor? My new slippers are ruined!' She got to her feet in one fluid movement and gestured at her toes with both hands.

Marigold caught Unity Olivier's eye, and they both turned away to hide their laughter. The ballerina's cat-like eyes narrowed to slits, and her right hand trembled by her side. For a moment, Marigold thought she was going to strike her. Then Mr Olivier stepped between them and snapped his fingers above his head. A moment later, a conductor in a blue and gold uniform appeared at his side.

'Michele is at your service, should you require replacement slippers, my dear Vivienne.' Something unspoken passed between them. Marigold glanced from one to the other curiously before Mr Olivier steered her away once more. "If you will excuse us, there are still a few guests I need to introduce to Lady Marigold.' Vivienne rolled her eyes, pouted, and turned her back on him.

Reluctantly, Marigold allowed Mr Olivier to lead her to the bar where a group of men were arguing about cricket. One of them was a tall man with wavy brown hair. He turned as Mr Olivier pushed his way into the centre of the group and she gave him a winsome smile.

CHAPTER FIVE

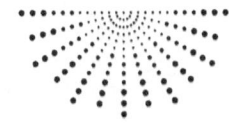

'Lady Marigold, may I introduce Inspector Gideon Loxley?'

She tried her best to keep her face impassive as Mr Olivier clapped a hand on Loxley's back with such force the Englishman nearly spilt his drink.

Mr Olivier didn't seem to care, and he winked at her. 'Don't let his youth and good looks fool you. He's one of the finest detectives in England, and we're very lucky to have him join us on this leg of our journey.'

Marigold feigned surprise. 'Inspector Loxley. We meet again.'

Loxley's eyes were bluer than she remembered, but they held just as much suspicion as the day she'd first met him.

'Lady Marigold, you do pop up in the most surprising places.'

His words sounded genuine, but there was something about his expression that made her suspect he wasn't at all surprised to see her.

He wore a short dinner jacket and a black bow tie. It was the modern style, but she still found it strange to see men without their white tie and tails at dinner.

The suit was well cut and fit him perfectly. Either the Inspector had expensive taste in clothes or a detective's salary went further than she knew.

Before she could consider it further, Mr Olivier said, 'You know one another? My goodness, is there anyone you aren't connected to on this train, Lady Marigold?'

'Inspector Loxley and I are only briefly acquainted.'

Loxley nodded and sipped his drink.

Mr Olivier laughed. 'How intriguing! I look forward to hearing more about it over dinner.'

Vivienne joined them, the beads on her gown sparkling in the candlelight. 'Rumour has it the Light-Fingered Lord is aboard the train. I hope you will keep us safe, Inspector.'

Loxley frowned. 'That's the plan.'

'I certainly hope so. When Aline told me about this light-fingered person, I was reluctant to come aboard. If anything happens to my precious jewels, I'll be heartbroken.' She patted the sapphires at her throat.

'Fear not, mademoiselle, you're perfectly safe on the Lunar Express,' Mr Olivier assured her.

'And yet thefts have occurred on each of the last three journeys on this train, have they not?'

Mr Olivier's left eye twitched. 'That was unfortunate, but we have increased security substantially. Inspector Loxley's presence is proof of that,' he huffed.

Vivienne snorted and opened her mouth, as though she wanted to argue, but her sister whispered something in her ear. She pursed her lips but said nothing further.

Unity Olivier cleared her throat to break the awkward silence. 'Is it true you're an adventuress, Lady Marigold?'

'That's a rather generous label, but I suppose it's true. I've travelled extensively since the war ended,' she demurred.

Loxley leaned towards her. 'For what purpose?'

She forced a smile. 'For work and pleasure. After the war ended, I wanted to see more of the world. As you know, most recently I was in Istanbul.'

'And before that?'

'I was in Kenya where important work is taking place to save animals such as elephants, lions, and tigers from English hunters.'

'What kind of work did you do during the war?' he asked.

She took another sip of champagne to hide her irritation at his questions. 'Secretarial work.'

'Goodness, Inspector, are we all to be questioned in this manner? Or is it only Lady Marigold who has caught your interest?' Vivienne said coyly.

She fluttered her eyelashes at him, and Marigold found herself torn between annoyance that Vivienne had intervened and relief at the distraction.

Loxley drained his drink and handed it to a passing waiter. 'I'm interested in everyone on the train, Miss Cosette. That's my job. I met Lady Marigold in unusual circumstances in Istanbul. Naturally, I'm curious to learn more about her.'

The announcement of dinner saved Marigold from further interrogation. A gramophone was playing jazz music at low volume, allowing the diners to carry a conversation as they made their way into the dining car in groups of two.

Soft golden light from the wall sconces and candles bounced off the bevelled glass wall panels separating the carriage, creating more intimate dining areas.

Marigold's stomach grumbled at the smell of freshly baked bread and roasted meat wafting from the kitchen car at the rear of the carriage. The tables were covered in crisp, white linen tablecloths. Highly polished cutlery was laid in perfect measurement on either side of each fine bone china place setting. A cream coloured rose in a bud vase adorned each table.

To her dismay, she was to dine at the Olivier's table and her seating companion was Inspector Loxley.

Loxley appeared as unhappy about the arrangement as she felt.

She paused beside the table. 'It seems we're being thrown together, Inspector.'

He held out her chair for her, but before he could reply, Unity Olivier took a sip of water, choked on it and was seized with a coughing fit. When she had recovered, she said, 'You're in for a treat tonight. Our chef, Mr Dubois, is very talented.' Her hands trembled as she unfolded her napkin.

Mr Olivier snorted as he took his seat. 'If only our chef would focus his efforts on his food instead of his hobbies, imagine what could be achieved.' He snapped his fingers at a waiter and ordered himself another drink.

Marigold took a sip of champagne and weighed up the pros and cons of kicking Mr Olivier in the shins. He really was insufferable. She wondered how his wife put up with him.

The door to the kitchen car opened and she glimpsed more chefs in white smocks and puffy hats holding fry pans full of flames.

The executive chef emerged from the kitchen and beamed at the guests. He was a short man with a round face and thinning, brown hair. He reminded her of a threadbare teddy bear she had refused to give up as a child.

'Good evening, ladies and gentlemen. It's a pleasure to cook for you tonight.' He spoke in English with a charming French accent. With a click of his fingers, a team of waiters emerged from the kitchen carrying trays full of steaming bowls of soup.

Mr Olivier frowned at the bowl in front of him. His nostrils flared as he summoned the chef.

'Does this contain garlic, Dubois?' He sniffed the bowl as though it were poisoned.

The chef balled his hands into tight fists at his side. 'No sir. I'm aware of your allergy. None of the dishes tonight contain garlic.'

Mr Olivier smirked up at him. 'One can't be too careful. I know how distracted you are with your little ice carving project.'

Anger flashed across the Frenchman's face, and Mr Olivier laughed before addressing Marigold and Loxley.

'Our chef has a preoccupation with ice-sculptures. We must hope his skills in that endeavour aren't reflective of the standard of his cooking tonight.'

'Rest assured, Monsieur, my food is always of the highest quality.' The chef was smiling, but there was something about his expression led Marigold to believe he would have slipped something stronger than garlic in Mr Olivier's soup, given the chance.

'I'm sure the food will be delicious as always, Chef Dubois,' Mrs Olivier tittered, giving him a nervous smile.

Marigold tasted the soup and marvelled at its velvety texture and rich flavours of tomato and fresh basil. There was no trace of garlic.

Each course was more delicious than the last, but Mr Olivier continued critiquing each dish and belittling the chef not only to the guests at his table, but to the entire dining carriage. Marigold kept her head down, avoiding eye contact to hide her discomfort at Mr Olivier's behaviour. She didn't find his brutal assessments amusing in the least, but across the aisle, Vivienne seemed to find everything Mr Olivier said exceedingly funny.

By the time the crème chocolate was served, she was hoping Unity would run off with Chef Dubois when the train arrived in Paris.

Mr Olivier and Vivienne were openly flirting across the aisle, and despite Loxley's best attempts to distract her, Unity's eyes kept straying to her wayward husband and the ballerina. Her expression was downcast, and she barely touched her food.

At the end of the meal, Mr Olivier tapped on a wineglass with his fork to get the attention of his guests.

'Let us retire to the lounge car for port and coffee,' he declared as though he were the ringmaster of a circus.

Marigold decided it was time to make her escape.

'I'm afraid I must bid you goodnight. It has been a very long day. Thank you for a wonderful evening,' she lied as she got to her feet.

Unity's face fell. 'Of course, my dear, but I was hoping you might join me for cards. Perhaps I can engage you in a game tomorrow?'

Marigold nodded and was about to depart when Loxley also rose and said goodnight. 'Lady

Marigold, may I escort you to your compartment?'

'Yes, make sure she gets back safely, Loxley,' Mr Olivier said, giving him a wink as he tapped the side of his nose.

Marigold's temper simmered on the edge of her limits of self-control.

She bid the table goodnight before she gave Mr Olivier a piece of her mind.

Loxley kept pace beside her easily with his longer stride. She quickened her step, hoping to arrive at her suite before he had an opportunity to question her further.

'Do you have any leads on the jewel thief?' she asked, slightly out of breath as they made their way down the corridor and crossed into the first-class sleeper carriage.

'If I did, I wouldn't be discussing it—unless you have something to confess?'

She stopped short and her jaw dropped. 'Are you suggesting I could be the Light-Fingered Lord?'

Loxley shrugged. 'The thief could be a Light-Fingered Lady. That's what I'm here to find out. I obtained background information on all the passengers on this train before we departed, and I have to say, yours stood out.'

'In what way?' She did her best to keep her

tone even. She had nothing to hide—about the jewel theft, anyway.

He paused, leaned against the wood panelled wall, and crossed his arms over his chest. 'You seem to have been involved in some less than legal dealings these past few years. I hope for your sake it doesn't extend to activities on this train.'

Her temper flared, and it was a moment before she trusted herself to speak. 'Are you accusing me of something?'

'I'm not accusing anyone at this stage, but I'm watching. You would do well to remember it.'

She narrowed her eyes and retorted in a tone she hoped was both icy and disdainful. 'Thank you for your company, Inspector. However, there is no need to escort me any further. I'm quite capable of walking on my own.'

She was about to turn on her heel and make what she planned to be a dramatic exit when a familiar, fluffy, white dog came trotting up the corridor.

'Pepper?'

The runaway lifted his head and met her eyes for a moment, then sidestepped her outstretched arms and took off at a run.

Loxley put his hands in his pockets and rocked on his heels. 'Do you need help?'

'No, thank you. You're far too busy with your theories and investigations.'

Before he could reply, she hurried up the corridor after Pepper.

CHAPTER SIX

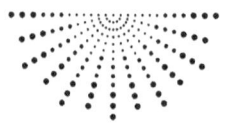

Marigold nearly collided with Hermione Carey as she crossed between the service and first-class carriages.

Hermione's right hand rose to her head. She patted her turban, as though to check it was in place, then glanced at Marigold's stockinged feet. 'Are you alright?' There was a hint of anxiety in her voice, and she blinked rapidly.

Marigold had kicked off her t-strap silver heels and discarded her shawl as she hurried along the corridor in pursuit of Pepper. She blew a stray curl out of her eyes and straightened her headpiece. She realised she must look a fright. No wonder Hermione was concerned.

With a delighted bark, Pepper left the corridor

and ran into a compartment. Marigold turned to Hermione with an apologetic smile.

'Yes, I'm quite well, but terribly sorry, I'm afraid I can't stop and talk. My dog has escaped, and I need to catch him quickly before he does any damage.'

Hermione gave her an uncertain smile. Marigold suspected she was trying to decide whether she should call for help or offer it. Fortunately, it was the latter.

'What kind of dog is he? I can help you search for him.'

Marigold scanned the empty stretch of corridor. Where could Pepper be hiding? She glanced back at Hermione. 'He's a little white terrier with a fluffy topknot, and his name is Pepper.'

Hermione smiled. 'My aunt had a dog named Pepper. Unfortunately, he was extremely unfriendly and loved to nip my ankles whenever my aunt wasn't looking.'

'My Pepper is friendly and never bites. But he's a dreadful thief. He adores shoes and goes in search of them whenever he gets the chance.'

'How did he escape?'

Marigold pursed her lips. 'I imagine he slipped out when someone opened the door. He's quite an escape artist.'

She edged along the corridor with her back to

the hard wood panels and stifled a gasp when she peered inside the compartment Pepper had entered.

He had a man's shoe in his mouth and was devouring it like it was the tastiest bone he'd ever eaten.

'Pepper, no. Put that down,' she hissed, creeping inside on her tiptoes.

Hermione followed, wrinkling her nose. The compartment was sparsely and plainly furnished. There was a banquette, a wooden chair, a washbasin, and a wardrobe. It was also unbearably hot and stuffy.

Piles of papers were balanced haphazardly on the shelf next to the bed and under the window. A man's clothes were strewn all over the floor and on the back of the chair.

It wasn't hard to see why Pepper had run into this compartment. It was a dog's dream come true.

Hermione stepped gingerly over a pile of books on the floor. 'What a dreadful mess. I wonder who this compartment belongs to?'

Marigold wrinkled her nose. 'Whoever it is, they need to open a window. It can't be healthy to breathe in all this stale air.'

Pepper was so intent on chewing the shoe, he didn't seem to realise they were there. Either that or he was ignoring them. After observing him for a moment, she was convinced it was the latter.

'Your dog is adorable,' Hermione cooed.

Marigold rolled her eyes. 'He's lucky he's cute because he's very badly behaved.'

'Do you want me to stand in the doorway? In case he makes a run for it?'

'That's a good idea. Thank you. I really appreciate your help, Miss Carey.'

'Hermione. Please call me Hermione.'

'Only if you call me Marigold. I haven't used my title since before the war. I find being plain old Miss Marigold Grey is a lot more fun than being a lady.'

Hermione gave her a shy smile. 'Alright then—Marigold—what's the plan?'

The crust of a baguette on a plate near the bed gave Marigold an idea. She picked it up between her thumb and forefinger and waved it in front of Pepper's nose.

The little dog immediately relinquished the shoe and jumped to snatch the crust.

While he gulped it down, she scooped him up.

'You've got to stop running off. You're going to get us both in big trouble,' she scolded.

Pepper whined, as if to say, 'Who, me?'

'Don't give me that look.' She tried to suppress a smile, but it was impossible.

'Thank goodness you've got him,' Hermione said, then she froze, and the colour drained from her face.

An angry male voice filled the compartment. 'What are you doing in here?'

Hermione's hands flew to her throat, and she gave a strangled cry. Marigold turned on her heel to see a tall, barrel-chested man standing in the doorway.

He had a round face, hooded eyes, and thin lips. His sandy blonde hair was slicked back behind his prominent ears. The Lunar Express' logo was embroidered on the left-hand pocket of his dark blue blazer.

Marigold gave him an apologetic smile while she tried to place his accent.

'I'm terribly sorry. My dog ran away, and we found him in here.'

'The door was open,' Hermione said, her voice barely a squeak as she moved to Marigold's side.

The man stepped into the room. His expression suggested their explanations hadn't improved his mood.

Marigold swallowed the flicker of fear rising inside her throat. Out of the corner of her eye, she saw Hermione's chin tremble.

'The door wasn't open. You broke in.' He pressed the call bell and pointed a red, swollen index finger at her. 'What were you doing in here?'

She decided his accent was French.

Marigold stepped closer to Hermione, who was now trembling from head to toe. 'I've already told you, the door was open, and we came in to retrieve my dog.'

Pepper growled and wriggled until she lost hold of him. He leapt out of her arms and launched himself at the man's legs.

Hermione cried out as the man lifted his foot and aimed a kick at Pepper's stomach. Fortunately, he missed.

Before Marigold could react, Pepper circled around the man's feet, weaving between them until he tipped sideways and had to grab the banquette to stop himself from falling.

Hermione shrieked and hid behind Marigold as the man pulled himself up. He swore loudly and directed several curses at Pepper as he pulled himself up to his full, towering height.

Someone cursed in the doorway. Another male voice. It was Mr Olivier. Much as Marigold loathed the man, she couldn't deny his arrival was welcome—and timely. Surely, he would make his employee see sense.

'Jorrisen, what's going on here?' He spoke as though his jaw was locked.

Mr Jorrisen's nostrils flared. He pointed at Marigold and Hermione. 'I have just caught these women robbing my room. I believe we have our jewel thieves. If you would be so kind as to call Inspector Loxley.'

Mr Olivier's face turned red so quickly, Marigold was concerned for his health. 'These women? Are you mad, Jorrisen? This is Lady Marigold Grey and Miss Hermione Carey. Both are first-class passengers.'

Mr Olivier's outraged voice was so loud it made Marigold's ears ring. Pepper let out a series of high-pitched barks, and she bent and scooped him into her arms.

In contrast to his employer's high colour, Mr Jorrisen's face grew pallid. 'Lady Marigold?' All the anger and indignation had gone from his voice, which now had an apologetic whine.

Mr Olivier turned to Marigold and Hermione. 'Monsieur Jorrisen is the deputy director of the Lunar Express and is normally known for his excellent customer service.'

Marigold forced a smile. 'I'm afraid my dog escaped from my suite and managed to get into Mr Jorrisen's compartment.'

'It wasn't his fault. The door was open.' Hermione emerged from behind her, but she was still shaking.

Mr Olivier glared at Mr Jorrisen. 'Obviously, there has been a misunderstanding.'

'My apologies again for my behaviour, Lady Marigold. Miss Carey,' Mr Jorrisen said in a choked voice.

Marigold gestured for Hermione to make an exit. She followed her, stepping over the mess on the floor. Mr Olivier moved aside so she and Pepper could pass into the corridor.

He bent in a half bow as she walked by him. She decided to take it as a sign of respect, although she suspected it might have been an opportunity for him to ogle her cleavage.

Tucking Pepper more securely under her left arm, she turned and met Mr Jorrisen's eyes.

'You may wish to get the lock on your compartment checked. The door was open. That's how my dog got in.'

'Of course, Lady Marigold. My apologies again for the misunderstanding.'

'On behalf of the Lunar Express, I would like to express my apologies for this unfortunate incident,' Mr Olivier said with a simpering smile.

Marigold redoubled her grip on Pepper as he began to squirm. 'Thank you. Now, if you will excuse us, it has been a long and tiring day.'

Mr Olivier bowed again. 'Of course. Please

don't hesitate to ring if there is anything you need.'

'Good night, gentlemen.' She almost choked on the last word. If ever two men failed to meet the definition of gentlemen, it was the two of them.

She set off down the corridor with Hermione at her side.

'That Jorrisen fellow is quite intimidating,' Hermione said when they reached the vestibule between the carriages. Her hands rose to her head, and she straightened her turban. Despite their adventure, she appeared unruffled. Marigold was sure the same couldn't be said for her appearance.

I'm so sorry you had to go through that.'

Hermione laughed. 'Don't be. It was quite exciting really, although I admit I was terrified when Mr Jorrisen first arrived. What a dreadful temper he has.'

'Yes, he was very unpleasant, but at least we got out of there before he realised what Pepper had done to his shoe. I must write him a cheque so he can buy a new pair.'

'Do you think Mr Jorrisen will get into trouble with Mr Olivier?'

'I think you can count on it. He seemed furious with him.'

The sound of raised voices drifted down the corridor.

'I don't think I'd like to be on the wrong side of Mr Olivier,' Hermione whispered, her eyes darting back up the corridor.

'Indeed. Once again, I'm sorry you got mixed up in this.'

Hermione gave her a mischievous smile. 'Don't be. I'm already looking forward to writing about it to my friend. This will cheer her up.'

'Well, that's one good thing, I suppose.' Both women winced as Mr Olivier's enraged voice drifted down the corridor.

Marigold tried to block out the tirade. 'Do you speak French?'

Hermione shook her head 'No. I'm afraid my only talent in school was copying the teacher's handwriting. I was dreadful at French, much to my mother's dismay.'

'Just as well,' Marigold muttered as Mr Olivier's blistering verbal assault continued.

Hermione's eyes widened. 'Is he being rude?'

'Dreadfully.' Marigold grimaced as Mr Olivier compared Mr Jorrisen to a donkey.

'I almost feel sorry for him,' Hermione said in a hushed voice.

'Almost?' Marigold's eyebrows shot upward.

Hermione shrugged. 'Don't worry. Then I remember how his foot struck out at Pepper, so whatever punishment Mr Olivier delivers is surely justified.'

The compartment door at the end of the corridor slammed shut and the windows in the corridor rattled.

Marigold opened the vestibule door. 'I think it's time we got out of here.'

CHAPTER SEVEN

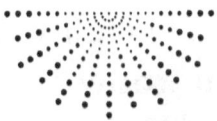

'That was without a doubt the most uncomfortable evening of my life.'

Elke glanced up from her book and did a double take as Marigold dropped Pepper and her shoes onto the bed.

'How did he get out?' She stared at the dog, clearly bewildered by his escape.

'That's what I was going to ask. I found him trotting along the corridor. Of course, he wasn't happy about being rounded up, so he ran. He got me into quite a bit of trouble,' She scratched Pepper behind the ears.

Elke walked to the bed and stood with her hands on her hips as she stared at the little dog.

Marigold suspected she was replaying the

evening in her mind, searching for the moment Pepper had made his escape.

Sure enough, after a prolonged silence, Elke snapped her fingers.

'Pepper must have run past the wagon-lit conductor when he arrived turn down the bed.'

Marigold tossed her gloves on the mahogany dressing table. 'You know Pepper. Any opportunity for freedom, he'll take it.'

Elke groaned 'I should have noticed he was gone, but I was reading one of Lady Clue's case files. I much prefer her books to that Sherlock Holmes man.' She returned to her chair and held up the book so Marigold could see the cover.

'Well, Lady Clues is real, not a fictional character,' Marigold said.

Elke snorted. 'Many do not believe a woman could solve the crimes she recounts.'

'Well, I don't need to be London's most famous detective to know I would have been better off staying in this evening,' Marigold said, rubbing her temples.

'It was bad?'

Marigold sighed. 'It was worse. Dreadful. Terrible. I can't think of enough bad words to describe how awful it was.'

Elke crossed her arms over her chest and

peered at Marigold over the top of her wire-rimmed glasses. 'What did you do?'

Marigold scowled. 'I didn't do anything.' She sat on the bed, fell back, and gazed up at the luggage rack overhead. 'In fact, my finishing school headmistress would have been proud of my decorum.'

She rolled onto her stomach and rested her chin on the back of her hands. 'Actually, she probably would have died of shock that someone other than me was the one behaving badly.'

Elke placed a bookmark in her book and set it aside. 'Then why was the evening so bad?'

Marigold examined her newly polished fingernails. 'There's a police detective from Scotland Yard on board. I met him briefly at the police station in Istanbul and he's now under the impression I may be a jewel thief.'

Elke snorted. 'But that is ridiculous. You have no interest in jewellery. What's his name? I'll go and tell him so.' She half rose from her chair, but Marigold waved for her to remain where she was.

'Thank you, but there's no need. It was just unexpected and unsettling. Also, you should know, Mr Olivier is no gentleman. He was dreadfully rude to the chef and then humiliated his wife by fawning over Vivienne Cosette, who, I assume, is his mistress—or if not, it's his intention for her.'

Elke sucked in her breath and gripped the arms of her chair. 'Vivienne Cosette is on the train? The ballerina?'

'Yes, but don't get too excited. She's quite unpleasant.'

'But just to see her in person would be exciting.' Elke got to her feet and performed a graceful twirl so out of character Marigold had to bite her lip to stop herself from smiling.

'I was delighted to meet her at first. Although I can't blame her for having a poor first impression of me. Still, she didn't have to react the way she did.' Marigold frowned at the memory.

Elke stopped twirling. 'What did you do?'

'Why do you naturally assume everything is my fault?'

'You are right, my lady.' Elke's tone was pious. 'I am unfairly suspicious and will brush away all previous memories of similar instances.'

Marigold bit the inside of her cheek. 'I wonder what it's like to have a respectful assistant.'

'Let us hope you never find out.'

Marigold rolled off the bed and poured herself a glass of water from the carafe on the dressing table. She sighed. 'I lost my footing and stumbled. A few drops of champagne—sprinkles, really—landed on Vivienne's satin shoes. The way she reacted; you would have thought I'd broken her toes.'

'Her toes valuable.'

'I agree, but they weren't in any danger—and neither were her shoes. By the time she'd stopped complaining, you couldn't even see the droplets. It didn't even leave a stain.'

'Perhaps the shoes were expensive?'

Marigold glared at her. 'You could at least pretend to be on my side.'

'I do not take sides—but I have been on the receiving end of your clumsiness.'

Marigold let her breath out in an exaggerated huff. 'I'm perfectly coordinated—most of the time.'

'If you say so, my lady.' Elke returned to her book, but Marigold was sure the corners of her mouth were twitching.

'Don't you want to hear about the rest of the evening?'

Elke lay the book face down in her lap. 'What else did you do?'

Marigold ignored the insult. 'The only thing I

had to do after that was endure the dinner, Mr Olivier and Miss Cosette's appalling behaviour aside, I was on my guard the entire time thanks to the police inspector.'

'Well, at least you were not bored.'

Marigold sat on the edge of the bed. 'I've decided I'm spending the rest of the journey in the suite. I never want to see any of those people again.'

'Where was Mr Bentley. Could he not save you from these people?'

'He was in the other dining room. I didn't see him all night, but I can't complain, at least he kept Clara away from me.'

Elke yawned, stretched, and got to her feet. 'I will retire to my compartment now, but I have laid out your clothes for tomorrow.'

'Thank you, but there's no need. You're not a maid.'

Elke snorted. 'I am aware, but we both know fashion is my area of expertise, not yours.'

Marigold played with the fringe on her skirt. 'I still don't see why I can't just wear my regular clothes. No one will notice, especially if I'm staying in the suite.'

Elke glanced at the wardrobe and bit her lip.

Marigold narrowed her eyes. 'What have you done?'

Elke ignored her, but she moved towards the wardrobe. 'I do not know what you are talking about.'

'I think you do.' Marigold took a step towards the wardrobe, but Elke blocked her path.

Marigold crossed her arms over her chest. 'I'd like to look in the wardrobe.'

Elke didn't budge. 'There is nothing to see except clothes.'

'Which clothes?'

Elke flattened herself against the wardrobe door.

Marigold plucked a feather from her headpiece and tickled the tip of Elke's nose with it. She sneezed, and Marigold wrenched the door open.

She skimmed the neatly hung rows of colourful dresses, skirts, and blouses. 'Where are my old clothes?'

'They are safe, but not needed for this journey.'

Marigold closed the wardrobe door and put her hands on her hips. 'Please tell me they are in a trunk, on a steamer, en route to England?'

'Most of them,' Elke muttered.

Marigold closed her eyes and took a deep breath. 'Well, what's done is done. I guess I'll just have to settle for being fashionable for a few weeks. Who knows, maybe you'll convert me.'

Elke's expression immediately brightened. 'That is my plan.'

'Why am I not surprised?' she rubbed her forehead.

'When you are the most fashionable lady on this train, thank me you will.'

Marigold laughed. 'The clothes will be fashionable, but not me. I'm a lost cause, Elke, but I appreciate your efforts.'

'I think you may surprise yourself, my lady.'

'There's really no need to keep calling me a lady. You know I don't think of myself like that.'

'But you are one and now mistress of Mayfair Manor. Perhaps the clothes will help you prepare for your new life?'

Marigold returned to the dressing table and unclipped her earrings. 'Being mistress of Mayfair is the last thing I ever imagined for myself. To be honest, Elke, I'm not sure I'll ever be ready for it.'

'You will be and the clothes are the start.'

Marigold frowned at her in the mirror. 'You know you don't have to stay, Elke. I want to—because honestly, I'm not sure how I'd cope without you—but a boring life in the English countryside isn't what you signed up for.'

Elke tapped her chin. 'I have always wanted to see England. If it's anything like I have read in Lady Clues, it will be far from boring.'

'I'm glad you think so because I keep having nightmares about being stuck at dinner parties with nothing to say and falling on my face at masquerade balls. I don't fit in with the people there, never have and having had a taste of freedom, I feel suffocated just thinking about it.'

'Then why are you returning?'

Marigold dipped her fingers into a pot of face cream and dabbed it on her cheeks. 'I have to, at least for a few months—to help Bentley. I owe it to him to make arrangements for the future of the house and to sort out this business with the skeleton in the wardrobe.'

Elke nodded. 'Ah yes, I had forgotten about the skeleton.'

'I wish I had.'

'So, you intend to stay in England for a short time and then resume your work for the Network?'

Marigold nodded. 'If they still want me. They're not too impressed at me running off at short notice.'

'They will take you back,' Elke said confidently. 'However, you may meet a handsome bachelor in the English countryside and decide not to return.'

Marigold snorted. 'Not likely. I haven't changed my mind about marriage. I value my independence too much.'

'There was an English gentleman asking questions about you in Istanbul,' Elke said slyly.

Marigold spun around. 'What? Why didn't you tell me?'

'I thought you were not interested in a romantic connection?'

'I'm not, but I still want to know who he was. What did he look like?'

Elke closed her eyes and screwed up her face. 'He was tall, perhaps a little over six feet, with brown hair, blue eyes, and a scar on his chin.'

'A scar on his chin? I think it was the Inspector I saw at the police station. The same one who now thinks I'm the jewel thief. His name is Gideon Loxley.'

'He is quite a handsome young man.'

Marigold ignored her suggestive tone. 'I don't like that he was asking about me. Trouble with the police is something I can do without.'

'Do not worry. I am confident he learned nothing about you.'

'That's a relief, but you should have told me,

Elke. It can't be a coincidence he's now on this train.'

'My apologies. It slipped my mind in the rush to get to the train station this afternoon due to your misunderstanding about the timing of our departure.'

Marigold turned back to the mirror and wiped off her make-up. 'I confess, the prospect of returning to England has me a little rattled; otherwise, I'd have a snappy retort.'

Elke reached for the door handle. 'You just need to sleep. Everything seems worse between sunset and sunrise.'

Marigold yawned. 'You're probably right.'

'I usually am.'

'Good night' Marigold said, laughing as Elke departed.

After changing into her nightgown, she crawled into bed, and reached for the slim volume of short stories on the shelf behind her head.

'Perhaps Lady Clues can distract me,' she told Pepper, but the little dog was already snoring on the pillow beside her.

After a few minutes of reading the same sentence repeatedly, she switched off the lamp and stared at the shadows on the ceiling.

Inspector Loxley's face floated before her eyes

and their conversations at the police station and on the train played in her mind like a film.

Why had he been asking about her in the market? What investigations had he made? And what had he learned about her?

CHAPTER EIGHT

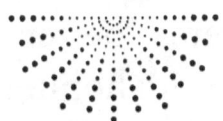

Despite her vow not to leave the suite for the rest of the journey, Marigold agreed to join Elke for breakfast in the dining car the next morning.

It was a decision she immediately regretted when she walked through the carriage and locked eyes with the one person she had been hoping to avoid. From the look on Clara's face, the feeling was mutual. She was breakfasting with her husband, who wore the same bored expression he'd had on the platform.

'Let's go return to the front of the carriage. There was a table there,' Marigold whispered to Elke.

'I am going to need more information about

this feud,' Elke said, casting a glance over her shoulder at Clara.

They took their seats and marvelled at the beauty of the passing scenery as the train sped by green fields, craggy, snow-capped mountains, and lakes with glass-like surfaces.

'Everything seems better when the sun is shining,' Marigold said, hoping to deter Elke from further discussion about Clara.

Elke stirred a lump of sugar into the fine bone china cup in front of her. 'And when there is excellent coffee.'

Marigold nodded and raised her cup to her lips. 'I asked Bentley to join us, but he's working again. I hope Mr Olivier is paying him well. It seems unfair when he's supposed to be a guest.'

'A man like Mr Bentley does not like to be idle.' Elke bit into a croissant and rolled her eyes in pleasure. She chewed rapidly and washed it down with a sip of coffee.

Marigold spread jam on a slice of toast. 'You're probably right, but after such a long time, I was hoping we'd have some time to become reacquainted.'

'Would you like tea, mademoiselle?' the waiter said as he pushed a trolley laden with a silver teapot, sugar bowl, and milk jug beside their table.

Marigold shook her head. 'No, thank you. I'm very happy with coffee for now.'

Elke wrinkled her nose at the teapot. 'I am happy with coffee always.'

'Tea is enjoyable if it's brewed properly—although English tea is an acquired taste. My father had a position in India, and I lived there until I was eight years old. When I returned to England, I couldn't drink the tea there for many years. It was another black mark against my name as far as my family was concerned.'

'There is coffee in England, is there not?' Elke said, staring at her empty cup in alarm.

Marigold laughed. 'Don't sound so worried. There will be. I'll make sure of it.'

'Why did your family care if you drank tea or not?'

Marigold shrugged. 'Uncle Thomas didn't, but my aunts and uncles don't like anything to be out of the ordinary. They already had to deal with an orphan who hadn't been raised in the English way.'

'They sound very unreasonable.' Elke gave the waiter a rare smile as he returned to the table with a pot of coffee and refilled her cup.

'Let's just say there's a reason I haven't seen them for the past decade. And I imagine they're very unhappy about me inheriting Mayfair Manor.'

'Your family will have to respect the wishes of your uncle. He wanted you to have the house.'

'They won't respect or like it, but they'll have to accept it. From what Bentley's told me, Uncle Thomas' will is unlikely to be overturned.'

'Why did your uncle give your cousin his title, but not the house?'

Marigold sipped her coffee. 'He didn't have any choice with the title. That goes to the next male in line, but he purchased the house, so he was free to do with it as he pleased.'

'But you were not expecting to inherit it?'

Marigold shook her head. 'Not at all. I just assumed he would leave Mayfair to Richard with the title.'

'What is he like, this cousin?' Elke said, pursing her lips as her hand lingered over a plate of pastries.

Marigold dabbed the corners of her mouth with a linen napkin. 'I haven't seen him in years. The last time was at Uncle Thomas' birthday ball just before the war.'

'The same ball attended by the skeleton in the wardrobe?' Elke said, lowering her voice to a whisper.

'Please don't remind me, and we don't know she was at the ball.'

Elke sliced a pastry in half. Glossy apple filling spilled onto her plate and the scent of cinnamon and sugar filled the air. 'But your family attended this ball?

'Yes, most of them. Not because they had any affection for Uncle Thomas. They were only there hoping to get his money.'

'I am not looking forward to meeting them,' Elke said through a mouthful of pastry.

'The upside is, if they don't visit, you may never have to,' Marigold said, looking up as an older couple walked into the dining car.

The man had an egg-shaped head and a moustache that almost reached the tips of each ear. Beside him stood a snowy-haired woman who's wrinkled hand rested on the striking emerald necklace covering her décolletage. The man tapped his silver handled walking stick against the doorframe, winced and rubbed his left leg. The woman looked at him with a mixture of concern and exasperation.

A conductor approached them, his eyes darting around the crowded dining carriage. 'Good morning, sir, madam. We are at full capacity. Perhaps you could try the alternate carriage?'

The woman raised her chin and the crepe-like

skin under her chin wobbled. 'Sir Fredrick's leg is troubling him, and he needs to be seated. Perhaps you could approach a party of two who may be willing to dine with us.'

The conductor tugged at the collar of his uniform. He turned and caught Marigold's eye. She gestured to the spare seats at her table and nodded. Relief washed across his face.

'This way, sir, madam. I believe the young lady is happy to offer seats at her table.'

When the elderly couple were seated, Marigold extended her hand. 'Good morning. I'm Marigold Grey, and this is my assistant, Miss Elke Müller.'

"I'm Sir Fredrick Haig and this is my wife, Lady Anne Haig.'

Lady Haig peered at Marigold and put a finger to her bottom lip. 'Did you say your name was Grey? Are you connected to the late Lord Harrington?'

Marigold's chest grew tight. 'Yes, I'm his niece.'

'Fine fellow," Sir Fredrick declared as Lady Haig reached across the table and patted Marigold's hand. 'My condolences. Lord Harrington was a wonderful man and his late wife was maid of honour at my wedding. I was sad to learn of his death.'

'Thank you. He considered Scotland his second home.' Marigold swallowed the lump in her throat as she recalled her uncle's enthusiastic retelling of his adventures in the Highlands.

A waiter arrived to take Sir Fredrick and Lady Haig's breakfast order. A squabble broke out between the two about what Sir Fredrick was allowed to eat. Lady Haig insisted his doctor had ordered fruit, tea and toast, while her husband was determined to enjoy a fully cooked breakfast. In the end they compromised on poached eggs on toast.

Lady Haig raised her teacup and turned to Elke. 'And you're German, Miss Müller?'

Elke set her jaw and pulled her shoulders back. 'Ja.'

Marigold held her breath, waiting for Lady Haig to reply, but she need not have been concerned.

The older woman's wrinkled face broke into a smile. 'I'm delighted to meet you.' She lowered her voice and her eyes darted around the carriage, then back to Elke. 'I have family in Germany. It hasn't been easy to admit these past few years.'

'But we quite like them,' Sir Fredrick said, giving Elke a wink.

'Miss Müller worked for the British government during the war,' Marigold whispered.

Lady Haig's eyes lit up. She leaned towards Elke. 'Really? Tell me more. Were you a spy?'

As Elke regaled Sir Fredrick and Lady Haig with her wartime adventures, Marigold's attention was once again drawn to the front of the carriage where a young woman with dark hair stood twisting her hands. She was dressed in a plain brown skirt suit and lace-up shoes. Her only jewellery was a rose gold broach pinned over her heart.

'I need to order a tray of breakfast,' she called to the attendant. Her voice carried across the dining car and conversations paused.

'Poor Renée. Vivienne Cosette is a nightmare to work for. If I didn't already have a lady's maid at home, I would offer her a position,' Lady Haig said, shaking her head.

Elke's eyes widened. 'You know Miss Cosette?'

'I have been unfortunate enough to be in her company long enough to know although she's a beautiful dancer, she's a thoroughly unpleasant young woman.' Lady Haig pursed her lips and raised her eyebrows as she nodded, first at Marigold and then at Elke.

Marigold sipped her coffee and listened as Renée gave the waiter her order. It included hot black coffee, orange slices, and a glass of water with lemon.

'Would Mademoiselle like to sit at a table?' the waiter said as he finished writing in his notepad.

Renée shook her head. 'I only need to order breakfast for my mistress.'

The waiter put his notepad in his pocket. 'Then you don't need to wait. A tray can be brought to her room.'

Renée's bottom lip wobbled. 'My mistress always eats breakfast in bed. Please, can I have a tray made up so I can take it to her as quickly as possible?'

'Certainly, mademoiselle, it can be arranged, but next time you can place your order with your conductor directly from your room. There is no need to come all the way into the dining car'

'Thank you. I apologise if I have broken protocol, but my mistress insisted.' Renée's eyes were shining with tears.

The attendant nodded and turned to leave

'I'm sorry for any inconvenience I have caused,' Renée called as she followed him to the back of the dining car.

Marigold watched her with concern. 'The poor girl seems terrified of Vivienne.'

'Prima donna by name and by nature,' Lady Haig said with a sniff.

Elke made a tutting noise. 'It is dreadful she treats her maid that way.'

Lady Haig raised her eyebrows. 'She doesn't treat her own sister much better. I saw them on the platform yesterday before the train departed. She speaks to her like she's hired help.'

'Perhaps she is?' Elke said as she eyed another pastry.

Marigold buttered another slice of toast. 'There's quite a large age gap between them. They may only be half-sisters.'

'Perhaps. It seems an odd relationship,' Lady Haig said as she sipped her tea.

Renée paced outside the kitchen door. Her level of agitation seemed disproportionate to a simple need for breakfast.

Marigold finished her toast and excused herself to Sir Fredrick and Lady Haig. 'I'm sorry to leave you so soon, but I have my dog in my suite and he frets if I leave him alone for too long.'

'Oh, it makes me miss my own darlings. I have a pair of Scottish terriers.' Lady Haig put a hand over her heart.

Sir Fredrick snorted. 'She spoils them worse than the children.'

Marigold laughed. 'I understand. Pepper is my family, too.'

The dimples in Lady Haig's cheeks danced. 'It

was a pleasure to meet you both. Perhaps we can dine together before the train reaches Paris?'

Marigold rose from her chair. 'I'd like it very much. Good day to you, Sir Fredrick, Lady Haig.'

'What a pleasant couple.' Elke said as they left the dining car and headed for the first-class carriage.

As Marigold paused to fix the buckle of her shoe, Elke let out a cry of alarm.

Marigold looked up 'What is it? What's wrong?'

But before Elke could answer, a body came flying towards her and crashed into the door.

CHAPTER NINE

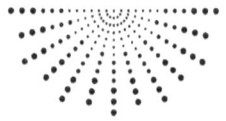

'M r Olivier!' Marigold's hands flew to her cheeks as she recognised the figure sliding down the wall and onto the floor.

Elke hurried to his side and checked his pulse. 'He is alive.'

Mr Olivier groaned, and his eyes opened. He tried to get to his feet, but his legs wouldn't hold him.

Marigold turned to a man standing nearby. He was watching Mr Olivier with an impassive expression.

'What on earth is going on?'

Mr Jorrisen's face flushed. 'It was an accident.'

'Accident?' She raised her eyebrows.

Elke helped Mr Olivier to stand. He cleared

his throat and straightened his coat. 'We were discussing security measures on the train, and I'm afraid in demonstrating that, things got a little out of hand.'

Elke eyed him dubiously. 'More than a little.'

'We take security very seriously,' Mr Jorrisen said, but there was a distinct lack of concern for his superior officer in his voice.

Marigold glanced from one man to the other. 'If everything is alright, then we'll be on our way.'

Mr Olivier nodded and smoothed down his hair. 'Perfectly alright, Lady Marigold. My apologies again for alarming you. Perhaps I can escort you back to your suite?'

Marigold forced a smile. 'Thank you, but I don't want to take up your valuable time.'

'It's no trouble, but if you're sure?'

She confirmed it was, and she and Elke set off down the corridor of the first-class carriage.

Once they were out of earshot, Elke said. 'That was no demonstration.'

'Definitely not. It's odd though. Last night Mr Olivier appeared to be the intimidating one.'

'It appears Mr Jorrisen is also capable of defending himself.'

'More than capable. Poor Miss Carey was shaking like a leaf when he caught us in his compartment.'

'Luckily we can put some distance between him and ourselves for the next hour.' Elke pointed to the window and Marigold realised the train was losing speed.

'A stop. How fortunate. Pepper will be dying to get outside to stretch his legs.'

Elke stayed in the suite to read her book, but Marigold and Pepper were among the first guests off the train when it pulled into the small country station. Pepper almost dragged her off the platform in his enthusiasm to reach the grassy area beside the railway tracks.

The sun was so bright she had to shield her eyes with her hand. Despite the summer-like sky, the air was cool and crisp, and the slight breeze made her glad she had worn her coat.

The Lunar Express sat idle on the tracks, steam drifting lazily from its engine. Blue suited conductors shouted orders at workmen as they loaded supplies and luggage onto the train.

Passengers from all classes walked along the platform, enjoying the fresh air and winter sunshine.

A young boy, perhaps eleven or twelve at the most, sat on the edge of the platform watching Pepper frolic in the grass. His brown coat was too short in the sleeves, had patches on the elbows, and it only fell to his knees. He had sandy coloured hair and a heart-shaped face with a charming collection of freckles across his nose.

He threw Pepper a stick and the little dog leapt to retrieve it 'What kind of dog is he, miss?' His accent was English with a hint of Turkish.

Marigold sat beside him. 'Pepper is a Dandie Dinmont terrier.'

The boy wrinkled his forehead. 'A dandy what?'

'Don't be rude Seb.' A girl, a few years older with a pale face, walked over to the boy and whispered something in his ear.

She too had freckles across her cheeks, and her curly brown hair had a hint of red in the sunlight.

Marigold smiled. 'That's alright. Not many people your age have heard of dogs like Pepper.'

'How did he get his name, miss?'

'Nearly one hundred years ago, a man named Sir Walter Scott wrote a book called Guy Mannering. One character in the book, a Mr Dandie Dinmont, was a farmer who owned pepper and mustard coloured terrier dogs.'

'And that's why he's called Pepper?' the boy said, furrowing his brow.

She laughed. 'You're right. Well done.'

The boy beamed back at her, but like the girl,

his face was gaunt and there were dark circles under his eyes.

'My name is Marigold, which seems boring by comparison.'

'My name's Sebastian and this is my sister Flo… Florence.' His sister gave him a reproachful look.

His face fell. 'Sorry miss, I'm not supposed to talk to strangers.'

'That's good advice. You're lucky to have such a wise sister, Sebastian.'

'Thank you, miss.' He flashed her another heartfelt smile.

'Were you in Istanbul on holiday?' She couldn't hide her curiosity about their origins. Their accents suggested money—old money—but their clothes were at odds with her assumption.

Florence bit her lip. 'That's right, miss. We were visiting our aunty and uncle.' Her tone was light, but she blinked rapidly as she spoke.

'How lovely. I too was visiting Istanbul, but alas, now I must return to England.'

Sebastian's eyes widened. 'You don't like England, miss?'

Marigold shrugged. 'I like it well enough, but I'll miss eating Turkish delight.' She gave him a wink and was rewarded with another toothy smile.

'Our mother used to buy it for us, but our stepfather...' Sebastian started to say.

'We should get back on board. We don't want to be late.' Florence's eyes darted nervously from Marigold to the train.

'Indeed, we should.' Marigold gently tugged Pepper's leash. The little dog gave her a look that suggested he knew exactly where they were headed, and he dug his claws into the ground.

She frowned. 'Come along, Pepper. You can't stay here all day. You'll be left behind.'

'Can I carry him for you, Miss?'

'Sebastian,' Florence's voice held a warning note.

'It's alright Florence. Sebastian would be doing me a favour. I'm afraid my shoes aren't made for walking through grass.'

Sebastian turned to his sister. Her eyes softened, and she nodded.

As they walked back along the platform, Marigold glanced at the girl. Both children were clean and tidy, but their worn clothes and thin faces concerned her.

'What carriage are you travelling in?'

'Third-class, miss,' Florence said, her voice trembling slightly.

'With your mother and step-father?'

Florence shook her head. 'No, it's just me and Sebastian.'

Marigold was careful not to let her surprise show on her face. 'Just the two of you. On your own?'

Florence nodded. 'Yes, miss. I'm sixteen and can take care of the both of us.'

Marigold smiled. 'I'm sure you can. You seem like a fine young lady, Florence.'

A pink rash crept up the girl's neck.

'Here you go, miss.' Sebastian handed over Pepper's leash as they reached the train.

'Thank you, Sebastian. It seems Pepper has made a new friend. Perhaps you could visit him on the train. He gets bored in my suite, and I'm not nearly as much fun as you.'

Sebastian turned to his sister. 'Could I?'

Florence bit her lip. She glanced from Sebastian to Marigold and then to Pepper, who was nudging the boy's leg with his nose. She nodded. 'I suppose it can't hurt. So long as it's no bother, miss.'

'None at all. I shall tell the conductor to admit you anytime you'd like to visit.'

Sebastian gave Pepper a final pat, then he and Florence boarded the third-class carriage.

Marigold continued up the platform, tugging a protesting Pepper on his leash. On the steps of the first-class carriage, she found Bentley waiting for her.

'There you are, my lady. I was beginning to worry.'

'Never fear, Bentley. My timekeeping skills have improved significantly since I was a girl.'

'I'm relieved to hear it.' He helped her carry Pepper on board and then brushed a few strands of dog hair off his coat sleeve.

They entered the deserted dining car, and she took a seat.

'Can I ask a favour, Bentley?'

He nodded and took the seat opposite her. 'Of course, my lady.'

'I've just met two young people on the platform. Siblings. A boy, Sebastian, about twelve years and his sister Florence, who claims she's sixteen but appears much younger. They are travelling in the third-class carriage, and I can't help but be concerned about them. Something doesn't seem quite right.'

'They are young to be travelling alone.'

Marigold picked up the finger vase on the table and sniffed the delicate pink rose. 'I've told them they can visit Pepper anytime they like, and I'll speak to the attendant, but can you also keep an eye out for them? In case they need anything.'

Bentley lay his hands flat on the tabletop. 'Of course, my lady. I'll ensure they are safe and well.'

'And fed, please. Make sure they are going to the dining car for meals. I'm worried they're hungry. Please organise to have their meals charged to my account, if that's the case.'

'I'll investigate and report back, my lady.'

Some of her worry about Sebastian and Florence eased, but her concern wasn't limited to them.

'I realise I've just asked you to do something for me, but please make sure you aren't working too hard, Bentley. You need some rest and relaxation as much as anyone.'

'Thank you for your concern, my lady, but I'm happiest when I'm of service, and based on what I have seen of the staff on this train, they need guidance.'

She set the vase down and raised her eyebrows. 'Really? Although I shouldn't be surprised if the way their superior officers behave is anything to go by.'

She told him of the altercation she and Elke had witnessed.

'Mr Jorrisen assaulted Mr Olivier?' Bentley said, his voice full of outrage.

'Yes. It was quite extraordinary. They both

tried to pretend it wasn't deliberate, but Elke and I are convinced it was.'

He sighed heavily and folded his hands in his lap as he sat back in his seat. 'I didn't like to say anything as I didn't want to alarm you, my lady, but I have had concerns about the behaviour of staff on this train from the moment we came on board.'

She stared at him. 'In what way?'

'I can't say for sure, it's just an observation of their attitude and behaviour.'

'And have you heard there's a potential jewel thief on board?'

He hummed with disapproval. 'Yes, my lady. I didn't want to worry you, but I understand additional security has been brought on the train for this journey to ensure everyone remains safe.'

'I'm not alarmed for myself. I don't own anything of value and have no interest in jewellery, but there's a police inspector on the train who thinks otherwise.'

Bentley's head snapped back. 'Do you mean Inspector Loxley?'

'Yes. The same one from the police station. It seems like a strange co-incidence I met him there and now he's on this train.'

Bentley glanced out the window, then back at Marigold. 'I admit it's unusual and even more so because I have since learned his family live not far from Mayfair Manor.'

Marigold grimaced. 'Oh no. He seems very unpleasant.' She tried to push away the unease creeping over her.

'What has he done to upset you?'

'He hasn't upset me at all, but he's suspicious of why I was at the police station in Istanbul and now seems to have drawn the conclusion I'm some sort of criminal.'

Bentley scowled. 'I'll speak to him, my lady, about being more respectful.'

'Thank you, but there's no need. I can handle myself around Inspector Loxley, but Bentley,' She checked over her shoulder to ensure they were alone. 'You don't think he's here because of the skeleton at Mayfair, do you?'

Bentley appeared momentarily taken aback, then his expression cleared. 'No, my lady. I told no one about my discovery and I'm confident no one else knows about it. It's just a co-incidence.'

Marigold got to her feet as the train whistle blew and the engine rumbled to life. 'You're right, I'm just being paranoid, but I can't help but feel uneasy.

CHAPTER TEN

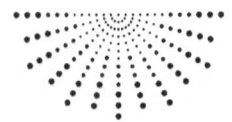

M arigold's afternoon of reading was interrupted by a knock at the door and the delivery of a note from Lady Haig. Her heart sank as she skimmed its contents.

'Bad news?' Elke said, as Marigold folded the note and placed it on the small writing desk near the window.

'Dreadful. Lady Haig has invited us to dine with her tonight.'

Elke raised her eyebrows. 'I thought you liked her. She seems like a pleasant woman.'

'I do. She's quite amiable, and I intend to invite her and Sir Fredrick to Mayfair.' she scooped Pepper into her arms and sat on the edge of her bed.

Elke frowned. 'Then what is the problem?'

'It seems Sir Fredrick's leg is troubling him, and he's not feeling up to attending the cocktail party Mr Olivier is hosting tonight.'

'And Lady Haig wants you to be her companion?'

Marigold narrowed her eyes. 'She's invited both of us.'

Elke resumed reading. 'Sadly, I am not able to attend.'

'Why not?'

'I am not well.'

Marigold put her hands on her hips. 'You don't appear to be ill.'

Elke kept her eyes fixed on her book. 'And yet I am certain a dreadful headache will befall me as the clock strikes seven this evening'

'That's some amazing detective work.' Marigold sat on the bed and picked Pepper up from the floor.

'Lady Clues is very instructional,' Elke said from behind her book.

Marigold rolled her eyes. 'I'm the one who hates social situations and much as it pains me, I shall have to accept Lady Haig's invitation. It would be rude to do otherwise when she knew my uncle and aunt so well.'

'Such a shame,' Elke tsked as she closed her book. She crossed the suite to the wardrobe and began rifling through the colourful collection of silks and beaded gowns.

'I know just the dress you should wear.'

~

AT SEVEN O'CLOCK, Marigold stood dressed in a gold sequined silk chiffon dress with a scooped neckline. She stepped into a pair of gold satin heels, wrapped a crushed velvet shawl around her shoulders, and frowned at herself in the mirror.

Her dark bob was offset by a gold, feathered headpiece over her right ear. She had never felt less like herself, but she had to admit, she looked the part of a lady.

The conductors were lighting the lamps as she emerged from her suite. She wrapped the soft shawl more tightly around her shoulders as there was a draft in the corridor.

She was in no hurry to reach the lounge car, but the sound of raised voices ahead slowed her steps further. Her heart sank as she caught a glimpse of Mr Olivier and Mr Jorrisen's reflections in the window.

They stood toe to toe in the vestibule between the sleeper and lounge cars. Mr Olivier's face was twisted, and his eyes were bulging. Mr Jorrisen was glaring at him, his expression dark and threatening.

Curious to learn more about the conflict between the two men and hoping this argument would end in a less violent manner, she backed away down the corridor and waited.

'I told you to wait, Jorrisen. That was the plan,' Mr Olivier said, his voice an octave higher than usual.

Mr Jorrisen sounded as though he was speaking through gritted teeth. 'I had to act. There was no time to consult you.'

Mr Olivier made a noise like a snarl. 'There is always time. The question is, what are you going to do now?'

'We'll think of something,' Mr Jorrisen said, his voice full of impatience.

There was a bone-jarring thud, and Marigold had a horrible suspicion it was a body slamming against a wall.

'No. You will think of something. This is your doing. You figure it out,' Mr Olivier snarled.

Mr Jorrisen's voice was raspy. Did Mr Olivier have his hands on his throat? 'Don't put the blame on me. It was your idea, and don't you forget it.'

'If you mess this up, I'll kill you,' Mr Olivier said, his voice climbing another octave.

'Not if I don't kill you first,' Mr Jorrisen growled.

There was the sound of a struggle, and just as Marigold had decided she had no choice but to reveal herself, she heard a third voice.

It was male, French, and high-pitched. 'Is everything alright gentlemen?'

'Mind you own business and get on with your duties,' Mr Olivier said harshly. His breathing sounded laboured.

Marigold heard the vestibule door open and then slam shut.

A moment later, a conductor came around the corner and almost collided with her.

'Mademoiselle, I- my apologies, I didn't see you there.'

Marigold raised her hand. 'Please don't worry about it. I shouldn't have been lurking, but I didn't want to interrupt the gentlemen's conversation.'

'A wise decision, Mademoiselle.'

Marigold peered up at him. 'Do Mr Olivier and Mr Jorrisen disagree often?'

'No, mademoiselle, I don't believe they do.' He tugged at his collar and his eyes darted to the clock at the end of the corridor.

'I'm sorry, I shouldn't keep you from your duties, and now, alas, I no longer have an excuse not to join the other guests in the lounge car.'

'Please let me know if I can be of service, mademoiselle.'

Marigold gave him a rueful smile. 'I may take you up on that offer.'

He nodded and set off down the corridor, standing aside to allow Lady Haig to pass.

She was wearing a forest-green silk coat over a beaded gown. A giant peacock feather was attached to the front of her black velvet headpiece.

'Lady Marigold, what a stroke of luck to run into you here.'

'Good evening, Lady Haig. I admit I was loath to enter the party alone and was hoping I might see you first.'

Lady Haig's pale eyes twinkled. She looked Marigold up and down and put a hand to her heart. 'You're a picture, my dear. Like a Dresden Shepherdess.'

'Thank you' Marigold hoped it was a compliment and made a mental note to ask Elke if she knew what a Dresden Shepherdess looked like.

Lady Haig gave her a wink, and they crossed between carriages. 'I'm grateful for your company this evening. Poor Freddie's leg is troubling him again, although, I suspect it particularly ails him when cocktail parties are on our social calendar.'

'Miss Müller also sends her apologies. She has a headache,' Marigold said, crossing her fingers.

They paused at the entrance to the lounge car, taking in the golden light cast by the brass lamps on the walls and the smell of candle wax mixed with perfume. A gentle piano melody floated above the clickety-clack of the train as it passed over the rails.

It was a peaceful, welcoming sight, but Marigold had a sudden urge to turn on her heel and return to her suite.

Lady Haig had other ideas. She stepped into the carriage with the poise of a queen.

As they walked past the baby grand piano Marigold searched the lounge car for Clara and was relieved not to find her there. She only hoped it remained the case for the rest of the evening.

Mr Olivier hailed them from the bar. 'Good evening, Lady Haig, Lady Marigold.'

His bow tie was slightly off centre, but there was otherwise no sign of his earlier scuffle. While Lady Haig made apologies on behalf of her husband, Marigold scanned the room for Mr Jorrisen.

She spotted him standing in a corner, clutching a glass of brandy. Unlike Mr Olivier, he was dishevelled. His hair was sticking up at the crown, his shirt appeared to be missing a button, and there was an angry red mark on his neck. His dark eyes glittered when they briefly met hers.

Mr Olivier clapped and rubbed his hands together. 'What would you like to drink? Our bartender has recently returned from America and is skilled in the art of cocktail making.'

Lady Haig's eyes widened. 'Cocktails? Those mixed drinks? Are they safe, Mr Olivier? I've heard they're made with ice.'

Olivier nodded. 'Quite safe, I assure you, Lady Haig. Our ice is made from water from the Swiss Alps. It's pure and free from contaminants.'

Her dimples danced. 'In that case, I shall try a gin sling. My younger sister, who lives in London, says it's her drink of choice.'

'And for you, Lady Marigold?' Mr Olivier said, his gaze dropping to her chest momentarily.

Marigold wrapped her shawl more tightly around her shoulders. 'Champagne please.'

Mr Olivier raised his arm and snapped his fingers to attract the attention of a nearby waiter.

The light caught the edge of his sleeve, and Lady Haig peered at his wrist. 'My goodness, Mr Olivier, what lovely cufflinks.'

He puffed out his chest. 'Yes, they were a gift from a Sultan, no less. He travelled with us recently and gave them to me as a token of his appreciation.'

'You shouldn't be wearing them. What if you lost them?' Unity Olivier said as she joined them. Her eyes lingered on the sparkling gems at her husband's wrists.

Mr Olivier scowled. 'Nonsense. Fine things should be worn. There is no point keeping them locked away.'

Unity opened her mouth, as if to argue, but her attention was drawn to the entrance of the lounge car where Vivienne was standing, looking every inch a famous ballerina.

Olivier cleared his throat. 'Excuse me ladies, I must say hello to Mademoiselle Cosette.'

Vivienne was wearing a black camisole with scalloped edging, under a gold beaded bolero tied under her bust with a black velvet ribbon. Unlike every other woman in the room, she wasn't wearing a dress.

She wore black silk faille pants and gold t-strap heels. A large silver filigree necklace with a crystal drop pendant fell just above her cleavage, and brass swing earrings hung from her ears.

Her blonde hair shone in the candlelight and all eyes were upon her as she entered the lounge car with a plainly dressed Aline at her side.

'She could at least try to be discreet,' Lady

Haig whispered to her as Vivienne swept past them on Olivier's arm, waving to selected guests as though she were royalty.

'It's not just Vivienne, though. Mr Olivier should have more respect for his wife.' Marigold's eyes followed Unity as she retreated to a settee near the window.

Lady Haig's face lit up. 'Oh, there's a familiar face.'

Marigold followed her line of sight and choked on her drink.

'Such a dapper young man,' Lady Haig said, her eyes shining as Gideon Loxley walked towards them.

Marigold couldn't argue with her assessment. Loxley was just as, if not more so, handsome as she remembered.

It was probably the tuxedo; she thought as she took another sip of champagne. Even the plainest of men were made attractive by a well-cut dinner suit.

Loxley bowed to them. 'Good evening, Lady Haig, Lady Marigold.'

'Good evening, Gideon. I trust all is well on the train?' Lady Haig said.

Loxley nodded. 'Where is Sir Fredrick?'

'His leg is troubling him tonight, but fortunately, I have this delightful young lady to converse with. I know you dined with her last night, so will not argue with my glowing assessment of her.'

Loxley's eyes met Marigold's. 'Indeed. On all occasions I have met Lady Marigold she has been very entertaining'

Lady Haig's smile widened. 'Really? Tell me, how did the two of you meet?'

'Lady Marigold provided translation services to me while I was in Istanbul,' Loxley said.

Lady Haig's face lit up. 'Fascinating. You speak Turkish Lady Marigold. How clever of you!'

Marigold smiled weakly. 'That's kind of you to say.' She drained her drink and searched for a waiter so she could order another.

Loxley clasped his hands behind his back 'Do you speak any other languages?'

She forced a smiled and crossed her fingers. 'French.'

In fact, she was fluent in several languages, but she rarely disclosed it, and had no intention of doing so now.

Fortunately, Lady Haig changed the conversation. 'How is your dear mother, Gideon?'

Loxley's expression softened. 'She's in good health and as earnest as ever in her efforts to marry off her children.'

Lady Haig laughed and turned to Marigold.

'Gideon's mother is an absolute delight, but her children stubbornly refuse to let her play the role of mother of the bride—or groom.'

'Do you have many siblings?' she asked, happy to keep the conversation off herself.

'Three brothers and three sisters, so my mother must not give up hope yet.'

When speaking of his family, there was a gentleness to his voice and his demeanour contrasted with what she had seen of him to date. She was about to comment on the size of his family when she became aware a hush had come over the guests.

Mr Olivier glanced nervously around the room. Vivienne was by his side, and she seemed determined to draw him outside the lounge car. Her voice had a hint of hysteria. 'I need to speak to you in private,' she hissed.

Mr Olivier gave his guests an uneasy smile. 'Excuse me ladies and gentlemen, I'll return momentarily.'

Lady Haig furrowed her brow. 'What on earth is going on?'

Loxley placed his empty glass on the table. 'I'm not sure, but if you will excuse me, I'll make some investigations.'

Olivier and Vivienne departed the lounge car and Marigold glanced at Unity. She was still sitting by the window, staring out into its blackened depths.

Lady Haig put a hand to her chest. 'Thank goodness Gideon is on board to keep order. His mother despaired when he joined Scotland Yard, but he seems to be doing quite well for himself.'

Marigold tried to ignore the raised voices drifting in from the corridor. 'She didn't want him to join the police?'

Lady Haig sighed. 'She lost her husband when Gideon was only sixteen and his older brother, the current Lord Cartwright, was eighteen. Then the boys and their younger brother went off to the war and, by some miracle, they all returned mostly intact. I suppose she thought her days of worrying were over. I know she's proud of Gideon, but she would prefer he had a less dangerous occupation.'

'She sounds like a wise and strong woman.'

Lady Haig smiled. 'She is, and you will no doubt meet her when you return to England. Kendrick Hall is not far from Mayfair.'

Marigold nodded, but her stomach was churning. The last thing she needed was Loxley being in close proximity while she tried to deal with a skeleton in the house. She hoped he didn't spend much time in the country.

She was about to enquire about this when

Unity jumped to her feet. Her face was flushed, and her eyes were narrowed as she set off across the carriage.

Marigold turned to Lady Haig. 'Would you excuse me for a moment?'

'Yes, go, dear. Mrs Olivier may need some support.'

Marigold nodded and hurried after Unity. She followed her out of the lounge car, where Mr Olivier and Vivienne were having a blazing row.

Loxley stood a short distance away and frowned when she joined him. 'What are you doing here?'

She shrugged. 'Same as you, seeing if there is anything I can do to help.'

'I don't think they need a translator for this exchange,' Loxley muttered as Unity put a hand on Vivienne's shoulder. The younger woman shook it off and turned on her.

'Don't touch me or you will regret it.'

Unity glared at the ballerina. 'Lower your voice. You're behaving disgracefully.'

'Stay out of it. It's none of your business.' Vivienne said, her voice full of venom.

Unity's face turned crimson. 'How dare you speak to me like that.'

'I'll speak to you any way I like.'

Unity turned to her husband. 'Are you going to stand by and let her treat me this way?

Olivier turned his back on both women for a moment. When he faced them again, his skin was mottled, and his hands were trembling.

'Mademoiselle Cosette, I think it's best you retire to your compartment.'

She gave him a look that could have frozen time. 'I'm not going anywhere.'

Mr Olivier's voice was low and full of desperation. 'Please, I'm begging you. I cannot have this discussion in front of my guests.'

'Leave. Now.' Unity said, lifting her chin.

Vivienne ignored her and turned to Mr Olivier. 'I won't be told what to do and I won't be banished to my compartment just because you don't like what I have to say. You will live to regret this moment.'

She jabbed her index finger into Mr Olivier's chest, then turned on her heel and returned to the lounge car, her eyes blazing.

Mr Olivier turned on his wife. 'I hope you're happy at the scene you've created.'

Unity burst into tears, and her legs went out from underneath her. Loxley caught her and led her to a seat in the lounge car, leaving Marigold alone with Mr Olivier.

The train director ran a hand over his face

and gave her a rueful smile. 'My apologies you had to witness another yet another scene. What must you think of me?'

'Aren't you going to check on your wife?'

Mr Olivier took a cigarette out of his coat pocket and lit it. 'It's best to put some distance between the two of us.'

Marigold frowned and took a step back to avoid being enveloped in a cloud of smoke. 'And Miss Cosette?'

'She's jealous of you.' he took a step towards her, backing her into the corner.

Marigold tugged off her gloves and put a hand up to halt his progress. 'I can't imagine why she would be, and I think you're quite close enough, Mr Olivier.'

He reached for her chin. 'On the contrary, I think I'm not close enough.'

She acted instinctively. Her arm rose, and she slapped him hard across the face.

A satisfying crack rang out, followed by a series of gasps from the lounge car. Then silence fell, and every eye was upon them.

CHAPTER ELEVEN

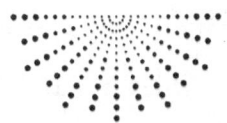

Marigold woke the next morning and immediately became aware of both stillness and silence. She shifted Pepper off her legs, pulled back the curtains and peered out the window.

Under leaden skies, the Lunar Express was sitting idle on the tracks next to what appeared to be the craggy side of a mountain.

The sky matched her mood. She'd had a restless night, reliving the events of the evening, culminating with her slapping the director of the train. She hadn't waited to see his reaction or to explain herself to the people in the lounge car. Instead, she had turned on her heel and swiftly returned to her suite.

'I'm beginning to think this train is cursed,'

she told Pepper. The little dog began scratching on the door, and she glanced out the window with a sigh.

After her behaviour the previous night, she was more resolute than ever about remaining in her suite for the duration of the journey, but surely at this early hour, she wouldn't see anyone.

After she had washed and fixed her hair, she peered into the wardrobe. On a hook inside the door, Elke had hung her outfit for the day.

She dressed swiftly in a red plaid tweed skirt suit. The double-breasted coat had a soft velvet collar and a belt with a gold clasp. She paired the suit with a pair of red shoes and matching felt cloche hat.

Looking in the mirror on the back of the wardrobe door, she had to admit it was a stylish outfit, but she longed for the ease and comfort of her old clothes

She put a hand on the window and cold spread across her palm. In the wardrobe, she found a thick, white wool coat and shrugged into it.

After pouring herself a glass of ice-cold water to relieve the dryness in her mouth, she pulled on her soft leather gloves.

The train was silent as she left her suite with Pepper on his leash. The lamps were still lit and through the window she could see the trees swaying in the breeze.

The wagon lit conductor sat at the end of the corridor, his chin on his chest. His eyes were closed, but he jerked upright when he heard her footsteps.

He cleared his throat and hastily put his hat on his balding head. 'Good morning, mademoiselle.'

'Good morning, Jean-Luc. What's happened to the train? Why have we stopped?'

The conductor got to his feet with a groan. 'I'm afraid there has been a rockfall overnight and we will be delayed until it can be cleared.'

'Oh dear. How inconvenient. However, I suppose it provides an opportunity for me to take Pepper outside for a stroll. Is it allowed?'

'Of course, mademoiselle. You can use the side door in the next carriage. I have laid out the stairs for this purpose, but just so you're aware, it's extremely cold outside.'

'Thank you, but I'm well prepared for the conditions.'

She bade him farewell and led Pepper through the carriage. Halfway along the corridor, a door opened, and Dennis Cosette emerged. He was dressed in a black suit and his hair was slick with oil. His citrus-scented cologne tickled her nose.

Dennis's dark, hooded eyes met hers, and his top lip curled. Then he turned and walked in the opposite direction.

'Someone's not a morning person,' she murmured to Pepper once Dennis was out of earshot.

The door next to Dennis's compartment opened, and Hermione Carey poked her head out. Her head was wrapped in a towel, and she wore a bathrobe.

'Oh, Lady Marigold...I mean, Marigold. I was expecting the wagon lit conductor. Do you know what's happened to the train?'

Marigold nodded. 'I'm afraid there's been a rockfall and we're going to be stuck here until they can clear it.'

Hermione's eyes widened. 'Oh no. Was anyone hurt?'

'Goodness. I didn't think of that. I don't think so, but perhaps the wagon lit conductor will have more information.'

Pepper barked and pulled on the leash. Hermione smiled. 'Good morning, Pepper. I'm sorry if I'm delaying your morning walk.'

'He's eager to get outside and I suppose we might as well make the most of it seeing as we don't appear to be going anywhere today.'

An odd expression crossed Hermione's face,

and she gripped the compartment door with both hands.

Marigold took a step closer. 'Are you unwell?'

Hermione's hand fluttered to her forehead. 'No. I'm quite well, just upset about the delay. I was due to meet a friend in Paris tomorrow. I hate to disappoint them, but it can't be helped.'

'So unlucky.' Marigold tried to feign disappointment.

Hermione narrowed her eyes. 'But you're not unhappy about it?'

Marigold smiled. 'You're very perceptive—and correct. I confess I don't mind the delay. My return to England is not by my choice.'

Hermione twisted the ring on the chain around her neck. 'That's right, you're returning to Mayfair for the first time since your uncle died. I don't blame you for not being in a rush.'

'Alas, the delay will only be temporary, but I have just started reading the new Lady Clues book, so I have plenty to keep me occupied while we wait for the track to be cleared.'

Hermione put a hand to her mouth to smother a yawn. 'Oh dear. Excuse me. I didn't sleep very well last night.'

Marigold smiled and smothered her own yawn. 'I won't keep you any longer.'

Hermione bent and patted Pepper on the

head. 'Goodbye Pepper, I hope you enjoy your walk.'

Marigold said farewell and made her way to the exit. The air outside was icy but refreshing after the stuffiness of the overheated train. The trees and bushes on the mountainside were full of birds chirping morning greetings to one another.

Pepper gave a yelp of delight and launched himself into a bush by the side of the tracks, pulling her behind him.

The sky was heavy with clouds and the wind made her eyes water, but she was enjoying the freedom of being on solid ground. She peered along the tracks, trying to see the rockfall, but the train was on a straight line of track, and she couldn't see anything beyond the front engine.

The squeak of the compartment door on its runners made her glance over her shoulder. Aline tentatively made her way down the steps. She wasn't wearing a coat.

Once she reached the ground, Aline removed a silver case from her pocket and took out a thin, brown cigarette. Her hands were trembling as she struck a match. Why on earth hadn't the woman worn a coat?

'Good morning, Madame Martin,' Marigold called.

Aline lifted her chin. 'Lady Marigold, I wouldn't have picked you for an early riser.'

Marigold frowned, wondering what had led her to draw that conclusion. 'I've never been one for sleeping late, but insomnia is my long-time companion. I suspect my attachment to coffee may have something to do with it, but I can't bear the thought of giving it up.'

Aline nodded. 'I too have a lifelong love of coffee.'

Up close, Marigold realised Aline was older than she had first thought. There were lines around her eyes and mouth and a smattering of white hair at her temples.

'My condolences on the loss of your uncle. Many years ago, I spent a summer in England, and I know he was highly regarded.'

Marigold swallowed the lump in her throat. 'Thank you. Did you meet him?'

Aline shook her head. 'I was unwell at the time and sent to convalesce with my aunt and she spoke of him often. When I was stronger, I wanted to study at Oxford, but then my mother died, and I returned to Paris to take care of Vivienne. I often think fondly of the wonderful gardens and grounds, though.'

'It must have been difficult for you. How old were you?'

Aline exhaled a stream of smoke. 'I was six-teen'. There was a catch to her voice.

'That's very young to have taken on such an enormous responsibility.' It seemed unfair Aline had given up her youth to care for someone as unpleasant as Vivienne.

Aline smiled. 'You would do the same, I'm sure. We protect the ones we love at all costs.'

Marigold nodded and tried to think of a way to change the subject without being rude. She was sure she would protect people she loved, but there hadn't been many of them in her life, and even fewer now Uncle Thomas was gone.

How lucky Vivienne was to have a sister as loyal as Aline to watch over and care for her.

'I was impressed with your slap last night,' Aline said, breaking her out of her reverie.

Marigold's cheeks grew hot. 'I know he's a friend of your sister, but I don't regret it.'

Aline exhaled slowly. 'He had it coming.'

'I won't argue. I just wish I could have avoided making a scene.'

'It was unavoidable. If it hadn't been you, it would have been Vivienne.'

Marigold was tempted to say Vivienne had done quite a good job at creating a scene of her own. She decided to probe the nature of the relationship between the ballerina and train director instead.

'What did Mr Olivier do to make her so angry?'

Aline rolled her eyes. 'What didn't he do? He'll be well advised to stay away from her today or he risks being hit over the head with a coffee pot— or worse.'

Marigold laughed. 'Speaking of coffee, I'm desperate for some.'

'I think it's too early for breakfast, but I'm sure the conductor can be persuaded to make some,' Aline said as she squashed the butt of her cigarette with the toe of her boot.

'Let me speak to the kitchen. You're half frozen. Go back to your compartment and I'll have a pot sent to you.'

Aline's teeth chattered as she nodded. 'Thank you. I'm in compartment twenty-two.'

After they had climbed aboard, Aline departed for the sleeper car, and Marigold tied Pepper to a brass post near the door.

'Stay here and behave yourself. I won't be long, and if you're good, I'll bring you back a treat.'

Pepper tugged at the leash, testing its strength. It must have passed, because he sat and kept his eyes on her as she walked backwards through the deserted dining car towards the kitchen. When she was convinced he wouldn't escape, she turned to face the kitchen door and let out a cry of alarm.

A young woman was pacing outside the door to the kitchen. Her long dark hair was neatly pinned above her neck.

When she lifted her head, Marigold realised it was Renée—Vivienne's maid. Her face was full of anguish, pale as the linen tablecloths, her pupils were dilated, and her hands were stained with something red.

Suddenly, Marigold could smell blood and fought the urge to retch.

'Are you alright Renée? What's happened?' She kept her voice low and calm despite the churn of emotions within her.

Renée's bottom lip wobbled. 'It wasn't me, mademoiselle, I swear it.'

Her legs gave way, and Marigold grabbed her by the elbows to support her while carefully avoiding the blood on Renée's hands.

'Oh, mademoiselle, I swear it wasn't me,' she wailed.

Marigold led her to a seat and tried to open the kitchen door, but Renée grasped her skirt and tugged her backwards.

'Don't go in there, my lady, it's horrible.'

Marigold frowned at the red streaks on her coat and tugged free of Renée's grip.

'Stay here.' She took a deep breath and slid the door open.

Renée had been right. It was a dreadful sight, but not the worst she'd seen, not by a long way.

She clapped a hand over her mouth.

Slumped on the kitchen floor was the body of Rueben Olivier. He was lying in a pool of blood with an ice pick sticking out of his chest.

Above him, an ice sculpture of a woman with a fruit basket on her head was slowly dripping onto the floor.

CHAPTER TWELVE

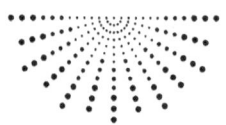

It took several seconds for her training to kick in, then Marigold backed out of the kitchen and closed the door.

Jean-Luc, the handsome, dark-haired wagon lit conductor, stood next to Renée. She was sobbing in the corner with her head buried in her arms. Relief washed over his face when he spotted Marigold.

'I wasn't sure what to do.'

She put a hand on his arm. 'Do you know Inspector Loxley?'

The wagon lit conductor nodded. 'Yes, mademoiselle.'

She took a deep breath. 'I need you to bring him here as quickly as you can, please. And also,

Miss Müller, who is in compartment number sixteen. Please tell them there has been a murder.'

Jean-Luc's eyes bulged, but he nodded, and with a last uncertain glance at Renée, he left.

On his way out, he passed Mr Jorrisen. The deputy director's eyes fell on Pepper, who had broken free of his leash and was enthusiastically chewing a man's shoe. Jorrisen's face turned puce.

Before he could say or do anything, Marigold cleared her throat. He peered into the dining car. 'Is everything alright?'

Marigold shook her head. 'No. I'm afraid it's not.'

His gaze moved to Renée's blood covered hands, and he stiffened. 'What's happened to her? Have you called the doctor?'

Marigold shook her head. That was a sensible idea. She should have thought of it. 'No, could you please organise for him to come immediately?'

She decided not to tell him what was on the other side of the kitchen door. Loxley could be the one to break the bad news.

'One moment, please.' he strode from the carriage, giving Pepper a disgusted look as he walked by. She heard him hail a nearby conductor and instruct him to summon the doctor.

'He's dead, isn't he?' Renée said through her sobs.

'I'm afraid so.' Marigold patted her on the shoulder as Loxley strode into the carriage.

She hadn't expected him to arrive so soon. Evidently, he was a morning person. Despite the early hour, he was already fully dressed, although his hair was damp and curling at the ends. He wore his usual frown. 'What's happened?'

Marigold got to her feet. 'I'm afraid there's been a murder.' She was surprised how cool and detached she sounded.

A muscle in Loxley's left cheek twitched. 'A murder? Who is it?'

She tilted her head towards the door. 'The body is in the kitchen.'

Loxley pulled a monogrammed handkerchief from the inside pocket of his coat, wrapped it around his hand, and opened the kitchen door.

Marigold peered around him. The scene in the kitchen hadn't improved.

'Mr Olivier?' Loxley said, a hint of surprise in his voice as he stared at the body.

She averted her eyes. The image of the body was already seared into her mind. She didn't need to refresh it.

She focussed instead on the ice sculpture. Large droplets were falling from the woman's feet and creating a puddle near Mr Olivier's head.

She kept her eyes on the ice-sculpture. Chef Dubois was an incredibly talented artist.

'Lady Marigold?'

Loxley's voice brought her back to the present. She blinked. 'Yes?'

He frowned. 'I asked how you discovered the body?'

Another drop of water splashed to the floor, and she forced herself to focus. 'I was outside the train with my dog. I came inside to see if I could order coffee, but in the dining car I saw Renée.'

Loxley glanced at the door. 'Miss Cosette's maid?'

Marigold tried to hide her surprise he knew who Vivienne's maid was. If he had investigated the passenger's personal details so closely, she had good reason to be concerned what he knew about her.

'Yes. She was pacing in front of the kitchen door. She appeared distressed.'

'How could you tell?'

She thought back to the moment she'd first seen Renée. 'From her body language, mostly. Her shoulders were hunched, and her head was down. It wasn't until I was closer that I noticed the blood on her hands.'

'Did she say anything?'

Marigold nodded. 'She said she hadn't done it.'

'Did you ask her what it was she hadn't done?'

Marigold stifled a sigh. She was rapidly tiring of his questions. Surely, they could wait until poor Mr Olivier's body had been removed from the kitchen.

She glanced at his body and felt a sliver of sympathy for the train director. Her encounters with him hadn't been pleasant and his morals had certainly been questionable, but no-one deserved to die like this.

'Did you ask her what it was she hadn't done?'

Marigold narrowed her eyes. 'I heard you the first time, Inspector. I'm just wondering why it's necessary for me to answer all these questions now. Surely there will be time for that later?'

'There is no better time than just after a crime to question a witness.'

She stifled a sigh. 'Very well. No, I didn't ask her, but it was clear to me she was referring to something that had happened in the kitchen. Her eyes kept darting in that direction. Her hands were covered in blood.'

Loxley's voice was a steady monotone. 'And then?'

'And then I entered the kitchen and found Mr

Olivier like this.' She gestured to Mr Olivier's body on the floor.

'The first time you saw the body was when you came into the kitchen this morning?'

'Obviously. How else would I have found the body?'

Loxley's nostrils flared. It appeared his calm demeanour was cracking, and she was getting to him after all. 'Did you touch anything?'

She glanced at the ceiling, pretending to think it over, then she began to count on her fingers. 'Yes, a few things. The body, the murder weapon, the ice sculpture...'

Loxley cut her off. 'This is no time for sarcasm. A serious crime has been committed, and I don't need you making a difficult situation worse by not cooperating. Especially as your role in its yet to be determined.'

Marigold put her hands on her hips. 'My role? I had no role. I'm just the unlucky person who came searching for coffee and found a body.'

Loxley's eyes were fixed on Mr Olivier. 'How unlucky for you it was the morning after you publicly slapped him.' He knelt and examined the train director's body more closely while Marigold paced the room.

Surely, she wouldn't be a suspect because of one little slap?

'His watch is broken. I suspect he put up his arm to protect himself. It didn't help sadly, but at least it provides us with a time of death,' she said, unable to help herself.

Loxley stared at her. 'You seem to know a lot about it.'

Marigold shrugged. 'Not really, but I read a lot of detective books. I know how important it is to note these things.'

'Lady Marigold, this is not fiction, and you would do well to save your observations for your statement,' Loxley said through gritted teeth.

She sighed. 'You're going to interview me? Whatever for?'

'In case you haven't noticed, and it appears you haven't, this is a murder scene, your presence makes you a witness and you were last seen slapping the victim.'

'So, I'm a suspect?'

'One suspect.' He got to his feet.

'But this is ridiculous. Why would I kill Mr Olivier?'

'It will be up to you to provide that explanation, Lady Marigold. Now, if you would be so kind as to wait outside so I can do my job?'

Before she could think of a withering reply, the door swung open, and Chef Dubois walked in.

The smell of cigarettes clung to his white chef's uniform. His eyes fell on Mr Olivier's body, the ice pick, and then to the melting ice sculpture on the table.

'Oh no, no, no, no, Josephine,' he wailed. He hurried to the ice sculpture and began assessing the damage.

'Mr Dubois, please stay back. This is a crime scene, and I cannot have you touching anything,' Loxley snapped.

'But what about Josephine?' Chef Dubois wrang his hands, his face was full of anguish.

Loxley blinked slowly and pinched the top of his nose. 'Who?'

Marigold pointed to the ice sculpture. 'I assume this is Josephine.'

'I need to get her in the cool room before she's gone. What's she doing out here?' Chef Dubois wailed.

A muscle in Loxley's cheek began to twitch. 'Mr Dubois, a man is dead in your kitchen, and you're concerned about a block of ice?'

The chef advanced on the Inspector. He was trembling, and when he spoke, his voice broke. 'A block of ice? Josephine is a masterpiece in the making.'

Marigold patted him on the arm. 'Don't worry, Chef Dubois, I'm sure it will be alright.'

'Both of you need to leave immediately,' Loxley said, pointing at the door.

She shook her head. 'The thing is, Inspector; I think Chef Dubois has a point. If we don't move Josephine into the cool room, she'll continue to melt, and she might be evidence.'

Loxley looked at her for a long moment, then exhaled slowly. 'Very well but put on gloves if you have them and touch nothing else.'

Marigold nodded at Chef Dubois. He opened a drawer and pulled out two pairs of white serving gloves.

The door opened again, and Marigold bit back a laugh as Elke walked in wearing a blue medical gown, mask, and cap.

Loxley's eyes bulged and rubbed his forehead. 'Who are you?'.

'Doctor Johnson is not feeling his best this morning. I believe he drank too much wine last night and is suffering the consequences. I can help in his absence.' Elke took a step towards Mr Olivier's body.

Loxley put a hand up to stop her. 'Are you a doctor?'

Elke tipped her head to one side and narrowed her eyes. 'Technically, no, but I have read many medical books.'

'Leave. Immediately. All of you,' Loxley said, pointing to the door.

Marigold stepped forward. 'Inspector, this is Elke Müller, my assistant. I think you'll find she has considerable skills that may be of use. She worked in many hospitals during the war.'

Loxley spoke through gritted teeth. 'Lady Marigold, your role in this matter has come to an end.'

Elke slipped under his arm and crouched next to Mr Olivier's body.

Marigold searched for something she could use to distract Loxley until Elke had time to complete her examination. 'There's no need to be rude, Inspector. I've had quite a shock, you know. Discovering a body isn't pleasant.'

He put his hands on his hips. 'I'm aware. However, you seem to be coping extraordinarily well. That's something we shall discuss when I interview you.'

Chef Dubois raised his hand and waved it until he got Loxley's attention. 'I need to move Josephine before it's too late. I need my staff to help get her back in the cool room,' he wailed.

Loxley rubbed his forehead and glanced at Mr Olivier's body. Fortunately, Elke was back on her feet.

She moved to Marigold's side. 'Perhaps we should return to our compartments, my lady.'

Loxley set his jaw. 'For once, I agree with you.'

He opened the door and gestured for the two conductors lurking in the dining car to approach. 'One of you please assist Chef Dubois to move his… ice sculpture. And the other can escort Lady Marigold and Miss Müller to their compartments.'

'You will regret this. I could have been of use,' Elke said, shaking her head as she passed by him.

Loxley rolled his eyes. 'Believe it or not, I'll take the chance.'

CHAPTER THIRTEEN

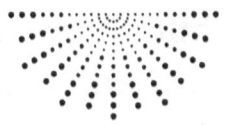

Marigold took her time retying Pepper's leash, her eyes on Loxley, as he walked over to Renée and sat opposite her. His voice was calm and sympathetic.

'Now, Miss?'

'Seydoux. Renée Seydoux.' She dabbed at her eyes with a napkin. She trembled as she met his gaze.

'Miss Seydoux, Mr Olivier is dead, and his blood is on your hands. I'm sure this is distressing for you, but I'm afraid I'll have to detain you in the boiler room until I can interview you.'

Renée's slim shoulders shook, and fresh tears welled in her eyes. 'Oh no, please, can't I go to my compartment? The boiler room is terribly scary. I heard it's haunted.'

Loxley put his hands flat on the tabletop. 'As you're in a shared compartment, I'm afraid you'll have to move into the boiler room and remain there until I can clear you of responsibility for Mr Olivier's death. Hopefully, it won't take long.'

Renée's chin wobbled and tears streaked down her cheeks, but she nodded. Her fear was palpable. Marigold's stomach churned.

Suddenly, she thought of a way to help. She called across the room, 'Miss Seydoux could stay in my suite with a guard outside. There's a spare bed in Miss Müller's compartment I can use.'

Elke shook her head. 'You cannot do that. It wouldn't be appropriate.'

'Of course, I can. It's far better than a boiler room as a cell. I insist Miss Seydoux uses it.'

'No. Miss Seydoux can stay in my compartment, and I'll move into the maid's quarters in your suite, my lady.'

Marigold opened her mouth to argue, but the look in Elke's eyes made her change her mind. Instead of protesting, she nodded.

Loxley's eyes dropped from Marigold to Pepper, who had almost separated the sole of Mr Jorrisen's shoe with the leather upper. He flung it around in his mouth until the sole flew into the air and landed at Mr Jorrisen's feet.

The deputy director's face turned scarlet. His

chest rose with an inhaled breath, and she feared it was going to result in a stream of abuse for Pepper on the exhale.

Not that Marigold could blame him. The shoe appeared expensive, and if Pepper's enjoyment of it was anything to go by, it was also quite tasty.

Before Mr Jorrisen could say anything, Loxley got to his feet and turned to Jean-Luc. 'Take Miss Seydoux to Miss Müller's compartment and stand guard until I'm able to question her.'

Jean-Luc gestured for Renée to follow him, and the blood covered maid got shakily to her feet and took a few wobbly steps across the dining car. When she reached Marigold, she let out a half sob, half gasp.

'Thank you, my lady, and Miss Müller. You're both far too kind. I'm grateful. But please know, I didn't kill Mr Olivier. He was like it when I went into the kitchen.' Her eyes shone with tears as she reached for Marigold's hands.

Marigold forced herself not to recoil, but she couldn't help but stare at the dried blood on Renée's hands. It was also caked under her neatly trimmed fingernails.

'I'm sure it will all be straightened out quickly.'

Elke nodded 'And we shall have your things brought to you.'

Renée began to cry again as Jean-Luc led her out of the dining carriage.

Marigold watched her go, and frustration surged through her. She glared at Loxley, then turned to Elke.

'We must leave the Inspector to his task.'

'What about my shoe?' Mr Jorrisen said in a strangled voice.

Marigold raised her eyebrows. 'Mr Olivier is dead. I hardly think this is the time to talk about a shoe. However, rest assured, I'll ensure you're compensated for its loss.'

'Could I have a word?' Loxley said, tapping Mr Jorrisen on the shoulder. The deputy director glared at Pepper and then Marigold, before following Loxley to the back righthand corner of the carriage.

Marigold lingered and managed to overhear Loxley conveying the bad news. Mr Jorrisen sounded calm as he volunteered to inform Unity of the death of her husband.

'Lady Marigold, your presence here is no longer required,' Loxley called across the room.

She gave him a departing wave. 'We were just leaving.'

As she left the dining car, she collided with Bentley. 'My lady, what has happened? The conductor alerted me you had been involved in an incident in the dining car.'

Marigold patted his arm. 'Please don't worry, I'm fine, but I'm afraid something dreadful has happened.'

She paused as a man in his early sixties who was carrying a black doctor's bag brushed past them. He nodded and said good morning as he turned into the dining car. He didn't appear to be suffering from a hangover.

Elke met Marigold's eyes and shrugged. She shook her head. Elke would have some explaining to do when Loxley caught up with her, but she was more than capable of handling whatever he threw at her.

'Let's go back to my suite so we can talk properly,' she told Bentley.

As they walked, she filled him in on what had transpired.

'Mr Olivier is dead? And was murdered? I must say I regret we ever stepped foot on this train,' Bentley said with a deep sigh.

'Yes, it does seem rather cursed, doesn't it?'

'How did you become involved, my lady?'

'I was outside with Pepper, and when I came back to the train, I went in search of coffee for myself and for Aline Martin. Instead, I came across Vivienne Cosette's maid who was covered in blood.'

Bentley's thick eyebrows shot up. 'Her maid? Is she injured?'

She shook her head. 'No. She's just had a terrible shock. She was the one who discovered Mr Olivier's body first, you see.'

Elke cleared her throat. 'There is, of course, the possibility she is the killer.'

Marigold paused outside the door to her suite and waited for Clara Bligh and her husband to walk by. Clara glared at her and said something to Osbert that made him smirk.

Under other circumstances, Marigold would have called her out, but on this occasion, she let it go. There were bigger issues going on than revisiting her feud with Clara at that moment.

'I don't believe Renée is capable of murder,' she told Elke as she inserted the brass key into the lock.

'It is not what we believe, but what story the evidence tells,' Elke said sagely.

Once they were inside, Marigold turned to her. 'You found something on Mr Olivier's body, didn't you?'

Bentley stiffened. 'You examined Mr Olivier's body?'

'Only for a moment when Inspector Loxley

wasn't looking, and I suspect Elke found something,' she told him.

Elke nodded. 'Your instincts are correct. I don't believe the ice pick was the only murder weapon. I could smell something acrid in Mr Olivier's mouth.'

Marigold's eyes widened. 'Garlic? Was it an allergic reaction?'

Elke shook her head. 'No, my conclusion is the method of murder was poison.'

Marigold gazed out the window as she processed this information. A memory tickled the edge of her brain. After a moment, she turned back to Elke. 'Arsenic?'

Elke nodded. 'I believe so.'

Bentley rubbed his chin. 'But why would someone stab him if he was already dead?'

'Perhaps they were not sure if he had died,' Elke said with a shrug.

Marigold stroked Pepper's soft topknot and watched as fat snowflakes drifted by the window and stuck to the glass. 'Or maybe they wanted to frame someone else for his murder?'

Bentley drummed his fingertips on the writing desk under the window. 'Do you think Inspector Loxley suspects you and Miss Seydoux?'

Marigold nodded. 'He as good as said I'm considered one, but Mrs Aline Martin can confirm I was outside with her earlier, and the wagon lit conductor will confirm the time I left my suite this morning.'

Bentley paced beside the window. 'I think there are many others who will be on Inspector Loxley's suspect list as the day goes on.'

'Yes. And Mr Jorrisen should be at the top of it.' She poured herself a glass of water, hoping to wash away the bitter taste in her mouth.

Bentley cleared his throat. 'Also, I'm sad to say, because I quite like the man, but I imagine Chef Dubois will also be questioned.'

'He did have a peculiar reaction when he entered the kitchen. His only concern was for his ice-sculpture. He barely seemed to notice Mr Olivier was lying dead on his kitchen floor.'

Elke interlocked her hands and pointed her index fingers. 'He was in shock?'

Marigold scratched Pepper's ears. 'I don't know. I know he didn't like Mr Olivier, but to not be disturbed by his death seems a little odd.'

Bentley turned away from the window. 'I witnessed a terrible row between Chef Dubois and Mr Olivier last night after the dinner service was complete. The Frenchman was enraged by Mr Olivier's criticism of his cooking.'

Marigold frowned. 'Enough for him to kill him?'

Bentley sighed. 'I hope it isn't the case.'

'Vivienne Cosette must be a suspect, too. I don't know what was going on between her and Mr Olivier, but she threatened him after they fought last night.' Marigold knew she shouldn't jump to conclusions, but there was a certain satisfaction about adding Vivienne to the suspect list.

Elke sat with her legs crossed, tapping her foot in the air. 'And if the mistress is on the suspect list, so too must be the wife.'

Marigold frowned. 'I hadn't thought of her, but I guess it makes sense, although I would have suspected she wanted to kill Vivienne more than her husband.'

'One never knows what really goes on inside of a marriage,' Elke said quietly.

Bentley's mouth became a thin line. 'We must trust Inspector Loxley will conduct a proper and thorough investigation'

There was a knock at the door. When Marigold opened it, she found Nico, the conductor, standing in the corridor with a trolley laden with tea, coffee, croissants, and toast.

'I thought you might want some breakfast, mademoiselle.'

'Bless you, Nico. You're an angel.' She waved him inside.

'I know I shouldn't be hungry after what I've just seen, but strangely, I'm starving.' She took a chocolate croissant from the tray and bit into it. The pastry melted on her tongue, and some of the tension lifted from her shoulders.

'Shock triggers the survival instinct,' Elke said as she buttered a slice of toast.

Marigold turned to Bentley. 'On another matter, how did you get on with young Sebastian and Florence? Are they alright?'

Bentley balanced a teacup and saucer on his open palm. 'They are. You were right, my lady, they hadn't been taking meals on the train. I spoke to the conductor in third-class and arranged for them to eat in the dining car.'

She nodded and sipped her coffee. 'I can't help but worry about them. They're so young to be travelling so far on their own.'

'From what I have learned, their mother was English and married a Turkish man. Sadly, she died two years ago, and their stepfather hasn't made their life easy. They are travelling back to England in the hope of connecting with their mother's family.'

'I would like to ensure they do.'

Bentley put his cup on the tray. 'I share your

concern for their welfare. Leave it to me, my lady. I'll keep an eye on them.'

When the breakfast things were cleared away, Bentley excused himself to check on the staff. 'Under the circumstances, I should offer my services to Mr Jorrisen.'

Marigold sighed. 'You're a good man, Bentley, but please, be careful out there.'

CHAPTER FOURTEEN

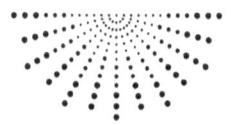

Once Bentley was gone, Marigold found it hard to settle. First, she picked up a book, but after she'd read the same page three times, she put Lady Clues aside.

Next, she tried playing solitaire, but again her mind wandered, and the cards ended up in a meaningless mess.

Finally, she got to her feet. 'I think I'll take Pepper for another stroll. The train doesn't seem to be going anywhere, and the fresh air might help clear my head. It's so hot and stuffy in here.'

Elke snapped her book shut. 'I will come with you. Some cool air would be pleasant. I do not understand why they are trying to roast us on this train. Surely there is a way to control the temperature?'

Marigold picked up her coat. 'If there is, they don't seem to be using it.'

They left the suite and some of the weight in Marigold's chest began to lift as they walked along the slightly cooler corridor. Outside the train, she could hear men's voices and the clink of metal on rock as the clearance team continued to chip away at the landfall.

Nico had told her the north dining carriage was closed, and all passengers were being served breakfast in their compartments. Future meals would be taken in the south dining car for the rest of the journey.

Silver trays and dirty dishes were piled outside several compartment doors. The corridor smelled of toast, curdled milk, and burnt sugar.

Poor Nico was hurrying along the corridor, stacking trays on a trolley. He wore a white apron with a coffee stain on the front and had beads of sweat on his forehead.

'You're doing a good job, Nico.' Marigold called to him.

He smiled at her over a stack of dishes. 'Thank you, mademoiselle. It's a most unusual morning.'

'I imagine it's difficult for you and the other staff to keep working in the midst of such a dreadful thing happening.'

Nico nodded. 'It's shocking indeed. But Mr

Jorrisen says we must uphold the good name of the Lunar Express. We must honour Mr Olivier by ensuring the guests are taken care of.'

Marigold picked Pepper up to stop him from sniffing around Nico's shoes. 'That's admirable, but please make sure you take care of yourself, too.'

He sighed. 'Most passengers are understanding of the current situation.'

'As they should be. It's not the fault of the staff the director of the train has been murdered,' Elke said, her voice full of anger.

Marigold shot her a questioning look.

Elke shrugged. 'What I mean to say is, the passengers should be glad they are being served under such difficult circumstances.'

Nico's cheeks flushed. 'Thank you, Miss Müller. It's a pleasure to serve you and Lady Marigold.'

He turned to collect another tray, and Marigold and Elke set off again.

Despite the heat pumping through the sleeper carriage, Marigold rubbed her hands together to warm them. 'Nico is very sweet. I must tell Bentley to keep an eye out and make sure he's treated well.'

Elke snorted. 'At this rate, you will have Mr Bentley taking care of everyone on the train.'

Marigold's cheeks flushed. 'Oh dear. I didn't realise I was doing that. The last thing I want is to add to his workload. I won't say anything about Nico. I'll just have to make sure Mr Jorrisen improves the way the staff are treated now Mr Olivier is gone.'

'You think Mr Olivier was the one responsible for the unhappiness of the staff?'

Marigold pulled on her gloves. 'I admit it could have been either of them, but with Mr Olivier gone, I guess we'll find out soon enough what kind of leader Mr Jorrisen is.'

'Who do you think the ungrateful and difficult passengers are?' Elke said as they approached the end of the corridor.

Marigold scowled. 'If I know Clara—and I do —she'll be one of the worst offenders.'

Elke frowned. 'You must tell me what went on at that boarding school.'

At the end of the corridor, a woman called Marigold's name.

Unity Olivier stood in the doorway of her suite. The new widow was dressed from head to toe in black. She wore a crushed velvet drop-waisted dress with black suede t-strap shoes and a feathered headband in her fair hair.

The smell of cigarettes wafting from her suite made Marigold queasy. She forced herself to speak. 'Mrs Olivier, I'm so sorry for your loss.'

Elke gave Unity a curt nod. 'I too am sorry.'

'Won't you come inside and sit with me for a moment? I find I simply can't bear to be alone.'

Despite her anguished words, Marigold noted the lack of tears as Unity dabbed her eyes with a lace-trimmed handkerchief.

'Of course, so long as you don't mind Pepper joining us. He's generally well behaved.'

Unity nodded and bent to pat Pepper. 'I like dogs. Rueben didn't. Perhaps I'll get one now. For company.'

Unity sat on the settee, and they took seats opposite her. Marigold cleared her throat. 'What a dreadful shock you've had. How are you, Mrs Olivier?'

'Please, call me Unity, and are you sorry he's gone? I hate to speak ill of the dead, but let's not pretend Rueben wasn't a dreadful man.' She twisted her handkerchief and gave her a sad smile. 'I suspect you know that, though. You saw the way he behaved the other night.'

Elke pulled a small bottle of liquor from her handbag. 'Would you like a drink?'

Marigold whipped her head around to stare at her. Where did you get that?' she muttered under her breath.

'I come prepared.' Elke walked over to the cabinet above the washbasin sink and took out three glasses. She poured a generous measure handed one to each of them.

Marigold sat back in her seat, enjoying the burn of the liquor in her throat. For someone who didn't usually drink, she certainly was doing a lot of it on this train.

'I understand you were the one who discovered Rueben's body.' Unity shuddered as she swallowed a mouthful of brandy.

'Actually, it was…' She stopped herself just before she made a potential faux pas. She had been about to say it had been Vivienne Cosette's maid who had discovered Mr Olivier's body. But if Unity thought Marigold had been the one to discover her husband's body, Mr Jorrisen must have told her it was what had happened. Had it been to spare her feelings? Or to avoid an emotional outburst? She guessed it was the latter.

'I was up early for a walk with Pepper. I went into the dining car to get some coffee. That's when I discovered what had happened to Mr Olivier,' Marigold said. Technically, all those things were true.

Unity let out a shaky breath. 'Mr Jorrisen said Rueben was stabbed.'

Not wanting to share details that might be

news to Unity, Marigold asked, 'Have you spoken to Inspector Loxley about it?'

Unity's expression darkened. 'Yes. I rather think he suspects me.'

'You? Surely not.' Marigold hoped she sounded more surprised than she felt.

'I suppose I can't blame him. I didn't do it of course, but I can understand why someone would. Oh dear, as a family friend, perhaps you're shocked to hear this.'

'It was my uncle who was acquainted with Mr Olivier. I only met him for the first time when I boarded the train.'

Unity's eyes dropped to the floor. 'He was embarrassed to have such a plain wife. He only loved my money—until it ran out.'

'I'm sure that's not true,' Marigold said, but she suspected it was.

'The irony is, of course, now I'll get everything. Not that Rueben had money. He couldn't hold on to it for long. But there's a sizeable life insurance policy I'll collect. No wonder the handsome Inspector suspects me.'

Elke put her empty glass on the table. 'Do you have an alibi?'

'Of sorts. I went for a walk after dinner last night and had an encounter with Vivienne

Cosette. Then I came back to my compartment and took a sleeping draft. I didn't realise Rueben hadn't returned until Mr Jorrisen knocked on my compartment door to tell me the news.'

Marigold pretended to sip her drink. 'I assume the exchange between the two of you didn't go well?'

Unity snorted. 'Oh indeed. Stupid woman. She had no idea what the real Rueben was like or that she was only one of his *lady friends*.'

'Did she say anything about Mr Olivier? She seemed very angry with him outside the lounge.'

Unity raised her painted eyebrows. 'You think she killed him?'

Marigold shrugged. 'It's not for me to say, but I can't help but be curious about why she was so angry with him.'

Unity took another sip of her drink. 'I despise the woman, but surely someone so slight couldn't have taken down a man the size of Rueben. He would have snapped her wrist in an instant.'

Marigold scratched Pepper behind the ears. 'I suppose, but surely she's more of a suspect than you?'

'That depends on who Inspector Loxley believes had the most reason to want Rueben dead.'

Unity drained her liquor glass. Her brusque

manner was at odds with the tragic figure she had presented in the doorway to her suite.

Marigold took a tiny sip of her drink and repressed a shudder. 'Do you think Vivienne will confirm your alibi?'

Unity shrugged. 'I suspect she'll need my alibi in return. We will have no choice but to help one another—painful though it will be.'

'Do you believe she had a role in Mr Olivier's death?'

Unity put her glass on the floor and rubbed her eyes. 'He had been receiving threats, but that wasn't new. I never imagined he'd be murdered.'

Elke leaned forward in her seat. 'Why was he receiving threats?'

Unity smiled, but her bottom lip trembled. 'My husband was a man who took money from people to fund his lifestyle. That made him unpopular.'

Marigold stared at her, wondering how much of Unity's grief was genuine and how much was for show. 'Is the Inspector aware of this?'

'Yes, I told him and showed him the most recent notes Rueben received. Hopefully, it will help the investigation.'

Elke rested her elbows on her knees and interlaced her fingers. 'Who do you think is the killer?'

Unity drained her glass and held it out to Elke for a refill. 'I'd like to say, Miss Cosette. She certainly had a motive, and I admit I'd get satisfaction from seeing her behind bars.'

Marigold nodded. 'What would Vivienne's motive have been?'

Unity shrugged. 'Something she said made me believe he had taken her money, too. It's what he did. Mr Jorrisen had similar grievances.'

'But enough to kill him?' Elke handed Unity another glass of amber liquid.

Unity downed her drink in one gulp and put the glass on the coffee table. 'I guess we will find out.' She yawned and got unsteadily to her feet. 'My apologies. I need to lie down before I embarrass myself further.'

Marigold stood and brushed off her skirt. 'You haven't done that at all, and if there is anything we can do to help, please don't hesitate to ask.'

Unity nodded. 'Thank you, Lady Marigold. That's kind.'

Elke walked to the door and blurted out, 'I hope you are not guilty.'

Unity's back stiffened, and her mouth became a thin, hard line.

Elke tried again. 'That is to say, I hope other people do not assume you are guilty.'

'Perhaps Bentley could give you a few pointers in diplomacy,' Marigold told Elke after Unity slammed the door to the suite behind them.

Elke shrugged. 'I only speak the truth. She does not have to like it.'

CHAPTER FIFTEEN

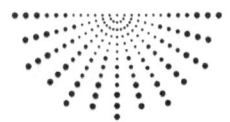

Inspector Gideon Loxley was a meticulous note taker.

It didn't surprise Marigold, but it irritated her. It was all she could do not to drum her fingers on the polished oak desk as she waited for him to finish documenting her words.

She felt more like her old self, having changed into a pair of white wool high-waisted trousers and a silk blouse with a gold rosette broach at her throat. Much as she hated to admit it, she quite liked the clothes Elke had purchased for her.

'Perhaps Ms Müller could take your dog for a walk?' He glanced pointedly at Pepper, who had interrupted his questioning for the third time by sniffing loudly around the office.

She smiled with false sweetness. 'I need to

keep an eye on him. He has a talent for getting into trouble.'

Loxley pursed his lips. 'It seems he takes after his owner in that respect.'

Pepper growled, and she reached into her handbag and fed him a biscuit. He settled at her feet, crunching it loudly.

Loxley gave a sigh that suggested his patience was wearing thin.

They were sitting in what had been Mr Olivier's office—a small room with oak-panelled walls and a thick red carpet. A photograph of a younger Unity and Rueben Olivier sat on the desk.

It was a wedding portrait, taken in a studio, and Unity's expression was wistful. Mr Olivier was scowling.

Marigold thought longingly of the lunch she'd missed as her stomach rumbled. She cursed the poor timing of Loxley's interview request, which had been delivered to her in the south dining carriage just as she had taken her seat.

There had been no official announcement about Mr Olivier's death. The passengers had only been told there had been an incident in the north dining carriage. However, gossip had spread the news throughout the train in a matter of minutes.

Loxley glanced up from his note taking. 'So, after Miss Cosette departed, you walked into the dining car?'

'Yes. That's correct.' She craned her neck to observe him making his notes. His penmanship was impressively neat.

'What time was this?'

She puffed out her cheeks and exhaled slowly. 'I'm not sure. I don't wear a watch and I don't recall seeing a clock.'

'And when you walked into the kitchen, you found Mr Olivier on the floor?'

She nodded. 'Yes. The ice pick was sticking out of his chest.'

'And there was no one else in the kitchen?'

Her eyes widened. 'I didn't conduct a search, but I didn't see anyone. I assume you would have found them if there had been.'

Loxley narrowed his eyes. 'How well did you know Mr Olivier?'

Marigold smothered a yawn. The early morning start was catching up with her and with her lunch delayed, her energy was flagging.

'Not at all. He told me he was an acquaintance of my uncle.'

'So, you had never met him before boarding the train?'

She shook her head, and Loxley made another note.

'I understand your uncle died recently,' Loxley said, his tone softening.

She nodded and swallowed the lump that suddenly appeared in her throat. 'Sadly, it's true.'

'My condolences. I didn't know him well, but my mother has always spoken highly of him.'

She reached into her handbag and fed Pepper another biscuit. 'It's odd so many people on this train seem to be connected in some way.'

Any trace of friendliness disappeared from his face and voice. 'That certainly seems to be the case where you're concerned.'

Marigold frowned. She hadn't intended to bring it to his attention, but admittedly, it was true.

'Actually, I meant Mr Olivier and Vivienne Cosette.'

Loxley placed his pen on the desk. 'I don't see how that's of concern to you.'

She smiled. 'I'm not concerned. Just interested.'

Loxley sat back in Mr Olivier's chair. His expression was unreadable. She met his unblinking stare.

Pepper chose that moment to pounce on her handbag in search of more treats. He dragged it across the room and its contents spilled onto the floor. To her dismay, one item landed at Loxley's feet. He bent down and picked it up.

'I'm interested in your explanation of this?' He dangled a pearl-handled pistol over the desk in front of her.

She kept her face impassive. 'A souvenir. From the war. Given to me by the bravest woman I've ever met.'

'You didn't think to declare you had a weapon on board?'

Marigold lifted her chin. 'Why would I? It's not like I have any intention of using it.'

Loxley glared at her. 'A man is dead.'

'Correct, and at first glance it appears he was killed by an ice pick. Not a gun.'

Loxley examined the weapon. 'Why would you bring a gun on board?'

'Miss Müller, and I have recently been to Africa, where we were outsmarting animal hunters. There was comfort in two women, alone, having a form of defence that didn't rely on our mental and physical abilities—considerable though they are.'

Loxley scowled. 'I'll have to confiscate it. I'll return it when we arrive in Paris.'

'Surely that's not necessary?'

There was a knock at the door and Jean-Luc

entered carrying a silver tray laden with a teapot, a pair of teacups, and a plate of madeleines.

Loxley thanked him, and Jean-Luc departed with a curious glance at her.

'There is no need for you to stay. That will be all—for now.' Loxley said as he poured himself a cup of tea and stirred a lump of sugar into it.

Marigold ignored him and poured hot, fragrant tea into the other cup, along with a generous splash of milk. She placed a shell shaped sponge cake on the saucer and sat back in her seat and took a bite.

'These are delicious.' She pointed to the madeleines before she fed the other half of the little cake to Pepper.

'Don't let me keep you,' Loxley said, frowning as Pepper devoured his treat.

She stared at him. 'If you have further questions, I'd prefer to answer them now.'

Loxley put his teacup carefully on its saucer. 'I have a few leads to follow-up, but I'll let you know if there's anything further.'

She drained her teacup, pushed back her chair, and stood, brushing a few crumbs off her trousers. 'I can't imagine why that would be, but of course I would be happy to cooperate. Before I go, may I ask you a question, Inspector?'

Loxley closed his notebook and nodded. 'What's it?'

'I was wondering if you had determined Mr Olivier's cause of death?'

He frowned. 'What a morbid question.'

She shrugged. 'Perhaps, but I'm curious.'

'The likely cause of death seems obvious.' He placed his pen, notebook, and her gun in the top desk drawer.

Marigold picked up her handbag and looped it over her arm. 'The ice pick? It does seem the logical explanation, but my assistant, you remember her Inspector—the one with the medical training you weren't interested in taking advantage of— she detected something interesting about Mr Olivier's body.'

The crease between Loxley's eyes deepened. 'As I recall, Miss Müller didn't have any contact with Mr Olivier's body, so I'm not sure how that's possible.'

She smiled and shrugged. 'Elke has many hidden talents. Trust me, Inspector, she detected the smell of bitter almonds in Mr Olivier's mouth. Furthermore, her conclusion is he was poisoned before he was stabbed.'

Loxley sighed, got to his feet, walked to the door, and opened it. 'Thank you for your theory,

Lady Marigold, but the medical examiner will advise the official cause of Mr Olivier's death.'

'Actually, it's Miss Müller who should get the credit.'

'Then I look forward to hearing more of her theories when I speak with her.'

'I'm sure she'll provide you with many valuable insights.'

'I'm a busy man, Lady Marigold.' He tapped on the door. 'Is there anything else?'

Marigold pretended she was considering the question. 'No, I believe that's all. Thank you, Inspector.'

'Good day, Lady Marigold.'

'I think you mean good afternoon, Inspector. It's after midday, after all.' She walked out of the office with Pepper in tow.

He slammed the door behind them, and Pepper barked in protest.

'I know. He's very rude, isn't he?'

Elke was waiting for her at the end of the corridor. 'Are you going to be arrested?'

Marigold frowned. 'No. Why? Did you expect I would be?'

Elke shrugged. 'You slapped the man, found his body, and the Inspector seems suspicious of you. I naturally assumed you would be arrested.'

Marigold scooped up Pepper to stop him from

attacking the wood panelled wall. 'Naturally? I'm afraid I don't see how you came to that conclusion.'

'That's because you're English. We Germans are far better at solving puzzles.'

Unsure where the conversation was heading, Marigold decided to change the subject.

'Let's take Pepper back to the suite and then return to the dining car for lunch. I'm starving.'

Elke nodded. 'I will stay with him while you dine.'

Marigold frowned at her. 'No, Elke, you should come with me. There's no reason you shouldn't be dining with the first-class guests now you're staying in my suite.'

Elke narrowed her eyes. 'I think perhaps you do not want to dine alone.'

Marigold laughed. 'Was I that obvious?'

'Yes.'

'It's true. I don't like to eat alone, but I also think you should dine with me.'

'What happened to dining in your suite for the duration of the journey?'

Marigold sighed and paused at the entrance to the first-class carriage. 'I'm not saying I like it, but it strikes me if we're going to stay up to date with whatever is going on, we need to be among the other guests.'

A compartment door at the end of the corridor opened, and a familiar male figure emerged.

Marigold caught Elke's eye and stepped back into the vestibule. From this vantage point, she was confident they couldn't be seen, but they had a clear view of the events in the corridor.

'Is that not Vivienne Cosette's suite?' Elke said, squinting through the bevelled glass of the door.

'Yes, it is.' Marigold's eyes widened as she spotted the ballerina lingering in the doorway. She was wearing a silk dressing gown and a matching turban.

'What is he doing in her compartment?' Elke whispered.

'I don't think he's there to make a delivery,' Marigold said, arching an eyebrow. She put Pepper on the ground. 'Well, well, well. First the train director and now his deputy. I wonder what Vivienne's connection is to each of them?'

Elke tapped her chin. 'It is interesting that the two people who were last seen having violent encounters with Mr Olivier should now turn out to be acquainted.'

Marigold pushed the vestibule door open, and they walked in silence through the first-class carriage.

'Perhaps Mr Olivier's fight with Mr Jorrisen was about Vivienne?'

'Maybe he discovered Mr Jorrisen was involved with her,' Elke said as they entered the suite.

'It could be, but Vivienne was furious with Mr Olivier last night. He must have done something. She wouldn't have been that angry at simply being discovered.'

Elke walked to the window and opened it a few inches. Cool air rushed inside, along with the faint odour of burnt rubber. 'People have killed for less.'

Marigold glanced at her curiously. 'How do you know?'

Elke held up her book. 'You only have to read Lady Clues to know a motive for murder can grow from the smallest insult.'

'The only way to know for sure would be to talk to Vivienne, and I don't think she would be open to that.'

Elke tapped her fingers on the cover of her book. 'That is true, but perhaps she can be persuaded if she thinks you know something she does not.'

Marigold stared at her. 'What are you proposing?'

Elke smiled. 'Let me fill you in on the plan.'

CHAPTER SIXTEEN

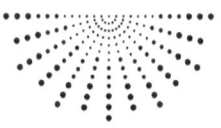

The next morning, Marigold and Elke arrived in the south dining car just after eleven o'clock. The sun had broken through the clouds. Rays of weak winter sunlight streamed through the carriage windows, making the glassware on the tables shine. Tiny particles of dust floated around them in the air.

The carriage smelt of wood polish and candle wax. There was a low murmur of voices coming from the kitchen, the sound of vegetables being chopped, and the clink and clang of pots and pans as lunch was prepared.

The decor was almost identical to the north dining car, but instead of crimson, the walls and carpet were midnight blue. The south dining car remained closed until further notice.

As Marigold and Elke walked the corridors, they'd heard whispers and seen the concerned faces of their fellow passengers. Compartment doors that only the day before had been kept open to view the passing scenery and parade of guests in their finery were now closed. People no longer lingered in the corridors but walked swiftly to their compartments with their heads bowed.

Mr Olivier's murder had sent fear through the train. Until more was known about what had happened to him and his killer was caught, people were being cautious.

It remained to be seen if Vivienne would be one of them.

'She's never going to fall for this.' Marigold drummed her fingernails on the polished tabletop.

Elke smirked. 'I think you will be surprised. Your note was very convincing.'

'My note?'

Elke nodded emphatically. 'Yes. I thought Miss Cosette was more likely to respond to you than me. After all, we have not been introduced.'

'I suspect the opposite is true. Vivienne is not at all fond of me—especially after I ruined her shoes.'

'I believe your note was persuasive enough to overcome that obstacle.'

Marigold frowned and lay her hands flat on the table. 'What did it say?'

'I said you had information about Mr Olivier and it would be in her best interests to meet with you,' Elke said, looking pleased with herself.

'And you think it will work?'

'I know it will, because here she is.' Elke inclined her head towards the entrance of the carriage.

Marigold stole a glance over her shoulder and watched Vivienne and Aline speaking to the waiter.

As usual, the sisters were at the opposite end of the fashion spectrum.

Vivienne was wearing a black silk blouse, wide-legged trousers, and a beret. Over this sombre ensemble, she wore a long, black satin coat with floral embroidery on the lapels.

She looked like a model in a Paris fashion boutique. Marigold assumed this was her version of a mourning outfit.

Aline was also wearing black, but where it highlighted and complimented her sister's beauty, it drained her face of the little colour she'd had in the first place.

Elke gave Marigold a triumphant smile. 'Raise your hand so they see you.'

'We're difficult to miss given we're the only ones in the dining car and from the expression on Vivienne's face, there's no chance she hasn't seen me.'

However, feeling slightly foolish, she lifted her hand and waved.

Aline acknowledged her with a nod and said something to her sister. Vivienne rolled her eyes, and for a moment Marigold feared she was going to turn on her heel and leave.

Something Aline said must have made an impact, because a few moments later Vivienne lifted her chin and made her way down the aisle to Marigold and Elke's table.

'I told you she would not be able to resist,' Elke said through her teeth.

Marigold forced a smile. 'Good afternoon, Vivienne, Aline. How nice of you to join us.'

Vivienne's beautiful face twisted into an ugly scowl. 'I don't know what game you're playing, Lady Marigold, but I'm here, as you requested. Please don't waste my time. Enlighten me as to this information you claim you have to share.'

A rush of insults filled Marigold's mouth, but she bit them back. It wouldn't do to lose her temper, but it didn't mean she couldn't enjoy Vivienne squirming a little.

'I don't know about you, but I missed breakfast and I'm famished.' She picked up a menu and pretended to read through it.

'Are you ready to order ladies?' the waiter said. He was a short, stout Frenchman with a thin moustache. He stood at the end of the table with his pencil poised over his notepad.

'Just tea,' Vivienne snapped, pushing her menu away.

'No wonder she's so bad tempered. Some food would help her mood,' Elke said in a low voice from behind the menu.

Marigold nodded and smiled at the waiter. 'May I have coffee and a pastry?'

'I'll have the same,' Aline said, earning herself an elbow in the ribs from Vivienne.

'As will I.' Elke collected the menus and handed them to the waiter.

Once he had departed, Vivienne got straight to the point. 'What do you know about Mr Olivier's death, and how does it concern me?'

Marigold widened her eyes. 'Goodness. Surely, we can have some polite conversation before we start discussing the distressing news about Mr Olivier.'

Vivienne clenched her jaw, and Marigold decided not to push her luck.

'I don't know if you're aware, but I had the misfortune to discover Mr Olivier's body.'

'How dreadful,' Vivienne said, not sounding the least bit sympathetic.

'It certainly wasn't pleasant.'

Vivienne examined her gloves and smoothed out an imaginary crease. 'I'm not seeing what this has to do with me.'

Marigold leaned forward. 'Has Inspector Loxley questioned you yet?'

Vivienne shifted in her seat. 'That's none of your concern.'

'I'm sure you think so, but I've always loved solving puzzles, and I think there's a big one here.'

Vivienne rolled her eyes. 'Oh, I see. You're playing detective, are you? Who do you think you are, Lady Clues?'

Elke sat up straighter and scowled at the ballerina's mocking tone.

Marigold couldn't hide her surprise. 'You read Lady Clues?'

Vivienne scowled. 'Of course not. I read literature, not newspaper fodder.'

'You could learn a lot from Lady Clues,' Elke muttered.

'I doubt it,' Vivienne said, her lip curling.

Marigold decided it was time to steer the conversation in a different direction.

'My question for you, Miss Cosette, is about whether you and Mr Olivier were involved with one another?'

Vivienne bit her bottom lip. 'What's it to you if it were the case?'

'It wouldn't surprise me, but after your performance the other night, I wonder if the two of you had a falling out large enough to motivate you to kill him?'

'That's ridiculous. Vivienne didn't kill Mr Olivier,' Aline spluttered, her cheeks flushing.

Vivienne slapped the table and the crockery rattled. 'What's the point of this? You said in your note you had information about Mr Olivier's death involving me. What is it?'

Marigold rested her elbows on the table. 'My information relates not to Mr Olivier, but to his deputy.'

Vivienne's face remained mostly impassive, except for a slight twitch in the corner of her left eye. 'Jorrisen?'

Marigold nodded. 'Yes. I saw him leaving your compartment yesterday.'

Aline's jaw dropped. 'You must have been mistaken.' She looked to her sister for confirmation, but Vivienne ignored her and instead leaned further across the table towards Marigold. She lowered her voice, and her eyes were steel daggers.

'He called on me to check on my welfare. You would do well not to read anything more into it than that—or to gossip about me.'

Marigold sat back in her seat and folded her hands in her lap. 'I don't gossip, but I can't help but think you're not being entirely honest.'

'Why would I lie?' Vivienne tugged off the glove on her right hand and began to twist the gold and sapphire ring on her index finger.

Aline mimicked the motion, although her fingers were bare.

Marigold was tempted to point out Vivienne had a reputation for deception—but she suspected it would see a rapid conclusion to the conversation—and she still had questions to ask.

'Mrs Olivier told us her husband was being threatened, blackmailed even. Perhaps you and Mr Jorrisen know something about that?'

Vivienne gave a bitter laugh. 'Unity would say anything to implicate me. The woman is delusional and pathetic. Rueben didn't share anything with her, including a bed. If he was being blackmailed, she would be the last person to know about it.'

Elke drummed her fingers on the table. 'You do not believe he was being blackmailed?'

Vivienne sighed loudly. 'I'm annoyed at being lured here under false pretences.'

'So, you do believe it?'

Vivienne peered down her nose at Elke. Her expression was sour. 'Who are you?'

Before Elke could respond, the waiter arrived with a trolley laden with tea and delicate cakes. Once he had laid the table, he bowed and departed.

Marigold inhaled the delicious aroma of coffee and forced herself to smile at Vivienne.

'My apologies. How rude of me not to have introduced my assistant, Miss Elke Müller.'

Vivienne wrinkled her nose as she watched Elke slather jam on a scone. She turned to Marigold. 'You have a German assistant?'

Marigold popped a tiny macaroon in her mouth, enjoying the explosion of sweetness on her tongue. She leaned towards Vivienne; her eyes narrowed. 'You're correct on both points. Elke is my assistant, and she's German.'

Vivienne pulled her gloves back on. 'Whatever do you need an assistant for?'

'Miss Müller is my friend as well as my assistant. She's the cleverest woman I know. I'm lucky she chooses to work with me.'

Vivienne snorted. 'But what do you do? You're a lady of leisure, are you not?'

'Far from it. I have many things to keep me busy.' Marigold kept her tone light, not wanting to encourage Vivienne's interest in her. It was time to refocus the conversation and take back control. 'Are you sure there is nothing you want to confess, Miss Cosette?'

Vivienne's teacup clattered as she dropped it onto the saucer. 'Confess?'

'Yes. In relation to Mr Olivier's death.'

Elke nodded. 'A guilty conscience can weigh you down.'

'How dare you accuse me.' Vivienne pushed her chair back from the table and got to her feet. 'I can't believe I wasted my time on this. From now on, stay away from me. Both of you.'

'That should not be a problem,' Elke called as Vivienne stormed out of the dining car.

Aline glanced regretfully at her unfinished plate of pastries. 'She really is quite upset about Mr Olivier. It's unkind of you to speak to her this way.' She turned on her heel and hurried after her sister.

Marigold selected another macaroon from the pastry stand in the middle of the table. 'Well, that went about as well as I expected.'

Elke sipped her coffee. 'It was very enlightening though.'

Marigold watched the sisters leave the dining car. 'I'm guessing Vivienne hasn't paid a condolence call on Unity.'

'I wonder if Vivienne and Unity will confirm each other's alibi?' Elke mused.

Marigold stirred a lump of sugar into her coffee. 'I imagine they will have to.'

Elke pointed over her head. 'Here comes someone who may know the answer.'

CHAPTER SEVENTEEN

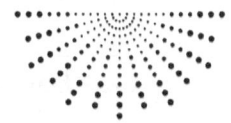

Inspector Loxley walked through the dining car, his eyes scanning the carriage.

'Ah, Lady Marigold, just the person I was looking for.'

She raised her eyebrows. He sounded unusually upbeat. 'Why? Do you have some new crime to accuse me of?'

Loxley checked his pocket watch, which was pinned inside his coat.

'Not unless you're ready to confess to one. I do, however, require your help.'

Marigold narrowed her eyes. 'My help with what, exactly?'

He put his hand in the pockets of his trousers. 'I need to ask Mr Jorrisen a few questions about his argument with Mr Olivier in the corridor. As the only witness to that incident, I would like you to be present to confirm his story.'

She put her elbows on the table and rested her chin in her hand. 'Really? It's almost as though you value my opinion.'

His left cheek twitched. 'Let's not get ahead of ourselves.'

Not wanting to appear too enthusiastic at the prospect of learning more about Mr Jorrisen's relationship with Mr Olivier, she paused and pretended to consider his request.

Elke kicked her foot under the table, and she sighed. 'I suppose I have no choice but to co-operate.'

'You may decline. Lady Haig speaks highly of you and insists you aren't likely to want to become involved. However, the evidence so far suggests the opposite.'

Marigold glanced at him. Was he making a joke? She couldn't read his expression or his tone. She decided to let it slide. 'When are you talking to Mr Jorrisen?'

'As soon as you have finished your coffee. Please meet me in Mr Olivier's office and don't talk to anyone in the meantime.'

She resisted the temptation to roll her eyes. 'I assume you don't mean Miss Müller?'

Loxley sighed. 'Just make sure she's the only person you talk to between now and then.'

He turned on his heel and departed.

'At least he let you finish your coffee,' Elke said, as the waiter appeared at their table with another plate of cakes.

Marigold inhaled the aroma of sugar and chocolate. 'I'm afraid Miss Cosette had to leave, and we can't eat all of these. I'd hate for such lovely cakes to go to waste. Perhaps you could have the remainder sent to her compartment?'

The waiter nodded. 'Certainly, mademoiselle. I'll arrange it.'

Marigold smiled. 'Merci, and please give our compliments to Chef Dubois.'

The waiter bowed. 'I'll pass on your kind words.'

Elke watched him go with a curious expression on her face.

'What is it?' Marigold said as she cut the side of a tiny chocolate cake with her fork.

Elke furrowed her brow. 'Inspector Loxley must not consider Chef Dubois a suspect if the man is still cooking lunch.'

'I hadn't thought of that. I'll see what I can learn when I go with him to question Mr Jorrisen.'

'Are you sure it's a good idea to accompany him?'

'You have reservations?'

Elke took a sip of water. 'Why would he ask you to go with him while he questioned Mr Jorrisen?'

'You don't think he was being honest when he said it was because I'm the only witness to the fight in the corridor? What other reason would he have?'

Elke drummed her fingers on the tabletop. 'I am not sure, but I think you should be careful. After all, the Inspector has not ruled you out as a suspect.'

'You think he's trying to trap me in some way?' Marigold lowered her fork. Despite the delicious cakes, suddenly she had no appetite.

'I just think you should be on your guard. I can think of no circumstance where a police officer has asked Lady Clues to participate in questioning a suspect.'

Marigold smiled. 'Much as we love our dear Lady Clues, we can't be guided by everything she writes. But you're right, now I think of it. It does seem odd.'

In truth, Marigold was annoyed she had taken Loxley's request at face value. Of course, the man had another motive for asking for her help. She should have known better. Thank goodness she had Elke watching out for her.

She frowned. 'I'll be careful, but it's a good opportunity to see what Mr Jorrisen has to say for himself about the fight with Mr Olivier.'

'And to learn what the plan was they were arguing about,' Elke said as she finished her scone.

Marigold nodded. 'Yes, I'd forgotten about that.' She dropped her napkin onto her plate. 'I think I'll go now. The sooner I find out what's going on, the better.'

She got to her feet, straightened her skirt, and tucked in her blouse

'Good luck,' Elke said.

'Let's hope I don't need it.'

As Marigold left the dining car, she saw Hermione sitting by a window writing a letter. She made a mental note to catch up on her own correspondence before the train reached Paris.

~

LOXLEY PAUSED outside Mr Jorrisen's compartment. 'Remember, you're here as an observer only. I'll ask the questions.'

Marigold rolled her eyes. 'What if he says something untrue or that differs from my recollection of the events?'

'Should it occur, make a note of it and tell me later.'

She opened her mouth to protest, but Loxley held up a hand. 'It's non-negotiable.'

She sighed loudly. 'Very well.'

In truth, she had no intention of keeping quiet if Mr Jorrisen gave her a reason to question something, but she decided to keep that to herself.

Loxley knocked on the door and after a few seconds, an unshaven, dishevelled Mr Jorrisen appeared. He frowned as he took in first Loxley and then Marigold.

'Inspector, you've caught me at a bad time.'

Loxley held his ground. 'We'll wait while you wash.'

Mr Jorrisen scowled and closed the compartment door. After a few minutes, he returned, his hair slicked back, smelling of pine cologne and wearing a clean shirt. 'Has something else happened?'

'No, I'm here to ask you some additional questions. I asked Lady Marigold to accompany me as she witnessed an argument you had with Mr Olivier in the vestibule between the first-class carriage and the lounge car the day before he died. An argument you failed to mention when we spoke yesterday.'

Mr Jorrisen's face screwed up like he'd swallowed a lemon. 'I didn't hide it deliberately. I simply forgot about it.' Turning to Marigold, he said, 'I didn't realise you had overheard us. My apologies.'

His words didn't match his tone—surly, with a hint of sarcasm, but she decided to play along.

'There's nothing to apologise for. I chose not to reveal myself to avoid embarrassment.'

Mr Jorrisen nodded and ran a hand over his chin. He turned to Loxley. 'Could we have this discussion in the lounge car? It should be empty at this hour, and I'm afraid my compartment isn't fit for company.'

Loxley nodded, and a few minutes later, they were sitting at an empty table.

'I imagine the loss of Mr Olivier has put a great burden on you,' Loxley said, shaking his head as a conductor enquired if they required anything.

Mr Jorrisen kept his head down. 'It has, but under the circumstances, I need to do my duty.'

Loxley took out his notebook. 'I'm sure your employer will be impressed by your efforts. Perhaps you'll be promoted.'

'It doesn't seem appropriate to be discussing this with Mr Olivier's body still onboard,' Mr Jorrisen said stiffly.

Loxley raised his eyebrows. 'And yet you had time when Mr Olivier was alive.'

'The argument Lady Marigold witnessed wasn't what you think.'

'Feel free to provide an explanation," Loxley said.

'It was a disagreement between colleagues. It happens. Surely you have disagreed with your peers, Inspector?'

'Yes, but unlike you, one of them has never been found dead shortly afterwards.' Loxley's words hung in the air.

Mr Jorrisen slumped in his seat. 'I didn't kill Olivier,' he whispered.

Marigold leaned towards him. 'Did he ever ask you for money?'

Loxley frowned at her. 'Lady Marigold, you're not here to ask questions.'

'My apologies, Inspector, but I understand Mr Olivier sought loans from several people on this train. I merely wondered if Mr Jorrisen was one of them.'

'He did owe me money, as a matter of fact, but you're right, I've since learned I wasn't alone in that.'

Marigold nodded. 'But that isn't what you were fighting about, was it? He was angry you hadn't followed the plan.'

Loxley slapped the table. 'Lady Marigold, if you don't stop asking questions, there will be consequences.'

Marigold rolled her eyes. 'You did bring me along, Inspector. I don't know what you expected to happen. I can't just sit here and say nothing.'

He glared at her. 'It will be in your best interests to try.'

She caught Jorrisen's eye, but he didn't engage.

Loxley cleared his throat and scowled at her before he returned his attention to Mr Jorrisen. 'As Lady Marigold has said, she overheard you fighting about a plan. What was it?'

'The plan was nothing of consequence,' Mr Jorrisen said, then, after a moment of silence, he muttered, 'It was to do with Mr Olivier's mistress.'

'Miss Cosette?' She earned herself another glare from Loxley.

Mr Jorrisen nodded. 'Yes, I don't suppose it's a secret the way they were carrying on in front of his wife.'

Loxley made a note in his book. 'And you disagreed with this behaviour?'

'Of course.'

Loxley tilted his head to one side and stared at Mr Jorrisen. 'Because?'

He scowled. 'I would have thought it was obvious.'

'Very well. Thank you, Mr Jorrisen. That will be all.' Loxley stood to leave and reluctantly, Marigold followed. Once they reached the corridor she said, 'I thought you were going to actually question him.'

Loxley turned to her, his face a stony mask. 'Lady Marigold, are you the detective on this case?'

'Not technically, but my assistant and I are doing quite a good job of unravelling it. We could help you a lot, you know.'

Loxley glowered at her. 'You and Miss Müller are skating on very thin ice. Stay out of my investigation or you'll both suffer the consequences.'

'Your problem is there are far too many suspects. You need to rule some of them out so you can focus on finding the actual killer. I suggest you start by exonerating me and Elke—and Miss Seydoux. I'm convinced she's innocent.'

'And what's this expert opinion based on? Your espionage efforts in the war or the illegal protest activity you've been involved in since then?'

Marigold stared at him; momentarily thrown he'd found out so much about her so soon. 'I recommend you read Lady Clues, Inspector. I would be happy to loan you a copy.'

'Lady who?'

'Lady Clues. She's London's most famous lady detective and writes the most entertaining accounts of her cases.'

'As I have told you before, I don't need to read fictional work. I work in the real world, and I assure you, I'm more than capable of solving this crime. However, if you don't cease your interference, you will find yourself under arrest. Do you understand?'

'Absolutely, but I fear you'll be sorry you didn't accept my offer of help.'

'I guarantee you the opposite will be the case,' Loxley said.

CHAPTER EIGHTEEN

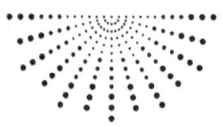

The Lunar Express was quiet in the late afternoon, with most of the first-class guests keeping to their compartments. There had been an announcement after lunch to inform the passengers the train wasn't expected to continue its journey until at least the next day.

Frustrated by the ongoing delay, Marigold and Elke were among the few who chose to stretch their legs—which gave them a legitimate reason to be at the entrance to the second-class carriage.

Outside Elke's former compartment—now temporarily home to Renée—a middle-aged conductor was sitting on a wooden chair. Every few minutes his head would slowly drift towards his belly, then his startle reflex would kick in and he would jerk upright.

'This should be easy,' Elke said, as the conductor's head drooped once more. 'If we wait long enough, he'll actually fall asleep, and then you can walk right in to talk to Renée.'

Marigold shook her head. 'He's only dozing. If I try to enter the compartment, he's going to wake up. Plus, how am I going to get inside?'

Elke reached into her pocket and withdrew a key. 'I always make sure I have a spare.'

Marigold shook her head and took it from her. 'You never cease to amaze me with your ingenuity.'

Elke shrugged. 'It is just common sense to be prepared.'

'I suppose you're right. You never know when you'll have to give up your compartment for a murder suspect.'

Elke had her eyes fixed on the conductor. 'I'll have to create a distraction so you can speak with Renée.'

'That sounds like a plan, but how are you going to do it?'

Elke put her fingers to her lips. 'I will think of something.' She started forward, but Marigold grabbed hold of her arm.

'Wait. You can't go until you know what you're going to do.'

'Trust me. I'll think of something.'

Her stomach churned as Elke set off down the corridor.

This section of the train was decorated less lavishly than first-class. The carpet was grey and showed signs of wear. The sconces on the wall were plainer, and the windows lining the corridor were smaller.

Just as Elke approached her old compartment door, she hunched over and clutched at her stomach. Her cry of pain was so convincing Marigold found herself taking an involuntary step forward.

The conductor sat up so fast he banged his head against the wall.

'What is it, madam?'

Elke continued to hold her stomach and moan. 'Help me, please. I need the doctor.'

The conductor glanced up and down the corridor, his face stricken.

'I'll get the doctor for you. Please, sit here,' he said, pointing to his chair.

Elke grabbed his arm and leant against him as she continued to writhe in pain.

'No, do not leave me alone. Take me to him,' she groaned.

The conductor peered at her helplessly and then at the compartment door.

'Come quickly then.'

They set off down the corridor with the conductor half carrying Elke.

Once they were out of sight, Marigold hurried to the compartment and opened the door with Elke's key.

Renée was curled up on the banquette, her eyes red rimmed and swollen.

She sat up quickly, her mouth falling open as Marigold slipped into the compartment and put a finger to her lips.

'Lady Marigold, what are you doing here?' Renée whispered.

She sat on the edge of the banquette. 'I wanted to make sure you were alright.'

Renée's eyes filled with tears. 'That's kind of you, my lady. You and Miss Müller have done more than I deserve.'

Marigold patted her hand. 'Don't be silly, it's the least we can do.'

Renée sighed. 'I think I'm in a lot of trouble, my lady.' Her bottom lip wobbled.

'I'm sure you'll only be detained temporarily, Renée. Has Inspector Loxley spoken to you yet?'

Renée nodded, and tears slid down her

cheeks. 'He has. I told him everything I could remember, but I'm not sure he believes me.'

Marigold frowned. 'What did happen yesterday morning? How did you come to discover Mr Olivier's body?'

Renée took a few deep, shuddery breaths. 'I came to the kitchen for a cup of tea.'

Marigold frowned. 'So early?'

Renée nodded. 'I always wake at dawn, my lady. I need to make preparations for Mademoiselle Cosette's day. She likes to have a cup of tea with honey when she first wakes. If she doesn't get it, she's likely to be in a terrible temper all morning and sometimes for the entire day.'

'Goodness. I'm a bear until I have my coffee, but I hope I'm not that bad. Did anyone see you leave your compartment when you went to get Miss Cosette's tea?'

Renée shook her head. 'No, my lady, but I didn't spend the night in my compartment. I stayed in the maid's quarters of Mademoiselle Cosette's suite. She wasn't feeling well last night, so I stayed to make sure she was alright and didn't need anything.'

Marigold raised her eyebrows. 'What time did you leave her suite yesterday morning?'

'I'm not sure, my lady, but if I had to guess, I'd

say it was close to six o'clock. The sun was just rising.'

Marigold made a mental note to check the timing with Elke. 'And did you see anyone when you left the suite? The conductor?'

Renée shook her head. 'No, my lady, the conductor wasn't at his station. He had been ill all night too, the poor man.'

'He and Miss Cosette were unwell?'

Renée flushed. 'I don't think for the same reason, my lady. I think the conductor ate something that didn't agree with him. He was pale and clammy when he came to turn down the bed last night. I felt sorry for him. He had to stay up all night, but my sympathy was lessened by his retching in the bathroom.'

'You must be a light sleeper to have heard him through the compartment door.'

Renée nodded. 'Yes, my lady. Any hint of noise or movement wakes me.'

'What about Miss Cosette? Why was she unwell?'

Renée's eyes dropped to her hands. She paused for a few seconds. 'I don't wish to betray my mistress's confidence if I can help it, my lady.'

Marigold gave her a reassuring smile. 'I understand, but I want to help get you out of here as soon as possible, Renée, so if you're able to tell me, I promise to be discreet.'

Renée bit her lip. 'I'd rather not say, my lady. I appreciate your help, but it has nothing to do with Mr Olivier's murder.'

'If you say so.' Marigold resisted the urge to keep pressing, but her curiosity about what had ailed Vivienne was overwhelming.

'Thank you, my lady,' Renée said, dabbing at her eyes with her handkerchief.

Marigold inclined her head towards the door, checking for any sign of the conductor's return, but there was only silence from the corridor.

Elke must have been giving a performance and a half to have distracted him this long. She pressed on with her questions while her luck held out.

'What happened when you left the suite to get Miss Cosette her tea?'

Renée got to her feet and paced by the window.

'I realised the train had stopped, and I was curious about what had happened, but I saw no one while walking to the dining car.'

'Why didn't you ring for the tea to be brought to you?'

'I did, my lady, but the poor conductor didn't respond. He was in the bathroom.'

'I see.' Marigold's stomach churned at the thought. She gestured for Renée to continue.

'As I approached the dining car I heard footsteps, but when I arrived, I couldn't see anyone.'

Marigold sat up straighter. 'Footsteps? Did they sound heavy or light?'

Renée chewed her lip for a few seconds. 'I'm sorry, I can't remember.'

'There's nothing to apologise for. I was just curious.'

'Now that I think of it, I think it might have been a woman's footsteps. They were fast and I think there was a tap, like a heel.'

'But you didn't see anyone or notice anything?'

Renée frowned. 'What kind of things, my lady?'

'Perhaps the smell of perfume or the rustle of a skirt?'

'No, my lady, I'm afraid I can't recall anything else.' Renée's shoulders slumped.

'It's fine, Renée. Please, continue with what you saw.'

Renée took a deep breath and her eyes filled with tears.

'I walked into the dining car, and it was empty, but there was a light under the door to the kitchen car. I called out, but no one answered. Then I opened the door and...'

She burst into tears and buried her face in her hands.

Marigold jumped to her feet and put her arm around the girl's shoulders. 'I'm sorry to have upset you.'

'It's alright, my lady, I know you're just trying to help me. It was such a dreadful sight.'

An image of the crime scene flashed before Marigold's eyes. 'Yes, I remember.'

'I thought he might still be alive, so I knelt at his side to check his pulse, but there was none.' Renée shook her head sadly.

'And that's how you got his blood on you?'

Renée nodded and glanced at her hands. 'I didn't realise it at the time. I panicked; you see. I ran outside, but then I didn't know what to do. I tried calling for help, but my voice was barely louder than a squeak. It was like a horrible dream.'

Marigold repressed a shudder 'How dreadful.'

'Then you arrived, my lady. It was such a relief to have someone else there.'

'Renee, when I came out of the kitchen, Jean-Luc, the night conductor was trying to help you. Where did he come from?'

Renée bit her thumbnail. 'I'm not sure, my

lady. One minute he wasn't there and the next, he was.'

Marigold nodded. 'He must have been passing by and recognised you.'

A tear slid down Renée's cheek. 'I guess so, my lady. You don't think he had anything to do with Mr Olivier's death, do you?'

'I'm sure he didn't, but I'll talk to him to see if he can recall anything to help prove you're innocent.'

'Oh, thank you, my lady. I'm so afraid the Inspector thinks I'm guilty.'

Marigold frowned. 'I know you were found at the scene, Renée, but is there any reason Inspector Loxley would suspect you? Did you know Mr Olivier?'

'He visited Mademoiselle Cosette occasionally, and I had seen him on other times we travelled on the Lunar Express.'

'Did you speak with him?'

Renée bit her lip, but before she could say a word, someone pounded on the door.

'Time is up. We must go now,' Elke hissed.

Marigold squeezed Renée's hands. 'I'm sorry, I have to go, but I'll keep trying to clear your name and I'll come back soon if I can.'

'Thank you, my lady,' Renée said quietly as

Marigold hurried to the door. She flung it open and nearly collided with Elke.

'The Inspector is coming,' Elke said breathlessly.

Marigold glanced down the corridor. It was empty, but she could hear footsteps approaching. She met Elke's eyes.

'Run.'

CHAPTER NINETEEN

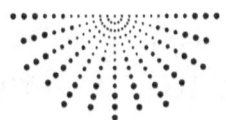

The last thing Marigold felt like was dinner in the dining car, but Elke had convinced her she might hear something to help Renée.

The train remained stuck on the tracks; the rescue team having been delayed by heavy snowfall. She'd spent the afternoon curled up by the window reading Lady Clues and watching as snow slowly covered the mountainside.

At seven o'clock she reluctantly changed into a dress with a red velvet bodice and pleated ivory satin skirt.

Thanks to Elke's hairdressing skills, her bob sat neatly around her chin and was offset by a jewelled headdress.

Marigold patted her hair. 'It seems wrong to

get dressed for dinner when a man lies dead on the train and his killer is among us.'

'Life goes on and the killer may reveal themselves in conversation. That's what Lady Clues always says. You must observe everyone closely tonight, my lady.'

Marigold frowned. 'I suspect you would be much better placed to attend this dinner than me.'

'Sadly, one of us must stay here with Pepper, he hates to be alone,' Elke said, patting the little dog on the head.

Marigold sighed and pulled on her gloves. I suppose I'd better get it over with then.

～

'LADY MARIGOLD, may I introduce a dear friend of mine, Madame de la Baume' Lady Haig said as Marigold took a seat at her table.

Madame de la Baume was a tall, thin woman with silver-streaked black hair, hooded eyes and thin lips painted with red lipstick.

Once they had exchanged pleasantries, her dark eyes narrowed as she examined Marigold's face. 'Why are you so pale?'

'Yes dear, are you feeling unwell?' Lady Haig said, reaching for Marigold's hand across the table. She was wearing a black lace dress and an enormous, feathered headpiece. Her emerald necklace was once again on display.

Marigold waited to reply as a waiter poured her a glass of champagne. She took a sip and smiled as the bubbles began to work their magic and relax the muscles in her neck.

'I didn't get much sleep last night, and it's been an eventful few days.'

Lady Haig nodded and lowered her voice. 'Yes, I heard you discovered Mr Olivier's body. How shocking.'

'Actually, it was Miss Cosette's maid, Renée, who found him,' Marigold said glancing around the dining car, but there was no sign of Vivienne.

'The poor girl, both for discovering the body and being Mademoiselle Cosette's maid. The poor girl can't put a foot right as far as she's concerned,' Madam de la Baume said with a sniff.

'Renée was very upset.' Marigold made a mental note to check in on the maid again after dinner.

'It's distressing all round. I can't wait to get off this train. I hope they can fix whatever the problem is soon. My nerves are frayed,' Lady Haig said, her voice breaking. She took a long sip of her cocktail and managed a shaky smile.

'Fear not, my dear, the Inspector seems to

have everything under control,' Madam de la Baume said, patting her forearm.

Lady Haig nodded. 'Loxley? Yes, we're lucky to have him.'

Marigold sipped her champagne. 'Unfortunately, he seems to think the worst of me. First, he accused me of being the jewel thief, and today he implied I had something to do with Mr Olivier's murder.'

Lady Haig gasped. 'But that's preposterous. Don't worry, my dear, I'll speak to him again and remind him who you are. He must treat you with more respect.'

'Thank you, but my ego will survive the insult.' Marigold hid a smile as she imagined Loxley's face as Lady Haig took him to task.

'I wish we'd never boarded this train. It seems to be full of criminals. We can't trust anyone,' Lady Haig said, glancing nervously over her shoulder.

Marigold frowned as Clara, Perry, and Osbert were seated at the table on the other side of the aisle.

Clara was wearing a lilac damask dress with silver tassels to her knees. Her blond hair was only just visible under her extravagant headpiece. It had a large splay of violet feathers secured with a burgundy velvet ribbon. A white fur wrap hung from her elbows. She looked every inch the glamorous film star.

Perry gave Marigold a flirtatious smile across the room, earning him an elbow in the ribs from his sister.

He ignored her and stood, almost colliding with Sir Fredrick who had just entered the dining car. 'Good evening, Sir Fredrick,' he said with a bow.

'Who are you?' Sir Fredrick shouted, glowering at Perry as he took a seat next to his wife.

Lady Haig spoke close to her husband's ear. 'It's Clara Bligh's brother, Peregrine. You must remember him, Freddie. He had quite a reputation in the village one summer before the war.'

Perry stood at the end of the table with his hands clasped behind his back. 'I hope my boyhood pranks won't be held against me, Lady Haig.'

She smiled and sipped her drink. 'I shall reserve judgement until I see what kind of young man you have grown to be.'

'Oh dear, I'd best be on my best behaviour then,' Perry said, giving Marigold a wink.

She rolled her eyes at him. 'Somehow I think your best behaviour might be the upper end of dreadful.'

Perry clutched at his heart. 'You must be kind to my poor heart, Lady Marigold.'

'I don't think your heart is what you should be concerned about young man. The look your sister is giving you is likely to kill you within minutes,' Madam de la Baume said, pointing across the aisle with a long, bony finger.

Lady Haig frowned. 'My goodness, she could at least try to hide the fact she doesn't like you, Lady Marigold.'

Marigold shrugged. 'I'm afraid there's a long-running feud between dating back to our school days.'

'With all Miss Bligh has achieved, you'd think she could put a childhood grudge to bed by now.'

Marigold sipped her drink and tried not to be offended when Lady Haig didn't refer to her accomplishments. But then again, had she known what she'd gotten up to during the war, perhaps she wouldn't be sitting here talking to her now.

'The two of you will have to settle your difference now you're neighbours,' Lady Haig said.

Marigold choked on her drink. 'We're what?'

Lady Haig frowned. 'But surely you know? It was all over the newspapers. Clara bought Ashcroft Abbey last year.'

Marigold's head suddenly felt full of fog. She turned towards the sound of Perry's voice. 'I for one am thrilled at this news. It means I'll get to see more of you Lady Marigold.'

She forced her mouth to form a smile. 'Wonderful,' she said, making a mental note to interrogate Bentley later.

'Terrible business on this train, isn't it?' Perry said, signalling to an attendant for a drink. 'Still, a murder will be quite a tale to entertain the boys at the club.'

'A man's death should not be fodder for gossip,' Sir Fredrick grunted.

Perry nodded. 'Of course, sir, I meant no disrespect, but I have to admit, I'm intrigued by what happened.'

'Let's talk about something more cheerful. This must be most distressing for Lady Marigold, given she discovered the poor man's body.'

Perry's eyes widened. 'Did you really?'

Marigold nodded. 'I was one of the first people on the scene.'

'Then please accept my apologies. It was crass of me to bring it up. I had no idea.'

She waved her hand. 'It's fine. Don't worry about it.'

Perry glanced around the room. 'Still, it's an odd feeling knowing there's a killer amongst us, isn't it?'

'Young man, you have a lesson to learn about discretion,' Sir Fredrick growled.

Lady Haig put a hand on her husband's shoulder. 'If you scold Peregrine, Freddie, you must do the same to me. I was just saying something similar. It's only human nature to be curious under the circumstances.'

'Did you know the man? Olivier?' Perry asked Marigold.

She sipped her drink to buy time before answering. Something in his tone put her on her guard.

'Not really. He was an acquaintance of my uncle, but we'd never met before I boarded the train.'

Perry nodded. 'And I heard someone stabbed him. What a terrible way to go.'

It appeared Lady Haig's indulgence of his youth, and her patience, had run thin. 'I must insist we change the subject. This must be distressing for Lady Marigold.'

'Thank you for your concern, Lady Haig, but I'm more curious than distressed by Mr Bligh's questions.'

Perry frowned at her. 'Curious?'

'Yes. I'm wondering why you're so interested in Mr Olivier's murder. Sometimes a killer likes to find out what other people know about their crime to make sure they aren't close to being caught.'

Perry stared at her for a moment, his face an impassive mask. Then he threw back his head and roared with laughter.

'I hardly think it's funny,' Madame de la Baume said with a frosty look.

Perry bowed to her. 'My apologies Madame, but I was just imagining my sister's face if I turned out to be the killer. I think she'd finish me off before I made it to the gallows.'

'Yes, I imagine she would,' Marigold said the corners of her mouth twitching.

Perry took a swig of his drink. 'Where did you come up with such a wild theory?'

Marigold shrugged. 'I have an interest in crime and I read a lot.'

Madame de la Baume's eyes lit up. 'Do you read Lady Clues, my dear?'

'I do indeed. She's a firm favourite of both me and my assistant.'

Perry rubbed his chin. 'Who is this Lady Clues?'.

'I'll send you a copy of one of her books, Mr Bligh. If you need stories for your club, you will find plenty in a volume of Lady Clues' cases,' Marigold teased.

Perry frowned. 'I'm afraid I'm not really one for books.'

Marigold rolled her eyes. 'Somehow, I'm not surprised.'

'Dancing is more my thing. What a shame we're not on a ship. At least you can have a bit of fun on one of them. This train is very dull—excluding recent unfortunate events, of course.'

A conductor approached the table and Perry excused himself.

'Lady Marigold, I have a message for you.'

She raised her eyebrows. 'Really? From whom?'

'From Inspector Loxley. He would like to speak with you as soon as possible'

Marigold frowned. Not again. What on earth could the insufferable man have left to ask her?

She turned to the Haigs and Madame de la Baume who weren't bothering to hide their curiosity.

'I can't imagine what Loxley needs to talk to you about at this late hour,' Lady Haig fretted.

'I'm sure it's just a few final details from the crime scene.' Marigold wished she felt as confident as she sounded.

'Tell Loxley I would like a word when he's finished talking to you,' Lady Haig said as Marigold prepared to take her leave.

She nodded, and her spirits rose slightly as she imagined Lady Haig giving Loxley a dressing down.

Mr Olivier's office door was open, and Loxley was standing by the window when she arrived. He turned at her knock and waved her inside.

'What can I do for you, Inspector?'

Loxley gestured for her to sit. He remained standing with his hands laced behind his back.

'As you're aware, I have been making further enquiries about a number of guests on the train, including you.'

'I imagine my dossier is rather interesting, or at least, I hope it is.'

'I admit it had some surprising information. You failed to mention you transferred Mr Olivier ten thousand pounds last month.'

Marigold's stomach dropped. 'I did what?'

'I think you heard me.'

'I did and you're mistaken.'

Loxley walked to the desk and held up a slip of paper. 'A letter was found among Mr Olivier's belongings confirming a bank transfer to him in your name.'

She swallowed hard. 'There has been a mistake, because I can assure you, I've never given anyone ten thousand pounds, and most definitely not Mr. Olivier.'

Loxley raised his eyebrows. 'It's difficult to argue with a bank record.'

'Someone must have given him the money in my name. You can check my accounts. There will be no such withdrawal.'

'Rest assured, I'll be checking, and if this transaction is confirmed, you will have some explaining to do.'

CHAPTER TWENTY

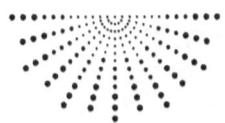

Marigold walked back to her suite in a daze. She couldn't fathom why someone would have deposited ten thousand pounds in Mr Olivier's bank account in her name. It had to have been a mistake, but how?

Lost in thought, she didn't see Hermione Carey until she collided with her.

Both women ended up on the floor, and Hermione's evening bag went flying. Marigold, who had the advantage of a burst of guilt fuelled adrenaline, bounced back to her feet first.

'Oh, Hermione, I'm so sorry. I didn't see you,' she cried as she helped the younger woman to stand. 'Are you hurt?'

Hermione's hand flew to her head, but her

black silk turban was still in place, as was her green silk evening gown. Marigold marvelled at the young woman's ability to remain presentable in any situation.

In contrast, Marigold had to tug her own dress up to maintain modesty and her headpiece lay across the floor on top of the contents of Hermione's evening bag.

'I'm uninjured, thank you, and the fault is half mine. I was lost in thought.' Hermione said bending to retrieve her bag from the floor.

Marigold dropped to her knees and picked up a newspaper clipping, a bundle of letters and a photograph with 'Dickie' written on the back.

Hermione crouched beside her and picked up a small glass vial with a cork on the top. In response to Marigold's questioning look she said, 'It's a sleeping draught. I got it in Istanbul. I have such terrible insomnia.'

'Me too. I'm jealous you have it.'

Hermione turned the vial over in her fingers. Her green eyes met Marigold's. 'You can have it if you'd like it.'

Marigold shook her head. 'Oh no. I couldn't, possibly.'

Hermione pushed it into her hand. 'I insist. My friend can bring another vial when she visits me next month.'

Marigold squeezed the little glass bottle. 'Only if you're sure?'

Hermione forced a smile. 'Yes. Please don't worry. I've misplaced my shawl and was on my way back to the dining car to retrieve it.'

'Would you like me to accompany you?'

Hermione shook her head. 'Oh no, there's no need. I'll just run in and get it.'

Marigold was about to bid her farewell when a glint of something shiny caught her eye. She bent and picked up a delicate gold ring with a square cut ruby.

'My ring,' Hermione said, snatching it out of her hand.

Marigold raised her eyebrows at the unexpected sharpness in her tone, and Hermione flushed.

'Oh dear, forgive me, dear Marigold. That was dreadfully rude of me, but I panicked. I didn't know my ring had come off my finger.'

'I can't blame you. It's a lovely ring.'

'It has a lot of sentimental value and I'm so scared I'll lose it with this jewel thief on board,' Hermione said, her cheeks still pink.

'I understand, and I won't delay you any longer.'

Hermione nodded and pointed to the glass vial in Marigold's hand. 'There's only enough there for one night. You'll need to drink it all to get the best effect'

Marigold slipped the vial into her evening bag. 'I'll do that. Good night.'

~

BENTLEY AND ELKE were playing cards when she walked into the suite.

They were sitting opposite each other, with Pepper watching from the floor like an umpire in a tennis match.

Marigold wouldn't have dared to say it out loud, but she couldn't help noticing how well they complemented each other. Bentley was wearing his usual brown, three-piece wool suit with a starched shirt and black tie. Elke wore a camel-coloured wool dress and brown, lace-up Oxford shoes.

Marigold sank to the floor next to Pepper and stroked his soft topknot. 'I'm glad you two are having a pleasant evening.'

Elke shot her a quizzical look. 'You did not?'

She snorted. 'Far from it. Something odd is going on. It's almost as though someone is trying to make me appear guilty of Mr Olivier's murder.'

Bentley glanced at her over his hand of cards. 'They what?'

She leaned over to view his cards. He had a full house. She felt a small flicker of pity for Elke. There was no one on earth with a better poker face than Bentley.

'Inspector Loxley seems determined to haul me off to Scotland Yard or the French police as soon as the train pulls into the station.'

Bentley frowned. 'It does seem strange, my lady. Why do you believe he holds such a negative view of you?'

'Given her title, wealth and their previous encounter in the police station in Istanbul, it is logical he would be suspicious of her,' Elke said, laying down a card as though it were a bomb.

'Why is it logical? I would say it's the opposite. It's completely irrational to suspect me of either crime.'

Bentley considered his cards for a moment, then looked up at her. 'I suppose a detective's mind works in different ways, my lady. He must consider all possibilities. We must try not to take it personally.'

'That's impossible, but Loxley's impression of me is the least of my problems. He claims I transferred Mr Olivier ten thousand pounds. Have you ever heard anything so preposterous?'

Bentley's poker face flickered. He put his

cards face down on the table and cleared his throat. 'Did you say ten thousand pounds?'

'Yes. Why? Do you know something about this, Bentley?'

He frowned. 'Not about you providing the funds, my lady, as I'm sure you didn't, but a few weeks before he died your uncle instructed me to make a bank transfer.'

Elke's eyes widened. 'Of the same amount?'

Bentley nodded, and Marigold's anxiety rose. 'Was the transfer to Mr Olivier?'

'I don't know, my lady. The name of the account was a business, not a person. It was unfamiliar to me.'

Elke re-organised her cards. 'It could be a coincidence.'

'Perhaps, but it seems a big one. I wonder who it was and what the connection was between Mr Olivier and my uncle.'

Bentley shifted in his seat. 'Your uncle never spoke of him to me, but Mr Olivier was a guest at Mayfair on at least two occasions I can recall. I'll make enquiries to see what I can learn about his business dealings, my lady.'

She frowned. 'How Bentley? On the train?'

'Much like the network of servants, my lady, conductors are a wealth of information—if you know how to ask in the right way.'

She nodded. 'Thank you, I would appreciate your help.'

'Mrs Olivier, Vivienne or Aline may have information,' Elke said.

Marigold chewed her lip. 'I agree and I'll try to speak with Unity again, but unfortunately, we may have burned our bridges with Vivienne.'

Elke slapped her cards on the table. 'Then we will talk to Aline.'

Bentley's face finally showed a hint of emotion. His eyes scanned the royal flush.

'You're a formidable opponent.' He shook his head and gave her a wry smile.

Elke gave a nonchalant shrug. 'I play to win.'

Marigold gazed out the window. There was a storm in the distance, and the sky was flickering with light. She got to her feet and paced around the suite.

'Perhaps Aline is worth talking to. She was quite personable when I spoke to her outside the train.'

'She's in compartment nine,' Elke said as she shuffled the deck of cards.

Marigold frowned. 'How did you find out Aline's compartment number?'

Elke held up a familiar book.

'Lady Clues advises the first step of investigation is to identify all suspects. I have drawn up a list, and while Aline is not a likely suspect, she may provide information about her sister—who I believe is the most likely person to have killed Mr Olivier.'

Marigold took the book and turned it over in her hands. 'I must read this one. It seems I'm going to need all the help I can get if I'm going to get off this train as a free woman.'

Bentley cleared his throat. 'Once again, my lady, I must raise my concerns about your involvement in any private investigation into Mr Olivier's murder.'

She gave him an apologetic smile. 'I know you have my best interests at heart, Bentley, but I'm afraid I can't sit here and do nothing while there is a killer on the loose.'

'Forgive me, but isn't it Inspector Loxley's job to find the killer?'

Marigold nodded. 'It is, but in this instance, I feel I need to act in my own self-interest—and in Renée's interest. I'm convinced she was just in the wrong place at the wrong time.'

'I'll do whatever I can to help you, my lady, but my concern for your welfare remains.'

'Thank you, Bentley. I know you're always in my corner, and it means the world to me. I promise not to do anything rash or dangerous.'

The crease between Bentley's eyes deepened.

'I hope so, my lady. That will make a pleasant change.'

Despite herself, she laughed. 'I forget you know me so well.'

'I do, but I'm used to seeing you in less serious situations. Being a suspect in a murder case is uncharted waters.'

'At least she's not the only suspect,' Elke said. She took a folded sheet of paper from her inside pocket and handed it to Marigold, who scanned the list of names, then handed it to Bentley.

His eyes widened as he read the list Elke had prepared 'There seem to be rather a lot of people on this train who might have wanted Mr Olivier dead —Unity Olivier, Vivienne Cosette, Renée Seydoux, Mr Jorrisen, Chef Dubois and...' He frowned at Elke. 'Lady Marigold.'

'Why am I on the list?' Marigold said, her voice full of reproach.

Elke shrugged. 'Just because you're on it, does not mean I think you committed the crime. I am merely thinking like Inspector Loxley.'

'Please don't,' Marigold said with a shudder.

'Chef Dubois was also a reluctant addition to the list,' Elke said sadly.

Marigold nodded. 'I suppose he must be a suspect. Mr Olivier belittled him in front of the guests the first night on the train and the kitchen was the scene of the crime.'

'And through his network, Chef Dubois could have had access to a supplier of the arsenic and slipped it into Mr Olivier's food or drink,' Elke said, folding the list of suspects and putting it back in her pocket.

Marigold looked at her dubiously. 'So he poisoned him, then stabbed him with the ice pick to cover up the actual cause of death?' Speaking Chef Dubois' motive out loud made it seem unlikely, but Elke didn't seem to share her view.

'Then he could point the finger of blame at someone else. A classic misdirection strategy.'

'Chef Dubois seemed quite distraught about the destruction of his ice sculpture, though,' Marigold mused.

Elke appeared doubtful. 'Perhaps he is a talented actor?'

Bentley frowned and pursed his lips. 'Why was the ice sculpture removed from the cool room in the first place? It makes no sense.'

Elke turned the Lady Clues book over in her hands. 'There are many questions about Chef Dubois, but also about Mrs. Olivier. I do not believe she can be discounted as a prime suspect.'

Marigold nodded. 'I agree, and she was quick to point the finger at Vivienne Cosette.'

'Plus, she seems to believe she'll be the sole beneficiary of Mr Olivier's will.'

Marigold stared at her. 'It seems like a reasonable assumption on her part. Why would she think otherwise?'

Elke shrugged. 'Until we know why Mr Olivier was killed, we should consider all possibilities.'

'I'm afraid I don't see why Mr Olivier's will would be a factor in his death,' Bentley said.

Marigold sighed 'Me either'

Elke gave an exaggerated sigh. 'You both need to read more Lady Clues' books. Mrs Olivier may have killed her husband to inherit his life insurance money, but so too might anyone else who was named—such as Vivienne Cosette.'

Bentley still seemed bewildered. 'But why would Mr Olivier change his will to include his rumoured mistress?'

Marigold snapped her fingers. 'He might have if she were pregnant.'

Elke nodded. 'Exactly and if that was the case, wouldn't it be an even greater motive for his wife to have killed him?'

Bentley rubbed his forehead. 'Even if it was, there's no reason Aline Martin would share her sister's secret with you. Surely it would make her more likely to conceal it.'

Marigold yawned. 'That's true, but there's only one way to find out. I think I'll rise early to-morrow to see if I can talk to her.'

'I will come with you to talk to her, my lady,' Elke said as she got to her feet.

'There's no need, Elke. I don't want to drag you further into this mess,'

'Mess is what I do best, and I believe we have encountered worse than this.'

Marigold couldn't argue with that.

CHAPTER TWENTY-ONE

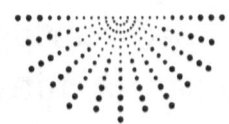

The next morning, Marigold and Elke left the suite just as the sun rose over the horizon. As they climbed down the steps to exit the train, they could hear the crank of machinery and the clink of metal on rock. Men's voices, French and Italian, drifted towards them. The smell of their cigarettes hung in the icy air.

'Perhaps it's a sign the track is being cleared at last.' Marigold huddled into her coat and rubbed her gloved hands together. Her breath floated in front of her in cloud-like puffs.

Elke stamped her feet as she looked around the deserted tracks. 'I hope so. The sooner we get off this train, the better.'

The cold didn't deter Pepper from taking a running leap into a frost-covered bush nearby.

Marigold followed him to make sure he didn't get into any trouble, blinking as her eyes stung from the cold. She heard Elke clear her throat. Aline Martin was making her way down the metal steps.

Unlike the previous morning, this time she was prepared. She was wearing a fur coat with a matching hat and a pair of mittens.

Aline met her eyes and smiled. 'Lady Marigold. We meet again.'

'Indeed. Unfortunately, the weather hasn't improved.'

Aline took off her mittens and lit a cigarette. Marigold made sure she stayed well away from the smoke to avoid it reaching her clothes. She could still smell it though and she fought the urge to retch.

'Good morning, Madame Martin,' Elke said, coming to stand beside her.

Aline looked wary. 'Miss Müller? Isn't it?'

Elke nodded, and Aline took a deep breath. 'I want to apologise to you both for Vivienne's behaviour in the dining car.'

'You have nothing to apologise for,' Marigold said, tugging Pepper away from a sparrow hopping along the railway tracks.

Aline waved away her words. 'It's what I do. Vivienne insults people and I repair relations with them.'

Marigold raised her eyebrows. 'She's lucky to have a sister like you.'

Aline shrugged. 'That's what family does. It's not so special.'

Elke looked like she wanted to argue, but Marigold shook her head and turned back to Aline. 'Speaking of Vivienne, I wonder if we could ask you a few questions.'

Aline let out a raspy laugh. 'You're still playing detective I see Lady Marigold.'

'It's more I'm trying to help someone—and myself if I'm being perfectly honest.'

'Ask away. I feel like I know you, even though we have only just met.'

Marigold raised her eyebrows. 'Really? Why?'

'I heard Mr Olivier tell my sister many stories about your uncle and his country estate.'

Marigold crinkled her forehead. 'Mayfair Manor?'

'Yes, the man never stopped talking about his visits and his connections to the British upper-class. He seemed fond of you.'

Marigold exchanged a surprised glance with Elke. 'I'm not sure why. I don't recall we met before I boarded this train.'

Aline took a long draw on her cigarette. 'I

guess it will remain a mystery. Unfortunately, we cannot ask him.'

She nodded. 'So, you knew Mr Olivier well?'

'He was an investor in my sister's ballet company,' Aline said through her teeth.

'And her lover?' Elke said.

Aline's eyes narrowed, and her face hardened. 'You like to ask inappropriate questions. It's not likely to lead to answers.'

Elke crossed her arms over her chest. 'It's not like it was a secret she had a motive for killing him. Perhaps you did too?'

Aline's face flushed. 'I think I'll leave now.'

Marigold shot Elke a warning look. This might be their only chance to talk to Aline alone. They couldn't afford to get her offside so soon.

She smiled apologetically at the French woman. 'If Vivienne had a motive, then we would have something in common. The Inspector also seems to think I'm a suspect.'

Aline's angry expression faded. 'Really? Were you involved with Mr Olivier, too?'

Marigold tried not to let her horror at this suggestion show on her face or in her voice. 'No, definitely not.'

'I only ask, as I was sure he had another woman, and I believe his wife thought the same,' Aline said with a shrug.

Marigold stared at her. 'Did Vivienne suspect, too? I heard she had an altercation with Unity the night Mr Olivier died?'

Aline's eyes dropped to the ground. 'She told me they had words and Mrs Olivier was beside herself. Completely irrational.'

'And yet, because of this fight, Vivienne and Mrs Olivier are now each other's alibi.'

Aline looked up and met her eyes. 'That's true. It's ironic.'

Marigold stamped her feet, trying to regain some feeling in them. 'I can't help thinking about what you said about Mr Olivier investing in Vivienne's ballet company.'

Aline raised her eyebrows. 'It's not so unusual for a dancer to have a patron.'

'The thing is, it doesn't seem like Mr Olivier had any real wealth. He was just in a cycle of borrowing and paying back people to fund his investments.'

Aline lit another cigarette. 'I'm afraid Vivienne didn't care where he got the money as long as he delivered it. The company couldn't have survived without it. I supposed she'll have to find a new patron now.'

Marigold stepped back to avoid the smoke. 'What about Mr Jorrisen, Olivier's deputy? Do you know him well?'

Aline looked uncomfortable. 'Jorrisen? We've spoken a few times.'

Marigold took a deep breath. 'The day of the murder, I heard Mr Jorrisen and Mr Olivier having a terrible row.'

Aline eyes widened. 'And you think he might have killed Mr Olivier? To get his job?'

'Perhaps, but I'm not the detective on the case. I'll leave it to Inspector Loxley.'

'Not if I have anything to say about it,' Elke said under her breath.

Marigold suppressed a smile and turned her attention back to Aline. 'You said Vivienne would have to get a new patron. You don't expect her to be named in Mr Olivier's will?'

Aline's eyebrows darted upwards. 'His will? I don't imagine he would have included her. Vivienne may have believed she was special, but I know how men like Mr Olivier operate. He would have found someone younger and more beautiful before long.'

Marigold nodded as two maids emerged from the train with thick woollen scarves wrapped around their necks. 'I imagine Vivienne is missing her maid?' She inclined her head towards the two maids.

Aline snorted. 'I have no doubt she's missing having someone to order around,'

Marigold's temper rose. 'She's not concerned about Renée?'

Aline shrugged 'I'm not sure she's thought about her much beyond the inconvenience of not having her around.'

Elke looked at her curiously. 'How long has Renée been working for Vivienne?'

Aline exhaled a long, smoky cloud. 'I would say, two years.'

'Vivienne must have been happy with her work.'

'She liked her well enough until we arrived in Istanbul. They had a falling out there. I'm not sure what happened between them, but I have had my suspicions.'

There was a long pause in the conversation while Aline took a last draw on her cigarette.

When Elke went to retrieve Pepper from the depths of a frost covered bush, Marigold turned to Aline.

'I want to clear my name and Renée's. Would you be willing to help me?'

Aline frowned. 'Why do you need to clear your name? You said you didn't know Mr Olivier before you boarded the train.'

'Being one of the first people at the scene of the crime means I'm under suspicion. Inspector Loxley also has some information about me so I can't be excluded.'

'How unfortunate.'

'It is, but I'm confident I can prove my innocence. I'm more concerned about helping Renée.'

Aline dropped her cigarette butt and stepped on it. 'Why? She's nothing to you.'

Marigold tried to hide her annoyance at Aline's coldness. 'Renée is a young woman who I believe was in the wrong place at the wrong time. The only reason she was there was to get Vivienne a cup of tea. She shouldn't pay for it with her life.'

Aline frowned. 'Tea?'

'Yes. She told me she went to the dining car to bring Vivienne her morning cup of tea.'

Aline snorted. 'I don't think so. Vivienne only drinks coffee first thing in the morning.'

'Are you sure?'

'I'm her sister. I think I would know.'

'Why would she lie?' Marigold replayed her conversation with Renée in her head. The young woman had sounded so genuine. Had she been mistaken?

'Renée is a keeper of secrets. There were things going on and she kept them from Vivienne, but I knew what she was up to.'

Marigold looked at her in surprise. 'You think Renée was involved with Mr Olivier?'

Aline wrinkled her nose. 'I don't know for certain, but I caught them having a whispered conversation on more than one occasion. It roused my suspicions and perhaps Vivienne's too.'

'Did you hear what they were talking about?'

Aline shook her head. 'No, it was the night before we boarded the train. Mr Olivier dined with us at the hotel, and I saw them talking in the lobby, but it was too noisy for me to hear what they were saying.'

'Did you tell Vivienne you'd seen them?'

'There was no point upsetting her further. She was already angry Mrs Olivier was going to be on the train.'

Marigold pursed her lips. 'Yes, I can imagine how distressing it must have been.'

Elke finally extracted Pepper from the bush and tucked him under her arm.

'I take it Mrs Olivier rarely travelled on the Lunar Express with her husband?'

Aline shook her head. 'It was a surprise to Mr Olivier too, from what Vivienne told me. Or so he led her to believe. Personally, I suspect Mrs Olivier planned the whole thing to confront Vivienne.'

'How did Vivienne find out Mrs Olivier was going to be on the train?'

Aline sniffed. 'From me. I confronted Renée after I saw her talking to Mr Olivier. I wanted Vivienne to be prepared.'

'How did she react?'

'How do you think? She was angry and upset.'

Marigold took Pepper from Elke and stroked his head. She met Aline's eyes. The French woman seemed to read her mind.

'Vivienne didn't kill him.'

'How can you be so sure?'

Aline took her mittens out of her pocket and pulled them on. 'Because I know my sister, plus she has an alibi.'

'What about Renée? Do you believe she could have killed him?' She wasn't sure she wanted to hear the answer, but it had to be asked.

'Without a shadow of a doubt,' Aline said. She smiled as Marigold and Elke exchanged a shocked look. 'You're surprised?'

Marigold nodded. 'Renée seems like a nice young woman.'

Aline scowled. 'Looks can be deceiving.' She turned back to the train. 'This has been interesting, but now I must return to my sister.'

Marigold shivered. 'Yes, it's very cold. We need to go inside too, before Pepper turns into an icicle.'

'Perhaps we shall meet again tomorrow at sunrise.' Aline sounded hopeful.

Marigold smiled. 'Perhaps, but let's hope by then the train will be on its way to Paris.'

'Indeed. Good day to you both,' Aline said as she climbed the stairs.

'What an enlightening conversation,' Elke said once Aline disappeared into the train.

Marigold sighed. 'It was and, in more ways, than one. I'm afraid for the first time I understand why Inspector Loxley thinks Renée is a suspect.'

CHAPTER TWENTY-TWO

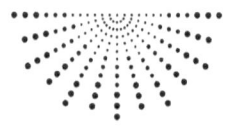

'**B**entley, would you be able to create a diversion?'

'Certainly, my lady. I have done so for your uncle on many occasions. However, I have the distinct impression I don't want to know why you need one.'

They were in her suite, and a plan was brewing in her head. Bentley was right. He wasn't going to like it.

'She needs you to distract the guard outside my original compartment,' Elke said, not looking up from her crossword.

Marigold raised her eyebrows. 'How did you know I wanted to talk to Renée?'

Elke glanced at her half-read copy of Lady Clues. 'It is the logical move for a detective and questions remain about her connection to Mr Olivier.'

'I really must finish my book. Lady Clues is very instructional.'

Bentley frowned. 'But you aren't a detective, my lady. Might it be best for you to leave the investigation to the Inspector?'

'I would, but unfortunately the wretched man now suspects me of being involved in two crimes and someone is encouraging that line of enquiry. There's no time to waste. I need to clear my name, and the only way to do is to find out who killed Mr Olivier.'

Bentley sighed. 'I fear your uncle wouldn't approve.'

'I'm sure he would if he knew I was at risk of going to the gallows?'

Bentley recoiled. 'My lady, you shouldn't say such things.'

'Perhaps not. I'm sorry. I didn't mean to upset you, but this is serious.'

'Of course, my lady. Whatever help I can provide, I will.'

Marigold paced in front of the window. 'Any luck learning about Mr Olivier's business dealings?'

Bentley shook his head. 'No, my lady. But I'll continue to see what I can discover.'

'Thank you, Bentley, and I'm sorry to be roping you into this.'

He bowed. 'As always, I'm here to be of service.'

Elke put her crossword aside. 'We should go while people are enjoying their afternoon rest.'

Marigold frowned at her. 'You've done enough Elke, there's no need for you to come along.'

Elke opened the compartment door. 'There is if you intend to return.'

'Was that an insult?' Marigold asked Bentley.

'I believe so, my lady, but with Miss Müller, sometimes it's hard to tell.'

'Time is ticking,' Elke said, tapping her wrist, even though she wasn't wearing a watch.

Marigold rolled her eyes but left the compartment. Bentley followed and locked the door behind them.

They walked through to the second-class carriage, but her plan to talk to Renée was immediately dashed by the sight of Inspector Loxley entering the compartment.

She stifled a cry of frustration. 'Well, that's that. We might as well go back to my suite,'

Bentley cleared his throat. 'Not so fast, my lady.'

She looked at him hopefully. 'What did you have in mind?'

'With Loxley engaged for the foreseeable future and Mrs Olivier in the dining car, it occurs to me there is an opportunity to discover more about Mr Olivier's financial interests.'

She looked at him in surprise. 'Bentley, you're not suggesting we break into the Olivier's suite, are you?'

'It depends on how you choose to frame it.'

She laughed. 'You've certainly come a long way in ten minutes, but we're on the same page. That's exactly what we should do.'

Elke reached into the pocket of her cardigan. 'And I have the brandy in case we need it.'

Marigold frowned at her. 'Why would we?'

'In case Mrs Olivier returns, we can say we came back for it.'

'It's unlikely to be a convincing excuse for why we're breaking into her compartment, speaking of which. How will we get in?'

Elke held up a key.

'Let me guess, a master key? Where did you get it?'

'Its best you don't know, my lady. So you can't incriminate yourself.'

Marigold shook her head. 'Just when I think

I've learned everything about you, I'm surprised all over again.'

'That is my goal,' Elke said.

Bentley appeared at the end of the carriage and beckoned them forward. 'The coast is clear. I'll keep a lookout. If I see anyone approaching, I'll begin a coughing fit and seek their help so you may make an escape.'

Marigold bit back a laugh. 'You seem to have a knack for this, Bentley.'

'I'm really not sure what's gotten into me, my lady.' He shook his head as though he couldn't quite believe it himself.

Elke inserted the key in the Olivier's door. It clicked open, and they slipped inside, closing the door behind them.

The suite had a lingering smell of Unity's floral perfume. It made Marigold queasy, and she longed to open a window, but there was no time to lose.

Elke began searching through the dresser drawers while Marigold scanned the top of Mrs Olivier's desk.

'Anything?' Elke whispered.

'No. I was hoping to find a diary or ledger, but neither is here. Most likely Loxley took them.'

Elke tapped her chin. 'Perhaps we need to break into his office to see them?'

'That's a step too far. I'll need to be desperate.'

Marigold tried the handle of the interconnecting doors. 'Unlocked. At least we'll have an escape route if Unity unexpectedly returns.'

Elke frowned. 'I do not think hiding in her dead husband's compartment is exactly an escape route.'

'Let's hope we don't need to use it,' Marigold said grimly.

Elke walked over to Unity's wardrobe and began rummaging through the dresses and shoes stacked on the floor. 'Hopefully now Mr Olivier is gone, Mrs Olivier can start dressing more fashionably.'

Marigold rolled her eyes. 'Not everyone likes fashion.'

'Says the woman who now spends ten minutes every morning checking her reflection in the mirror.'

Marigold scowled. 'That's not true.'

'We both know it is, my lady.'

'Sometimes I think you only call me that to get away with being rude,' Marigold grumbled as she turned her attention to the dressing table.

Mrs Olivier's wardrobe had been untidy, but her jewellery collection was perfectly organised.

In a rose-coloured velvet jewellery box, the

size of a shoe box, each pair of earrings was neatly separated by a tiny square box.

An unusual pair of diamond earrings caught Marigold's attention. She picked them up and examined them over by the window.

'What do you have there?' Elke said, walking over to her.

Marigold held them up to the light. 'These earrings have no backing. They're just the diamonds.'

Elke frowned. 'Perhaps they are to be repaired?'

'Maybe, or it could be the other way around. They could be ready to be constructed.'

She replaced the diamonds in the jewellery box and opened the adjoining door.

Mr Olivier's room showed traces of a search. The wardrobe door was unlatched, the dresser draws were not fully closed and the cushions on the settee were stacked against the wall. There was a lingering smell of cigars and cologne.

Elke began searching the pockets of Mr Olivier's dinner jackets. 'Ah ha,'

Marigold looked up. 'Please tell me it's something that will help.'

Elke scanned the letter she'd withdrawn from the pocket of a dark blue suit. 'It is a letter from Mr Olivier to your uncle.

'What does it say?'

'Your uncle says it was a pleasure to meet Mr Olivier and Miss Seydoux, and he'll consider their proposal.'

Marigold's jaw dropped. 'Renée went to Mayfair with Mr Olivier?'

'So, it would appear, my lady.'

Marigold scanned the letter, then took a deep breath. She'd deal with that situation soon enough. For now, she needed to concentrate on completing the search. She went to the dressing table where Mr Olivier's collection of cufflinks were stacked in a crystal bowl. She didn't need to rummage through them to find what she was looking for. Sitting on top was a set of cufflinks with the stones missing.

She held them up, and Elke's eyes widened. 'Mrs Olivier stole her husband's diamonds?'

'I don't know if stole is the word. What was his is surely hers now, but it's a peculiar thing to have done.'

'Yes, removing the diamonds would not have been easy,' Elke said as she examined the empty cufflinks.

Marigold paced the room. 'If Inspector Loxley knew about this, surely he would have taken both the diamonds and the cufflinks as evidence.'

'Unless he left them here for a reason.'

Marigold shook her head. 'I doubt it. He wouldn't have noticed the cufflinks. I only saw them because I was with Mr Olivier when Lady Haig commented on them. He told her they were a gift from a sultan.'

'Why would Mrs Olivier need to remove the diamonds?' Elke said, peering at the pieces of cufflink.

Marigold clasped her hands together and put a finger to her lips. 'Perhaps she needs to use them to make a payment.'

Elke's eyebrows rose. 'You think she hired someone to kill her husband?'

'It's possible.'

'This really is worthy of a Lady Clues case,' Elke said her eyes widening.

Marigold jumped as a trolley rattled past outside the compartment. 'Let's get out of here before we get caught.'

They made sure everything was as they had found it, then eased the door open enough to check the corridor. Marigold caught Bentley's eye.

'All clear,' he whispered.

'Good work, Bentley. Now we need to go back to plan A,' Marigold said as he joined them.

'Plan A, my lady?'

She filled him in on what they'd found.

He frowned. 'I don't recall Mr Olivier visiting with Miss Seydoux. It must have occurred on a day I was running errands for your uncle.'

'It's very strange, but I'm hoping Renée has information about why Mr Olivier had a receipt for ten thousand pounds in my name.'

'It's indeed a mystery, my lady, and I saw Inspector Loxley returning to his office, so the time is right to question Miss Seydoux.'

'I'm willing to incapacitate the guard, if necessary,' Elke said, cracking her knuckles.

Marigold exchanged an alarmed look with Bentley. 'Thank you, but there's no need, Elke. I'm very fond of Nico, and I have a plan.'

'Do you require my presence?' Bentley said, straightening his shoulders.

Marigold shook her head. 'No, thank you. It's better for me to talk to Renée alone.'

She watched as Bentley and Elke walked back to her suite, then approached Nico.

'Good afternoon, Nico. Miss Müller left some clothes in her compartment. Would it be possible for me to collect them for her?'

Nico's face flushed. 'I'm afraid I can't allow it, my lady.'

She lowered her voice and leaned towards him. 'I understand, but it's an emergency, you see.

She requires fresh under-garments, so if you could retrieve them for me, I would appreciate your help. They are...'

'There's no need to describe them, my lady. Please go in, but be as quick as you can.'

She nodded. 'Of course, thank you so much.' She flashed him a smile and slid the door open.

Renée was lying down, a cold pack on her forehead. Her eyes were red rimmed.

'Lady Marigold, what are you doing here?' She rubbed her neck as she sat up.

'I wanted to talk to you, Renée, about your visit to Mayfair Manor with Mr Olivier.'

Renée's bottom lip trembled. 'How did you find out?'

She held up the letter. 'This is a letter from my uncle. He wrote to Mr Olivier and mentioned how delightful it was to meet you.'

Tears slid down Renée's red cheeks. 'It's not what it seems, my lady.'

'What does it seem like?'

Renée swiped away a tear. 'There wasn't anything romantic between us.'

'If not his mistress, what were you to him?'

There was a knock on the door before Renée could respond.

'Lady Marigold, I must insist you exit the compartment. Inspector Loxley has said there are to be no visitors,' Nico called, his voice an octave higher than usual.

'I'm sorry. I'll be as fast as I can. I just can't locate Miss Müller's brassiere.'

There was a strangled sound on the other side of the door. Marigold smiled as she imagined the conductor's face getting redder by the second. Poor Nico.

She turned back to Renée. 'Did Mr Olivier ask Uncle Thomas for money when you visited him?'

Renée shook her head. 'I don't know, my lady. The gentlemen went outside for a walk. I stayed in the library.'

'So, you don't know anything about ten thousand pounds being transferred to Mr Olivier in my name?'

Renée's eyes widened. 'Ten thousand? My goodness, no, my lady. I'd tell you if I did.'

Marigold bit the inside of her cheek to hide her frustration. 'You were telling me you weren't one of Mr Olivier's mistresses, despite visiting Mayfair with him.'

'You don't believe me, do you?' Renée said, putting her head in her hands.

'It depends on what information you provide next.'

Renée's bottom lip wobbled. 'I'm afraid if I tell you what we really were to each other, it will make me look even more guilty than I do right now.'

'Tell me what's going on. If you're innocent, I'll help you.'

Renée gave a tremulous sigh. 'I wasn't Mr Olivier's mistress. I'm his daughter.'

CHAPTER TWENTY-THREE

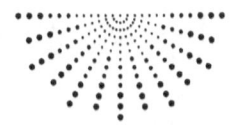

Marigold emerged from the compartment and flashed Nico a smile. 'My apologies for taking so long. Miss Müller and I appreciate your help.'

Nico heaved a sigh of relief. 'It was nice to see you again, Lady Marigold, but I cannot let you back into the compartment. I'm sorry.'

She nodded. 'Of course, Nico, and it's me who should apologise. I promise I won't need to go back in.'

'And there is no need for either of us to mention to Inspector Loxley you were there.'

She tapped the side of her nose. 'Definitely not. It will be our secret.'

Nico looked relieved, and a pang of guilt hit her for putting him in a difficult situation. It had been unavoidable, but she intended to keep her word. The next time she spoke to Renée, she hoped it would be when the maid was on the other side of the compartment door.

With renewed determination, she set off down the corridor.

'Well?' Elke said when Marigold entered the suite.

Marigold sighed. 'Things just got more complicated.'

'I cannot imagine how that is possible, but please, enlighten me,' Elke said with a snort.

'She is his daughter.'

Elke's head snapped back. 'Miss Seydoux?'

'That's right, and I don't know where this leaves any of us now.'

Elke rubbed her forehead. 'I see what you mean. Does it make her more likely to be guilty or less?'

'I'm not sure.'

'What did she say about him?'

Marigold sighed and looked out the window. There was a hint of blue sky in between the clouds. She hoped it was a good sign.

'Apparently, she only found out he was her father a few years ago. She tracked him down in Brussels and followed him to Paris last year. He was the one who got her the job with Vivienne.

Now she's terrified she'll look more guilty if anyone finds out.'

'Just because she's his daughter doesn't mean she had a motive.'

Marigold turned away from the window. 'It seems unlikely, and to be honest, I don't want her to be the murderer. She's a nice girl.'

Elke tut-tutted. 'According to Lady Clues, they are the ones we should suspect the most.'

THEY RETURNED to Marigold's suite and Elke immediately settled herself in the armchair and opened her book. Pepper gave Marigold a pleading whimper and with a sigh, she shrugged into her coat and put on her hat.

'Come on then, let's get some fresh air.'

Outside, the rescue effort appeared to be moving at speed. Her spirits lifted at the prospect of them getting moving again.

However, her relief was tinged with a hint of anxiety. Once the train restarted its journey, her time to prove Renée's innocence—and find Olivier's real killer would start to run out.

She huddled into her coat as the wind picked up. A group of children were tossing a ball across the tracks at the rear of the train, and Pepper strained on his leash to reach them.

'I know you'd like to join in, but it's not a good idea. They don't want their ball eaten, and we both know you can't be trusted not to run off with it,' she told Pepper.

The little dog gave her a pleading look and she was about to capitulate when she heard a boy say, 'Oh, it's Pepper.'

'Hallo, miss.' He dropped to his knees, and Pepper began licking his face.

'How are you, Sebastian?'

'Happy now, I've seen Pepper—and you miss, of course. It's very boring with the train not moving.'

'Yes, I agree. What are you doing to entertain yourself?'

Sebastian glanced over his shoulder and put a hand up to his mouth. 'Don't tell Flo, but I like to go exploring. I've made it all the way up to the first-class carriage miss. I even snuck into the kitchen car where the murder happened.'

She raised her eyebrows. 'Really? How?'

'I go at night, miss. I see lots of interesting things going on.'

'What kind of things?'

Sebastian looked up at her while Pepper

climbed over him. 'Lots of shouting and people having secret meetings.'

'Goodness, how intriguing. Perhaps you'll be a detective when you grow up.'

'Maybe. I have to be careful, though. There's a real detective on the train and he's nearly caught me a few times.'

'Yes, do be careful, Sebastian, but tell me more about the shouting and the secret meetings.'

'I saw Clara Bligh having a big row with him two nights ago.' Sebastian pointed to Mr Jorrisen, who was standing across the tracks smoking a cigarette.

Marigold heart thumped a little faster than usual and she tried to keep her face impassive. 'Really? Could you hear what they were saying?'

'Yes, miss, plain as day. They weren't bothering to keep their voices down, which surprised me, but they were in the fancy car with the piano and no one else was there, so they must have thought they wouldn't be heard.'

'That's the lounge car, Sebastian. What were they talking about?'

'About the murder, miss. Miss Bligh was really angry with the man. She kept saying he should have stuck to the plan.'

Marigold glanced at Mr Jorrisen. 'And what about the man?'

'He kept telling her not to blame him for what she'd done.'

'I wonder what it was all about?'

The boy shrugged. 'I don't know, miss, but he's a very angry man. I saw him being very mean to Mr Du-bow, too.'

She frowned. 'Mr Du-bow?'

Sebastian laughed. 'That's what he told me to call him. It's not his real name, but it's funny. He's the chef on the train and he found me in the kitchen one night, but he wasn't even mad. He gave me some eclairs to take back to Florence. I've never had anything so delicious, miss.'

'Chef Dubois?'

Sebastian beamed. 'That's his real name. I like him a lot. If I don't become a detective, I might become a chef when I grow up.'

'Perhaps you could be both, and I'm glad Chef Dubois was kind to you, but what did Mr Jorrisen do to him?'

Sebastian's shoulders slumped. 'I was afraid, miss. I heard yelling in the dining car and when I peeked around the door, I saw Mr Jorrisen with his hands around Mr Du-bow's neck. His face was very red, and his eyes were like...'

Sebastian mimed, his eyes popping out of his head.

'That's terrible.' Marigold glared at Mr Jorrisen.

'It really was miss. I was about to run for help when Mr Jorrisen dropped Mr Du-bow to the ground and stormed out. He opened the door so fast I only just got out of the way before it hit me.'

Marigold frowned. 'I don't think it's a good idea for you to be roaming around the train.'

'Don't worry about me, miss. I know how to take care of myself.'

'I'm sure you do, but there's some dangerous people on this train and I'd hate for anything to happen to you.'

Sebastian's face creased with worry. 'Don't tell Florence, miss. She doesn't know I've been sneaking out.'

Marigold patted his hand. 'I won't but promise me, instead of walking around the train at night, you'll come and visit me and Pepper.'

Sebastian sighed. 'The nice man you sent who told us to eat our meals in the dining car said we could visit, but Florence said it wouldn't be proper.'

'It's quite the opposite. Let me talk to Florence,' Marigold's eyes searched the exterior of the train and located her sitting on a step.

'Only about visiting Pepper.' Sebastian's voice had a note of panic.

She smiled. 'I said I wouldn't tell her about your night-time adventures, and I meant it. I always keep my word, Sebastian.'

'Me too, miss.'

Florence jumped down from the step as Marigold approached.

'Miss Grey says we can visit Pepper any time we like,' Sebastian told his sister.

'It's not Miss Grey, it's Lady Grey,' Florence reprimanded him.

'Actually, it's Lady Marigold, but I'd much rather you called me Marigold.'

Florence's eyes widened. 'Oh, we couldn't miss. It wouldn't be proper.'

'I find proper things are usually very dull.'

The corners of Florence's mouth turned upwards. Even the hint of a smile transformed her face. Marigold's heart went out to the girl with too many responsibilities for her age.

'I was just saying to Sebastian, Pepper is not allowed out of my suite unless I'm with him and he's very bored on his own. I'd love it if you and Sebastian would come and play with him.'

Florence chewed her lip. 'I suppose it would be alright. If we were helping you, miss.'

'You would be, but it wouldn't be a favour. I'd pay you, of course. Taking care of Pepper is most definitely a job.'

'Oh, we couldn't take your money, miss,' Florence said.

'Let's start with you coming to visit, and we can talk about it later.'

Florence nodded. 'Yes, miss.'

'Speaking of Pepper, I don't suppose you'd be up for coming back to my suite now, would you? I need to talk to Miss Bligh, and he's had quite enough excitement for one day.'

'Of course, miss, we can take care of him.' Sebastian said.

She smiled. 'I'd be most grateful.'

They entered the train, and Florence strode ahead. Marigold hung back with Sebastian.

'Sebastian, in your travels around the train, you haven't noticed what compartment Miss Bligh is in, have you?'

The boy nodded. 'I have, miss. She's Flo's idol, and I was hoping I could get her to sign something for me, but I've had no luck so far.'

'Perhaps I can help. Can you tell me what number compartment she's in?'

'Yes miss, it's compartment twelve. Could you ask her to sign this?' Sebastian held out a photograph.

It was a photograph of Clara, but it wasn't a studio portrait or a clipping from a magazine. It appeared to be a private photograph. Clara was dressed in a white silk dressing gown and draped over a chaise lounge.'

Marigold tried to keep her tone even. 'Where did you get this photograph?'

Sebastian looked uncomfortable. 'Actually, miss, I found it on the first day of the train. It was in the pocket of the man who was murdered. I saw it fall out when he was looking for his cigarettes.'

Marigold's stomach dropped. 'You're sure it fell from Mr Olivier's pocket?'

Sebastian nodded. 'Yes, miss.'

'Thank you, Sebastian. Can I keep this? I'll try to get it signed for you.'

He nodded and Marigold quickened her step to catch up with Florence.

Elke looked up from her book as they entered the suite. She scanned the children warily.

Marigold suppressed a smile. 'Florence, Sebastian, this is Miss Müller. She is my assistant.'

Florence's eyes lit up as she realised what Elke was reading. 'Lady Clues?'

Elke nodded. 'You have good taste in books, young lady.'

'My mother loved her cases. We used to read them together.'

Marigold's heart hurt. 'I'm sure Miss Müller

would be happy to let you borrow some of her books. Wouldn't you Elke?'

Elke nodded. 'Of course. There is no point having books sitting on a shelf if they can be read.'

'Florence and Sebastian are going to stay here with Pepper while you and I speak with Miss Bligh about her friendship with Mr Olivier.'

Elke's eyebrows rose. 'Miss Bligh?'

Marigold nodded and held up the photograph.

Elke arched her eyebrows. 'This should be interesting,' she said as she closed her book.

CHAPTER TWENTY-FOUR

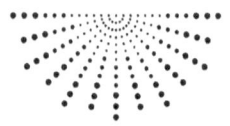

Marigold knocked on the polished wood of compartment twelve. The door opened and Clara appeared, draped in the doorway, a feather boa around her neck. She was wearing a cream satin dressing gown like the one she was wearing in the photograph.

When her smoky eyes took in Marigold and Elke, she gave a squark and hurriedly tied the dressing gown around her waist. She crossed her arms over her chest and looked at them through narrowed eyes.

Marigold didn't bother to hide her amusement. 'I'm so sorry to call unexpectedly, but we were hoping we could have a chat.'

Clara scowled. 'I can't imagine what we'd have

to talk about.'

'It seems unlikely, doesn't it? But you see, someone is trying to frame me for Mr Olivier's murder, and I'm hoping you might be able to help me.'

Clara frowned. 'How? The murder is nothing to do with me. I don't know anything about it.'

Marigold pushed past her. 'You may have convinced Inspector Loxley, but I suspect you know more than you're letting on.' She held up the photograph and Clara's expression soured.

'Who are you?' Clara demanded as Elke followed Marigold into the suite.

'My name is Elke Müller, and I am Lady Marigold's assistant.'

Clara's eyes widened and she mouthed 'Assistant?' before closing the door with such force it rattled on its runners.

Her compartment rivalled Mr Jorrisen's for mess and disorder. For someone so beautifully presented, she seemed to place little value on her lovely clothes and jewellery.

Beaded silks and satins in jewelled tones lay crumpled on the floor or slung over the furniture. A pair of diamond earrings were among other pieces of jewellery scattered over the dressing table, and necklaces were tangled and twisted.

Marigold and Elke cleared the settee, so there was space for them to sit.

Clara paced in front of the window. 'Where did you get the photograph?'

'From Mr Olivier's compartment.' Marigold decided it was close enough to the truth not to matter.

'And you think we were connected?'

Marigold nodded. 'That's the logical conclusion. A man rarely has a photograph of a woman other than his wife tucked away in his underwear drawer unless he has something to hide.'

Clara wrinkled her nose. 'I could deny it. The mere fact he had a photograph proves nothing. He could have gotten it from anywhere, but I suspect you have other reasons for believing I was involved with Mr. Olivier.'

'A witness has relayed to me you had an argument with Mr Jorrisen the night of the murder. You were heard telling him he should have stuck to the plan.'

Clara rolled her eyes. 'This isn't school Marigold. You're not a prefect anymore. Mind your own business for once in your life.'

Marigold gave her a cold smile. 'I'm aware of the time and the place. What I also know is the night before his murder I overheard an argument he had with Mr Jorrisen, and they were also talking about a plan.'

Clara scowled. 'And now you think I was involved in his murder, otherwise, why would you be here?'

'As I told you, my motive is to clear my name.'

'Well, I can't help you. I don't know anything about Rueben's death.' Clara's face and voice were impassive, but her hands shook as picked up a cigarette case.

Marigold pointed to the cigarettes. 'Would you mind not smoking? It makes me rather ill.'

Clara glared at her but put the cigarette box back on the dressing table.

Marigold nodded her thanks. 'Were you with Mr Olivier the night of the murder?'

'I can see you won't be dissuaded, so I won't waste my time trying to convince you of my innocence, but as a matter of fact I was with him and before you ask, he was alive when I returned to my compartment. Both my husband and the wagon-lit conductor can vouch for me.'

Elke narrowed her eyes. 'Did you tell Inspector Loxley you were with Mr Olivier?'

Clara heaved an impatient sigh. 'Why would I? I did nothing wrong, and I don't want to get dragged into a scandal about his death.'

'Yes, I imagine it would be very damaging for

your career,' Marigold said, her tone was light, but when she caught Clara's eye, she thought she saw a flicker of fear. They stared at each other for a long moment until Elke cleared her throat and asked, 'Did Mr Olivier ever talk to you about threats he was receiving or perhaps of someone blackmailing him?'

Clara gave her an incredulous look, then tossed her head and laughed. 'Blackmail? Who would blackmail Rueben? The man didn't have two cents to rub together. He was always borrowing money. If there were threats against him, that would have been the reason.'

Marigold leaned forward, resting her elbows on her knees. 'If Mr. Olivier had no money, why were you with him?'

Clara looked as though she'd eaten something sour. 'Rueben might not have had money, but he had connections and I could rely him upon to ensure I always travelled in style.'

There was a loud knock at the door, and Clara jumped. 'Who is it?' she called, her voice falsely bright and cheerful.

'Inspector Loxley. I would like a word.'

'One moment,' Clara said before she rounded on Marigold. 'What have you told him?'

Marigold shrugged. 'Nothing. Believe me. I

stay as far away from Inspector Loxley as I do from you.'

'How will you explain what you're doing here? Loxley knows we despise one another' Clara hissed.

Marigold frowned. 'How does he know?'

'Perry told him. He said the Inspector was asking a lot of questions about you.'

Marigold exchanged a worried look with Elke. 'Have you spoken to him yet?'

Clara shook her head. 'No. I've been avoiding him, but perhaps we can make a deal?'

Marigold's eyes widened. 'That's something I never imagined I'd hear coming from you but go on.'

There was a second knock, this one louder than the first. 'Miss Bligh?' Loxley sounded exasperated.

Clara tied her satin robe more tightly around her waist. 'You keep your mouth shut about me and I'll do the same about you.'

Marigold bit her lip, but she nodded. 'Fine.'

'I hope you know what you're doing,' Elke said out of the corner of her mouth as Clara opened the door.

In contrast to her casual attire, Loxley wore his usual grey pinstripe suit and was holding a notebook.

'Inspector, I wasn't expecting you,' she said, her voice breathy and flirtatious.

'Really? Because I have sent you several notes trying to organise an interview. Did you not receive them?'

Clara waved a hand over her shoulder at the mess on the floor behind her. 'I'm afraid I left my maid back in London. I'm just not coping without her.'

Loxley frowned as he scanned the inside of the compartment and his eyes narrowed when saw Marigold and Elke.

'Lady Marigold, Miss Müller, I didn't expect to find you here.' His voice was heavy with suspicion.

Marigold got to her feet, careful not to slip on a magazine. 'We were just enjoying some girl talk.'

Loxley frowned. 'Girl talk?'

'Yes. You have sisters, don't you, Inspector? I'm sure you're familiar with how women love to chat.'

His scowl deepened. 'Lady Marigold, can I have a word with you, please? Outside.'

'Say nothing,' Clara hissed as Marigold walked out of the compartment.

Loxley closed the door behind her and crossed his arms over his chest.

'May I ask what you're doing here?'

'As I said, Miss Müller and I were spending some time with Clara.'

'And how exactly are you acquainted with Miss Bligh?'

'She and I are old friends.'

'Are you really?'

'Yes.' She knew he didn't believe her, but nothing short of the sky falling was going to make her admit it.

'And Miss Müller is also a friend of Miss Bligh?'

She nodded. 'Indeed. They have so much in common.'

Loxley raised his eyebrows. 'Such as?'

'Books, art, you know, the usual things,' she said airily.

'Which of Miss Bligh's films is your favourite?'

Marigold, who had watched none of them, gritted her teeth, but she maintained her smile. 'Oh, I like all of them.'

'But surely there must be one you like more than the others?'

'Yes, but I couldn't possibly choose one'

'I see.' It was clear from his tone he knew she'd never watched one of Clara's films.

'Can I return to the compartment now?'

'Be my guest.' He stepped aside. 'But Lady Marigold,'

She looked back at him.

'Be careful who you speak to about Mr Olivier's murder. It may come back to haunt you.'

~

'I'VE NEVER MET A MORE INFURIATING man,' Marigold told Elke as they walked back to her suite.

Elke snorted. 'He certainly knows how to get under your skin and you under his.'

She stopped and looked at her. 'What do you mean?'

Elke shrugged. 'First you meet in Istanbul and now on this train and his family home is close to Mayfair Manor. It is like destiny.'

She looked at her blankly. 'Destiny? It's bad luck, that's what it is.'

'Perhaps, under different circumstances, the two of you might have become friends.'

'Friends? The man suspects me of murder—among other crimes. Mark my words. We will never be friends.'

The inside of her suite looked like Clara's. Cushions were scattered on the floor and Pepper was racing from Sebastian to Florence, clearly having the time of his life.

'What is going on here?' Elke said, looking around the suite in horror.

Marigold laughed at her outraged expression. 'Don't worry about it. Mess is easily rectified. The most important thing is they are all having fun.'

Elke frowned and retreated to her armchair. She picked up her Lady Clues book and sat down with a huff. She smiled as she heard her mutter, 'Fun?'

'Hello miss,' Florence said, giggling as Pepper licked her face.

Her heart turned over. The girl looked so happy and content. She wished she could make it a permanent state.

Sebastian wriggled out from under the settee. 'Did you get the photo signed by Miss Bligh?'

Marigold's stomach dropped. 'Not this time, but I promise I'll go one better and organise for her to meet you the next time you come to visit Pepper.'

Sebastian's thin face lit up. 'Really miss?'

'Of course. I told you, Sebastian, I always keep my word.'

'We don't want to be any trouble,' Florence said, her serious expression returning.

'You absolutely aren't trouble. Pepper is delighted. He'll be so disappointed when it's just me and Elke left to be with him.'

Florence and Sebastian exchanged glances. She frowned. 'Is everything alright?'

Florence nodded slowly. 'Yes, miss. You've been so kind to us and Sebastian told me the Inspector thinks you might be a suspect in the murder. I know it's not true and we might have something to help you.'

Marigold's mouth went dry. 'What do you have?'

'The night before last, I woke to find Sebastian missing. It was late, almost midnight, so I went to look for him and I think I know who killed Mr Olivier.'

Marigold sat on the edge of the settee. 'Who do you think it is?'

'You don't know he did it,' Sebastian said, clearly agitated.

'I have to tell Lady Marigold Seb. It's the right thing to do.'

'You don't need to tell me anything if you don't want to, Florence, but if it's about the murder, you might need to speak to Inspector Loxley.'

She recoiled. 'Oh, no, miss. I don't want to involve the police. I'll just tell you.'

Marigold glanced at Sebastian. 'Is it alright with you, Sebastian?'

He buried his face in Pepper's neck, but he nodded.

Florence took a deep breath. 'I looked everywhere for Seb, and I was getting so worried. I knew he'd been in the kitchen car the night before. He'd brought back eclairs, and I wondered if he might be there again.'

She gave her an encouraging nod. 'And was he?'

Florence shook her head. 'No. I found him hiding under a dining car table. There were two people in the kitchen. One of them was Chef Dubois. The other was a woman.'

She sighed. 'Mrs Olivier?'

Florence's eyes widened. 'How did you know, miss?'

She winked. 'Just a lucky guess, but what were they doing?'

'That might be a dangerous question,' Elke said from behind her book.

Florence's cheeks flushed. 'It was anything inappropriate, miss, but it was clear Mrs Olivier and Chef Dubois were on friendly terms.'

'Could you hear what they were saying?'

Florence nodded. 'Mrs Olivier said, Rueben made my life hell, and I dreamed sometimes of one of his enemies killing him, but they were just fantasies. I never wanted this to happen.'

'Was she crying? Did she sound upset?'

Florence shook her head. 'No miss, her voice was cold, hard as nails, really. To tell you the truth, I didn't believe she didn't want her husband dead. It sounded like she really was glad he was gone.'

She recalled Mrs Olivier telling her, 'Let's not pretend he wasn't a terrible person.'

'What about Chef Dubois? What did he say?'

'He was speaking in French, so I couldn't understand a lot of it, but he was telling her they were now free to be together.'

CHAPTER TWENTY-FIVE

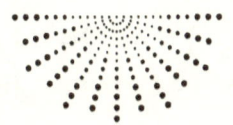

'Chef Dubois and Mrs Olivier conspired to kill her husband.' Elke shook her head.

Marigold shook her head. 'We don't know for sure.'

They were walking back to her suite after settling Sebastian and Florence into their compartment for the night. If she had her way, they would have stayed in her suite, but Florence had insisted they couldn't impose.

She'd done her best to try to convince them otherwise, but eventually had given up. However, she had insisted on making sure they were safely tucked up in their compartment for the night.

Elke had rolled her eyes at this and muttered comments about the dangers of emotional attachment. She knew she was right, but she couldn't help being protective of Florence and Sebastian.

As they crossed back into the first-class carriage, Elke said, 'So what now?'

She looked out the window for a moment. 'I don't know about you, but I'm rather peckish. Perhaps Chef Dubois can rustle something up for us in the kitchen.'

'Are you going to confront him?'

Marigold shook her head. 'No, but it can't help to see what he's willing to share.'

They walked through the train, keeping an eye out for Loxley. Fortunately, there was no sign of him as they entered the dining carriage.

There were still a few guests lingering over coffee and dessert while the waiters discreetly cleared tables around them, no doubt hoping they would hurry and retire to their compartments so they could do the same.

Despite the lateness of the hour, the kitchen was busy. Pots and pans were being washed, while an assembly line of kitchen hands dried dishes and polished glassware. Someone was singing in French and the smell of soap mingled with coffee.

In a back corner, two rotund men in white

aprons were kneading dough while arguing about the best restaurants in Paris.

Marigold and Elke stood watching the chaos for a moment, then Chef Dubois looked up from an animated discussion he was having with a waiter. His face lit up when he recognised them.

'Lady Marigold, to what do I owe this honour?'

She smiled at his enthusiastic greeting. She had a pang of guilt for the real reason they were there, and she pushed it aside. Much as she liked the man, what Florence had seen and heard had elevated him in the list of likely suspects.

'Chef Dubois, we were wondering how Josephine is?'

The Frenchman's smile widened.

'Oh yes, mademoiselle, she's back to her best after the unfortunate incident. Would you like to see her?'

She nodded. 'That would be wonderful, wouldn't it, Elke?'

Elke shot her a surprised glance but gave a quick nod to Chef Dubois.

He led them through the kitchen and into the cooler. She rubbed her bare arms, wishing she had worn a shawl—or better still—a coat.

She shivered, and not just because of the temperature. Meat hung from the ceiling on hooks like coats in a closet. Blocks of cheese were stacked on shelves and bottles of milk and cream sat in chests filled with ice.

At the far end of the room stood Josephine. She looked no worse for wear.

'She looks wonderful,' she told the chef.

Chef Dubois patted the ice-sculpture as though she were a beloved pet.

'I wasn't sure she would last the journey, especially with the delay, but when the temperature dropped to below zero, my spirits rose.'

Elke tilted her head as she examined the ice-sculpture. 'How long will she last?'

'In this temperature, maybe a few more days. Just in time for the competition, if I'm lucky.'

'She really is magnificent.' Marigold gazed up at the intricate detail on the sculpture. It truly was a work of art.

'I don't like to brag, but she's one of my finest pieces of work,' Chef Dubois said, but he was obviously bursting with pride.

'I think I will move to a warmer location,' Elke said through chattering teeth.

'Of course, this way,' Chef Dubois said, gesturing for them to follow him out of the cool room.

Marigold blinked as her eyes adjusted to the bright light of the kitchen.

Chef Dubois clapped his hands. 'Can I get you something to warm you? Coffee? Or something to eat?'

Marigold smiled as her stomach rumbled. 'That would be wonderful. I'm afraid we missed dinner.'

The chef looked around his kitchen. 'I'm feeling peckish myself. Perhaps an omelette?'

'It sounds lovely,' Marigold said and Elke nodded enthusiastically at her side.

Chef Dubois gave them a half bow. 'It would be an honour to cook for you and Miss Müller.' He snapped his fingers and ordered his staff to begin preparations for their meal.

'Please, let me see you to a table so you don't have to suffer from the noise and chaos of the kitchen.'

He led them to a small office off the kitchen with a table in the centre. He snapped his fingers again, and a waiter appeared out of nowhere with a tablecloth and silverware. Within seconds, the table was set with three place settings and a candelabra.

Her eyes widened. 'My goodness, this is most impressive.'

Chef Dubois beamed. 'I always make time for our special guests.'

She caught Elke's eye as she opened her linen

napkin. It was time to see what Chef Dubois had to say about Mr Olivier.

'It's a welcome change from the way we've been treated by Inspector Loxley.'

The chef waved his hands in the air. 'Oh, my lady, you wouldn't believe the questions he has asked. He has interrogated me and my staff. Even during the war, I didn't experience such harassment—my apologies, Miss Müller.'

'There is no need for it, Chef Dubois,' Elke said, waving her right hand dismissively.

Marigold frowned. 'But surely, he can't think you or your staff had anything to do with Mr Olivier's death?'

Chef Dubois shook his head. 'I hope not, my lady.'

Marigold rested her elbows on the table. 'Mrs Olivier must be very upset about it too.'

Chef Dubois' smile faltered. 'Madame Olivier?'

'Yes, the two of you are friends, are you not? She speaks fondly of you.' she crossed her fingers under the table.

'Does she?' He looked pleased and sat up a little straighter.

'Yes. I assumed you knew her well?'

Chef Dubois leaned forward in his seat. 'She has an interest in cooking and was a regular visitor to the kitchen when she travelled with her husband. She has been quite lonely, you know.'

'I imagine she is now Mr Olivier is gone,' Marigold said.

Chef Dubois dropped his eyes to the table. 'She was lonely before he died, my lady. Sadly, her husband preferred the company of others.'

Marigold nodded. 'I noticed he seemed very fond of Vivienne at dinner.'

Chef Dubois lifted his head and met her eyes. 'I don't wish to speak ill of the dead, but he was a hypocrite, I'm afraid. He had his dalliances, but poor Unity paid the price for her friendship with me.'

'What do you mean?'

'He didn't want her talking to the staff or anyone on the train. He was very controlling of her.'

Marigold took a sip of water and tried to keep her tone light. 'Do you know why?'

'I suspect he didn't want her to know how much money he owed people,' Chef Dubois said bitterly.

Marigold frowned. 'Mr Olivier had borrowed money from my uncle. Did he take from you, too?'

Chef Dubois scowled. He lowered his voice and quickly checked over his shoulder to ensure he couldn't be overheard. 'I'm very sorry your uncle was also owed money. That's why I need to win this competition, for the prize money. Olivier promised me he would double my money, but he lost it all.'

'Is that why Inspector Loxley suspects you?'

He nodded. 'I have nothing to hide. I didn't kill him, but please don't think any less of me for saying I'm grateful to whoever did.'

The waiter returned and put three plates of fluffy omelette in front of them. She took a bite, savouring its salty goodness. There was silence for a few moments while they ate. Finally, she put down her fork and got right to the point.

'Do you have any idea who might have killed Mr Olivier?'

Chef Dubois snorted. 'The list of suspects is long, but personally, I hold suspicions about Mademoiselle Cosette and the deputy director.'

'Vivienne and Mr Jorrisen?'

He nodded. 'I heard them fighting the night before he was killed and watched her strike him. She's, how you say, a little unhinged.'

Elke pushed her empty plate away and dabbed at her mouth with a napkin. 'What were they fighting about?'

'She wanted money from him to fund her new

production. He had promised, but failed to provide the funds. She was very upset about it.'

She frowned. 'Did you tell Inspector Loxley this?'

'Of course, I had no reason not to and no loyalty to Mademoiselle Cosette.'

'Here he had a perfectly reasonable motive for Olivier's murder, and yet Inspector Loxley continued to accuse Miss Seydoux,' Elke said under her breath.

Marigold looked at him thoughtfully. 'What makes you suspect, Mr Jorrisen?'

Chef Dubois sat back in his chair and chewed his lip.

'Olivier took money from his mother. She was a guest on the train a few months ago. She gave him her life savings with the promise of high returns. She's now destitute. What greater motive could a man have?'

She nodded. 'And I heard them quarrelling the night of the murder.'

'I too, argued with him. Does Inspector Loxley really suspect me?' Chef Dubois said with a hitch in his voice.

She patted his hand. 'Don't worry, I'm sure if you were truly a suspect, Inspector Loxley would have had you removed from the kitchen. Your continuing presence here is proof he doesn't seriously suspect you.'

Chef Dubois heaved a sigh of relief. 'You're very kind, my lady.'

'And you're a marvellous cook.'

Elke yawned. 'I second that.'

'Thank you for showing us Josephine and for the wonderful omelette.' She got to her feet.

The chef gave them a quick bow. 'You're most welcome, mademoiselle. I hope you enjoy the rest of your journey.'

'Good luck with Josephine and the competition. I look forward to Elke and I visiting your restaurant in Paris soon.'

The chef walked them to the door, and they set off back to the suite.

Elke stopped to fix the buckle on her shoe and looked up at her. 'What did you make of it?'

Marigold sighed. 'I'm not sure. Chef Dubois is such a lovely man, but it's undeniable how much he loathed Mr Olivier, and now we know he had even more of a motive to kill him.'

CHAPTER TWENTY-SIX

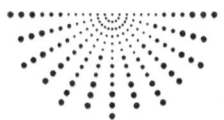

Hopes were high the next morning the train would soon be on its way.

Marigold spent most of the day outside with Pepper, Florence, and Sebastian, enjoying the unseasonably mild weather and sunshine.

She was in high spirits by the time the sunset and retired to her suite to get ready for dinner.

'For someone who swore they would not be leaving this suite, you have spent very little time in it,' Elke said as she handed her a black tulle gown with gold embroidery. It had a handkerchief-style hem and was trimmed with gold velvet ribbon.

Marigold dipped her head to hide her smile.

'It seems a shame to let the beautiful gowns you brought go to waste.'

Elke raised an eyebrow. 'Oh, I see. It's for the dresses. Not because you enjoy the company in the dining room?'

'It's a little of both. Some nights are more pleasant than others. I'm dining with Miss Carey this evening, so my hopes are high for some good conversation.'

'There is something a little odd about her though, don't you think' Elke said as she placed a feathered headpiece on her head.

'I think she's just nervous because she's travelling alone.'

'She's very fidgety. Always touching her hair. Perhaps you can have a word to her about changing her headwear. A simple headpiece would be more flattering to her than those turbans.'

Marigold rolled her eyes at Elke in the dressing-table mirror. 'Maybe she likes the turbans.'

'She would look better without them.'

Marigold picked up her beaded gold evening bag and headed for the door. 'I won't tell her you said that.'

The lounge car was crowded when she arrived. Word had spread the train would be on its way by morning and spirits were high.

The pianist was playing a jaunty tune, people were smiling, and there was a sense of optimism in the room she hadn't felt since the first day of the journey.

Clara was holding court at the bar with a noisy group, including Osbert and Perry. She caught Marigold's eye and gave a slight nod of her head, which Marigold read as confirmation she was sticking to her end of their deal. A niggle of doubt about the ethics of their agreement played at the corners of her mind, but she pushed it away.

Hermione was sitting on a settee on her own, sipping a cocktail. She was wearing a forest green velvet gown and a black silk turban with peacock feathers at the front. When her eyes met her, her shoulders relaxed.

'Good evening, Lady Marigold. I'm so glad you could join me.'

Marigold sat beside her. 'I'm very pleased to be here. It's wonderful to see everyone looking so happy.'

'Yes, it's been a horrible few days, but with any luck, we'll be on our way in the morning,' Hermione said, rising to her feet as Sir Fredrick and Lady Haig joined them.

'It's quite a party atmosphere in here tonight,' Sir Fredrick said once greetings had been exchanged and everyone was seated. He looked around the lounge car with a disgruntled expression.

'Don't begrudge the young ones a little fun, Freddie,' Lady Haig chided as she settled herself on the settee opposite Marigold and Hermione.

'They don't need any encouragement. These bright young people need a lesson in propriety.' Sir Fredrick curled his lip as he watched Perry Bligh drink a glass of champagne with his arm interlaced with a young woman in a red sequined dress with beaded fringe around her knees.

Lady Haig rolled her eyes at Marigold and Hermione. 'Ignore him, my dears. He's been reading the stories in the newspapers about the escapades of the young ones in London. I don't know why he does it. It only raises his blood pressure.'

'Lady Haig, may I compliment you on your lovely necklace?' Hermione said, pointing to the mass of emeralds around Lady Haig's neck.

'Thank you, my dear. That's very kind of you to say. It has been in my family for six generations.'

Marigold thanked a waiter as he delivered a glass of champagne to her. 'I'm glad you decided to wear it again.'

Lady Haig knocked on the mahogany table

beside her. 'Touch wood, my dear, but it seems the Light-Fingered Lord didn't board the train after...'

Before she could finish, the lounge car was suddenly plunged into darkness.

The piano fell silent, and voices rose in volume and levels of anxiety.

A man said, 'Strike a match.'

But before anyone had the opportunity to act on the instruction, a woman let out a blood-curling scream.

It didn't take her long to identify the woman as Lady Haig, and as a flare of light finally illuminated the back corner of the room, she realised what had happened.

'My necklace,' Lady Haig shrieked again as Sir Fredrick bellowed, 'What's happened? What's going on here?'

A chorus of voices, male and female, echoed Sir Fredrick's question as more flares of light appeared. Finally, the electric lights in the lounge car flickered back on. When they did, Inspector Loxley standing in the doorway.

Lady Haig stumbled to her feet, nearly tripping over Sir Fredrick. She held fast to her elbow, concerned she might fall.

A red line was growing darker by the moment

in the place where Lady Haig's grand necklace had sat just a few seconds earlier.

'Oh Gideon, my necklace. Someone has taken it and they must still be here. They can't have escaped so quickly,' Lady Haig said, clutching at her bare neck.

Loxley took her other elbow and helped her to steer the distressed woman back to the settee.

'Fear not, Lady Haig, we will find your necklace,' Loxley said, his eyes roaming around the shocked faces of the guests in the lounge car.

'You will have to search everyone.' She passed Lady Haig a handkerchief.

Loxley frowned, put his hands on his hips, and let his breath out in a low, even stream. Then he looked up at the expectant faces of the guests.

'Ladies and gentlemen. A terrible crime has been committed here just a few moments ago. Someone has stolen Lady Haig's necklace, and no one will leave this car until it's recovered.'

There were a few murmurs among the crowd —some supportive, some objecting.

Loxley cleared his throat. 'Can I please ask the ladies to move to the left side of the car and the gentlemen to move to the right.'

'May I ask why?' Perry Bligh said as he draped an arm around the girl in the red dress.

Loxley's mouth tightened. 'If I don't find the

necklace in my search of the carriage, I'm afraid everyone in this room will need to be searched.'

'But that's outrageous,' Dennis Cosette said, shaking his head.

'Perhaps, but it's necessary,' Loxley said, gesturing for the guests to split into two groups. He raised his eyebrows at her. 'That includes you, Lady Marigold.'

She fixed him with a cool stare. 'I was sitting directly opposite Lady Haig, and Miss Carey was right beside me. I'm sure both will confirm I didn't leave my seat.'

Lady Haig swatted Loxley with Marigold's handkerchief. 'For heaven's sake, Gideon, it wasn't Lady Marigold who took my necklace. The thief grabbed my necklace from behind.' She put a hand up to her neck and tears streaked down her cheeks.

'Look here, Loxley. Stop standing around and find out where the ruddy necklace is,' Sir Fredrick said as he patted his wife's shoulder.

Marigold raised her eyebrows at Loxley, and with an exasperated sigh, he gestured for her to sit.

Hermione clutched her arm. 'Do I need to be searched?'

She shook her head. 'No, you were sitting next to me, and I know you didn't move.'

'I'll be the one to decide who does and doesn't need to be searched,' Loxley said as he bent to search under the settee.

The men and women split into groups on either side of the lounge car. She scanned each guest, looking for some sign of guilt or innocence.

Lady Haig broke into fresh tears when Loxley announced there was no sign of the necklace in the carriage.

'Fear not, my dear. The culprit will be apprehended before this night is out and your necklace will be returned to you,' Sir Fredrick said as he glared around the carriage.

Loxley went first to the men's side of the carriage and performed a search of each gentleman. When he turned to cross the floor to the ladies, an elderly woman put up a hand to stop him.

'I appreciate your need to search each guest, Inspector, but I'm sure I'm not the only lady here who will not submit to a search by a gentleman.'

There were a few sniggers on the men's side of the carriage, and she fixed them with a fierce glare.

'Perhaps I can be of assistance?' She called from the settee.

Loxley's eyes met hers. She smiled when she read the defeat in them. He needed a woman to conduct the search of the ladies, and she was only one of three candidates for the job.

He scowled and gestured for her to join him. 'Very well.'

'I would prefer to be searched by you, Inspector,' Clara said, fluttering her eyelashes at him.

Vivienne stepped forward and nodded. 'I too don't wish to be searched by Lady Marigold. The last time she came near me she destroyed my satin slippers. I don't wish to risk whatever she might do to me given another opportunity.'

Loxley's left cheek twitched. 'Very well, anyone who is willing to be searched by me move to the right and those who wish to be searched by Lady Marigold, move to the left.'

The group of women split into two groups, and she quickly and respectfully searched the ladies who presented themselves to her.

Ten minutes later, there was still no sign of the necklace.

'Perhaps the culprit escaped the carriage after all,' Sir Fredrick said, looking around the carriage as though expecting to find a clue to support this claim.

'That's impossible. There wasn't time, and I was standing in the doorway when the lights went out. No one passed by me,' Loxley said.

Marigold's eyes roamed over Lady Haig's neck

and chin and then to the guests, who had now co-mingled.

'I know who it is and how they did it,' she told Loxley in a low voice.

He frowned at her. 'Enlighten me.'

She moved to Lady Haig's side and pointed to her neck. 'The thief moved behind her and removed the necklace with force, but to do so they had to brace themselves against her. They grabbed the side of her head and her chin.'

She pointed to the smudge of powder on the side of Lady Haig's face. 'The culprit will have powder on their hands and judging from the size of the mark on Lady Haig's face, I believe it was a man.'

Loxley looked at her for a moment, then asked the guest to hold their hands out. He walked between them, examining them carefully. Then he turned back to her. 'I see no powder.'

Marigold bit her lip and let her eyes roam over the guests again. Someone was concealing the necklace, but where?

An idea popped into her head, and she stood and crossed the room to a middle-aged English couple. She pointed to the man's dinner jacket. 'I think you'll find, Inspector, this gentleman wiped his hands on his coat.'

The man, who strongly resembled a walrus

with his round face and enormous moustache, narrowed his beady eyes. 'How dare you accuse me?'

Marigold stood her ground. 'I dare because you and your wife are the guilty party.'

'I advise you to tread carefully,' Loxley said in a low voice as he moved to stand beside her.

She tossed her head. 'There is no need for caution. This is no gentleman, and his wife is no lady. They are a pair of thieves.'

'You just searched us. Where do you think we're hiding the necklace?' the woman shrieked.

She bit her lip. 'It was very clever of you, but you should have chosen a different coloured wig.' She reached up and grabbed hold of the woman's hair.

Several people gasped and then the carriage broke into excited chatter as she pulled off the woman's wig to reveal Lady Haig's necklace.'

'How did you know?' Hermione said, once Loxley had detained the thieves in the boiler room and the excitement had died down.

'She had traces of powder in her hair and the wig wasn't on straight.'

'I just can't thank you enough,' Lady Haig said, patting her necklace.

'I guess this ends your suspicions about me

being the jewel thief,' she told Loxley as he joined them.

He frowned. 'I suppose it does.'

'Come on, Loxley, old boy, you could be a little friendlier. Lady Marigold's the heroine of the hour,' Sir Fredrick chided.

Loxley put his hands in his pockets. 'On this occasion the culprit was found, but in future, a more cautious approach should be undertaken lest an innocent party be accused by mistake.'

'You can just say thank you, you know. I won't make you eat humble pie for too long.'

Loxley got to his feet. 'I'm very glad this unfortunate incident was resolved so quickly, but I still have a murder to solve, so if you will excuse me.' He bowed and left the carriage.

'Goodness, I know he's under pressure to solve the murder, but he could have been a bit nicer to you,' Hermione said, smothering a yawn.

Marigold rolled her eyes. 'That was him being nice.'

CHAPTER TWENTY-SEVEN

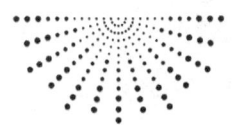

The train was moving when Marigold woke the next morning. She rubbed her eyes and tried to ignore the foreboding settling on her chest.

'Thank goodness we're on our way again, but it means the clock really is ticking now. I simply must find out who killed Mr Olivier.'

'Perhaps you need to join forces with Inspector Loxley,' Elke said as she climbed down from her bunk.

Marigold looked up at her and frowned. 'He's made it pretty clear he won't tolerate me inserting myself into the case.'

'That is what he says, but you will not be the only one feeling the pressure to solve this mystery before the train reaches Paris.' Elke shrugged into her dressing gown, tied it firmly around her waist, and gave her a knowing look.

Marigold ignored her and lay back against her pillows. 'There's so much information and too many suspects. I just can't piece any of it together.'

'I still believe Mr Jorrisen is the killer, but I admit there is no more proof it was him than anyone else,' Elke said.

Marigold sat up again and watched the green fields slide by the window.

'I'm going to have breakfast in the dining room this morning. This scenery is so beautiful. I want to make the most of it.'

Elke nodded and poured a glass of water. 'And I will have breakfast here this morning. I am determined to finish reading this Lady Clues case before the train arrives in Paris.'

'Thank goodness. I'm dying to talk to you about it.' She threw back the covers, and Pepper jumped off the bed. He settled himself in a sunny spot on the floor. She crossed the floor to the wardrobe and considered her choices.

'I think I'll wear this.' She held up a plum skirt, a purple and grey check silk blouse and a matching plum felt cloche with navy feathers and a velvet ribbon.

Elke raised her eyebrows and tipped her head

to the side. After a moment of deliberation, she said, 'You are getting better at this.'

'I could be quite the fashionable lady by the time we arrive in England.'

'That is my plan,' Elke said as she settled into an armchair with her book. She was so engrossed in the story she barely acknowledged her when she bade her farewell half an hour later.

Marigold walked slowly to the dining car and was surprised to find it nearly empty. The only other occupant was Hermione Carey, who was so engrossed in her letter writing she didn't look up.

Inspired by her dedication, she resolved to make a list of everyone she was overdue to correspond with as soon as she arrived in England.

After ordering coffee and a chocolate croissant, she gazed out the window and almost forgot where she was until she became aware of someone calling her name.

She turned and blinked as Inspector Loxley came into focus.

'Enjoying the view?' He was dressed in another pinstriped suit. How many of them did he own? She imagined a wardrobe full of perfectly pressed pinstriped suits and bit her lip.

'Yes, it's lovely to be on the move again. However, I suppose it leaves me even less time to convince you I didn't murder Mr Olivier.'

She couldn't read the expression that crossed over his face at first, but then she realised he was wrestling with something.

'Is everything alright Inspector?'

He looked at the empty seat opposite her and cleared his throat. 'May I join you?'

'As long as you're not here to arrest me, I suppose it can't do any harm.'

He sat opposite her and looked around the empty carriage. 'Where is Miss Müller?'

'She stayed in the compartment, determined to finish her Lady Clues book before the end of our journey.'

'This Lady Clues certainly has a hold over the two of you.'

Marigold bit back a retort in defence of her literary heroine. 'What can I do for you, Inspector?'

Loxley ordered toast and a pot of tea from the waiter, then turned to her. 'It has come to my attention I'm not the only one investigating the death of Mr Olivier.'

She raised her eyebrows. 'Really? Who else is investigating it?'

He sighed. 'You know as well as I do.'

She considered him for a moment. 'If I was investigating the case—which I'm not—of course, I would rule myself and Renée off the suspect list.

There's really no motive strong enough for either of us to have been the killer, and we also had a distinct lack of means and opportunity.'

'You sound very confident.'

'As you're aware, I do enjoy reading Lady Clues. I consider her quite a mentor.'

'If she were real, and on this train, who would she suspect?'

Marigold took a sip of coffee. 'At this point she would have narrowed the suspect list down to Vivienne Cosette, Mr Jorrisen, Mrs Olivier, and Chef Dubois.'

'I'm surprised, Miss Bligh, isn't on your list.'

She did her best to keep her tone light. 'Clara has two alibis. She's unlikely to be the killer.'

'Unlikely, but not impossible.'

'What aren't you telling me, Inspector?'

He raised his eyebrows. 'Almost everything. This is a police investigation, Lady Marigold. The information I obtain is not to be shared.'

'I see, but you're happy for me to share my information with you.' She couldn't keep her annoyance out of her voice.

Loxley sipped his tea. 'Correct. That's how police investigations work.'

Marigold scowled. 'Very well. Regarding Mrs Olivier, why would she remove the diamonds from her husband's cufflinks?'

Loxley choked on his tea. 'How do you know about the diamonds?'

She rested her chin in her hands and met his eyes. 'I noticed them on her dressing table when Miss Müller and I went to visit.'

He put his teacup back onto its saucer. 'You recognised the diamonds?'

She nodded. 'Yes, they're quite distinctive.'

'I thought you said you had no interest in jewellery.'

'For myself, it's true, but I can still appreciate their beauty.'

'What makes you think the diamonds have something to do with the murder?'

Marigold sat back in her chair. 'It seems an odd thing to do and suggests Mrs Olivier intends to either sell them or use them for payment. The question is, which one?'

Loxley stirred a spoonful of sugar into his tea. 'Mrs Olivier has an alibi.'

'Yes, but it doesn't mean she wasn't involved in her husband's murder. She's significantly better off without him.'

'And she has a friendship with another suspect,' Loxley said.

Marigold raised her eyebrows. 'Chef Dubois?'

Loxley nodded.

'But he might not be her partner in crime. In

fact, I find it hard to believe it would be him. He's such a lovely man,' Marigold said

'Is this how Lady Clues solves crimes? By ruling out everyone she personally likes?'

'First impressions are usually correct,' Marigold said, folding her hands in her lap.

'For your sake, let's hope it's not true.'

Marigold laughed. 'Finally, we agree on something.'

The corners of Loxley's mouth twitched. 'What other theories do you have?'

'Why should I share my investigation with you?'

Loxley crumpled his napkin and placed it over his empty plate. 'You don't have to, but it will be in your best interest if you want me to exonerate you and Miss Seydoux. How else will I do it?'

She resisted the urge to kick him under the table. She hated being backed into a corner, but the train was rushing to its destination, and as much as she hated to admit it, Loxley was right.

'I know I said Clara wasn't on my suspect list, but I believe she may have played some role in the murder.'

'And yet, just yesterday, the two of you were the best of friends. How fickle friendship is among women.'

Marigold scowled. 'You know we aren't friends. We never have been.'

'Childhood grudges aside, why do you suspect her?'

She twisted a lock of hair around her pointer finger. 'If I tell you, I'll need your assurance I won't suffer any consequences.'

Loxley pinched the bridge of his nose and waved his hand for her to continue.

She took a deep breath and decided not to reveal Sebastian's role in the story. 'The thing is, I happened to be in Mr Olivier's compartment, and I came across a photograph of Clara hidden in his drawers.'

Loxley let his breath out in a long, slow stream. 'What kind of photograph?

'The kind a man might keep of a woman he was passionate about.' She opened her handbag and took out the photograph.

Loxley took it and stared at it for a moment, then met her eyes.

'Why didn't you tell me you'd found this before now?'

She sat back in her chair and crossed her arms over her chest. 'You were ready to arrest me for stealing from Mrs Olivier—with no proof, mind you—what would have happened if I'd admitted I'd found this?'

Loxley put the photograph on the table and drummed the fingers of his right hand next to it. 'Mr Olivier might have harboured feelings for Clara Bligh, but so do half the men in England. I see nothing to suggest she was involved with him. Perhaps your personal grudge is clouding your judgement.'

She snapped her handbag shut. 'I admit I thought the same thing at first, but I have a witness who saw the two of them having a heated discussion the night after the murder.'

Loxley raised his eyebrows. 'What witness?'

She shook her head. 'I'm afraid I can't disclose it, but it's not important. The main thing is, there is something between Clara Bligh and Mr Jorrisen they aren't admitting to.'

Loxley looked pensive. 'And?'

Marigold sighed. 'And it was apparent they knew each other quite well. Far too well for a newly married woman on her honeymoon.'

'I'm not sure where you're going with this theory,' he said with a frown.

She slapped the table. 'Doesn't it seem like a big coincidence Mr Jorrisen, a man who I witnessed multiple times threatening Mr Olivier, paid a call on Clara the night after the murder?'

'You think Jorrisen murdered Olivier because of a love triangle?'

'It's possible.'

Loxley took out his notepad and wrote something inside. 'What other theories do you have?'

She chewed her lip. She didn't want to involve Sebastian or Florence, but how else could she explain what they'd seen?

'You'll need to trust me, Inspector, when I say I have a source on the train who provided me with reliable information about Chef Dubois and Mrs Olivier.'

'First a witness and now a source? You've only been on this train for three days. How is it possible?'

'People like to tell me things.'

'And it has nothing to do with you asking them questions?'

'Do you want to know what I know or not?'

He blinked. 'Tell me.'

While he wrote in his notebook, she relayed what Sebastian and Florence had told her about the chef and Unity Olivier.

'Anything else?'

'That's all I know.'

Loxley tucked his notebook and pen in the inside pocket of his jacket. He got to his feet. 'Thank you for your company this morning. It has been very enlightening.'

She frowned at him. 'Does this mean you're going to clear Renée and I from the suspect list?'

Loxley paused. 'I'll consider it.'

She swore under her breath as she watched him leave the dining car. Either telling him what she knew was a masterstroke or a huge mistake.

CHAPTER TWENTY-EIGHT

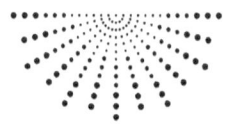

On the final night of the journey, Lady Haig hosted a party in the lounge car to celebrate Sir Fergus' eightieth birthday.

To Marigold's relief, she had insisted Elke attend. 'I'm very fond of her. Please tell her I expect to see her there.'

Elke hadn't shared Lady Haig's enthusiasm for her attendance.

'I still have five Lady Clues' cases to read. I do not have time to be attending a party.'

'Oh, come on. It won't be that bad.' Normally she would have agreed with Elke, but with the train journey coming to an end, she was eager for any opportunity to gather more clues.

Elke sighed and put her book aside. 'Pepper

will not be happy about being left alone for the evening.'

'Not to worry, I've asked Sebastian and Florence to stay with him.'

'Wonderful, I look forward to cleaning up the aftermath,' Elke muttered.

Marigold ruffled Pepper's topknot. 'But at least he'll have fun.'

Elke shook her head and continued grumbling under her breath as she left the compartment to bathe.

Marigold slipped out of her silk robe and stepped into a peach evening gown.

The dress had a sheer bodice sequin to the waist. The skirt consisted of tiers of scalloped beadwork in a shell pattern.

When she turned, the dress caught the light, and she couldn't resist doing a few twirls in front of the mirror. At this rate, she'd be a flapper by the time she arrived in England.

She poked her tongue out at her reflection. It was one thing to dress up on the train, but once she was at Mayfair, she'd be back to wearing more practical garments.

Elke returned to the compartment, having changed into a navy silk blouse and skirt. She snapped on a pair of pearl earrings and slipped a matching necklace over her head.

'I prefer to buy the clothes rather than wear them.' She scowled at her reflection.

Marigold smothered a smile. 'And yet you look lovely.'

Elke handed her an embroidered peach satin shawl. 'We should get this over with quickly.'

'We must try to hide our dismay from Lady Haig. I've grown fond of her,' Marigold said as she picked up her handbag.

Elke sighed. 'I too have a great deal of respect for her and will do my best to appear as though I am enjoying the evening.'

There was a knock at the door, and Marigold opened it to find Sebastian and Florence, their cheeks flushed and eyes bright.

Pepper jumped off the bed and launched himself at them.

'I think we can safely say we have been relegated in Pepper's affections,' she said with a laugh, watching as the little dog licked the children's faces. Their squeals warmed her heart. It was lovely to see them free from the burdens they carried, if only for a while.

Sebastian laughed as Pepper licked his chin. 'Thank you for letting us stay with Pepper, miss.'

She smiled. 'Of course. You're the only two I would trust to look after him.'

'You could be a film star,' Florence said. Her

hand reached out to touch one of the beaded shells on her skirt.

'How kind of you to say, Florence. I'm very lucky to have Elke to find dresses as lovely as this one for me. Left to my own devices, I'd probably be wearing jodhpurs and riding boots.'

'That is very true,' Elke said darkly, and Florence giggled.

'I've ordered you dinner. Nico will bring it to you shortly and there's a special treat for you too, Pepper.' She gave him a farewell pat.

Elke gave her a side glance as they left the suite. 'You have become very fond of those children.'

'They're easy to like, and I confess my anxiety is rising as the journey draws to a close. I fear what will happen to them when they return to England.'

Elke stopped to adjust her shoe. 'Perhaps you can help them find their relations.'

'As usual, you've read my mind. That's exactly what I plan to do. I just need to speak to Bentley about how we go about it.'

'Perhaps Mr Bentley will be reluctant to return to England. He seems very content working on the train.'

Marigold shook her head. 'That would never happen. Bentley loves Mayfair; it's his home.'

'And yours.'

Marigold sighed. 'Technically it is, but I confess, I'm still struggling to think of it that way. I've never had a home, and, in my imagination, I've always pictured a little stone cottage with a garden and fireplace. Not a two hundred room sandstone mansion.'

The lounge car was crowded and noisy when she and Elke arrived at the party.

The pianist was playing an upbeat tune she didn't recognise, but it made her want to tap her feet to the beat.

Lady Haig and Sir Fredrick's faces lit up, and they called to her. A rush of affection for them washed over her. Their simple enjoyment of life was both refreshing and inspiring.

She made her way over to them with Elke in tow. 'Good evening, Sir Fredrick, Lady Haig.'

'Oh Marigold, you're breath-taking,' Lady Haig said while Sir Fredrick nodded enthusiastically.

'She certainly is. Almost as lovely as my wife.'

Lady Haig blushed. 'Oh Fredrick, stop it.' She fanned herself with her hand.

'You also look very nice this evening, Miss Müller,' Sir Fredrick said, bowing to Elke.

Elke nodded. 'That is very kind of you to say, Sir Fredrick. May I wish you a happy birthday?'

He nodded. 'Indeed, you may, and you must have a drink so we can toast to my great age. He raised his hand and signalled to a waiter for more champagne.

Lady Haig's face lit up again. 'Oh, and here's dear Gideon. I'm so pleased you could come. I'm worried you're working too hard. Your mother wouldn't like it.'

Loxley took a gloved hand and kissed it. 'I'm counting on you not to tell her.'

'What news of the case, Gideon? Are you any closer to finding who killed Mr Olivier?'

Loxley glanced at Marigold. She raised her eyebrows. 'Yes, Inspector, please do update us on your progress.'

He put his hands in the pockets of his trousers. 'I'm confident the person responsible will be detained by the time the train arrives in Paris.'

'Is it Mr Jorrisen?' Lady Haig said, lowering her voice. She shot a glance across the room to where the deputy director was talking to Clara's new husband.

Loxley smiled. 'Let's talk about something more pleasant. How are Spick and Span?'

She caught Elke's eye and shrugged her shoulders. Lady Haig watched the exchange and laughed. She put a hand on her shoulder. 'They're our dogs, my dears.' Without further encouragement, she launched into a detailed description of her beloved pets and Loxley listened with what appeared to be genuine interest.

Elke nudged her in the ribs. 'Miss Carey is trying to get your attention.' She pointed over her head.

'Excuse me.' She raised her hand to acknowledge Hermione's greeting and crossed the room to join her.

Hermione was wearing a pale gold dress with flutter sleeves and a swirling pattern of silver beads on the bodice. Her gold satin turban was decorated with a feathers and sequins. She had a glass of champagne in her hand, which she attributed to the spots of colour on her cheeks and the glaze in her eyes. 'I'm sorry to have interrupted your conversation.'

She waved her hand. 'I'm glad you did. It's been lovely getting to know you too, but we mustn't lose touch. Promise you'll write to me and come to stay at Mayfair Manor.'

A strange expression crossed Hermione's face. Then she blinked, and it was gone so quickly she wondered if she'd imagined it.

Hermione cleared her throat. 'That would be lovely.' She dropped her eyes to the floor. 'I saw you talking with Inspector Loxley at breakfast this morning. I didn't want to intrude, but is everything alright?'

'Yes. Perfectly fine. The Inspector just had a few questions for me.'

Hermione shuddered. 'I hope he finds the person responsible for Mr Olivier's death soon. The thought of a killer walking among us is quite terrifying.'

'Yes, it's horrible, but it will all be over soon.'

Hermione nodded and looked over at her shoulder. 'Will you excuse me? Madame de Le Mason is signalling for me to join her, and I don't dare disobey her.'

Marigold laughed. 'Of course, but promise me we'll exchange addresses before the train arrives in Paris so we can write to one another.'

Once Hermione was gone, she returned to Elke and the Haigs, but when she turned around, she found herself face to face with Loxley.

'Lady Marigold, a word, please.' He gestured to the back corner of the lounge car.

'This is a party, Inspector, and I've already told you all by best information.'

'That may be so, but I found a rather interesting piece of information about you when I searched Mr Olivier's compartment.'

Marigold stared at him for a moment and tried to keep her face impassive. 'About me?

Goodness, surely, you've found out everything there is to know by now.'

'It seems your interest in criminal investigations might be more than a simple interest in detective books. My enquiries into your activities during the war have been blocked at every turn. It makes me wonder what the nature of them was.'

She blinked and took a sip of champagne. 'Wonder no longer, Inspector. I imagine the foreign office doesn't share its personnel files easily, but as a translator, mine wouldn't be very interesting.'

Loxley frowned. 'A translator?'

'Yes. Didn't I mention it?'

'No, you didn't.'

She took another sip of champagne. 'Silly me. It's not a secret after all, but you see, I have a natural talent for languages and speak quite a few of them. That's what I was engaged to do for the government, but alas, it sounds more interesting than it was.'

'Very well. If that's all there is to it, I'll leave you to enjoy the party.'

Marigold forced herself to keep her tone light. 'Won't Lady Haig be disappointed if you leave?'

'I think she prefers I solve the mystery of Mr Olivier's murder.'

She nodded and raised her champagne flute. 'So do we all.'

As he left the carriage, Marigold turned to put her empty glass on the silver tray carried by a nearby waiter. 'Lady Marigold?' he said.

'Yes?'

'Excuse me, mademoiselle, but I have a note for you.'

She watched him pick up a small cream envelope from the tray. Her name was written on the front in flowery script.

'Who's it from?'

He shrugged. 'I'm afraid I don't know, my lady. Someone placed it on the tray when I wasn't looking.'

She thanked him and turned away to open the letter. She scanned its content and snapped her head up, searching the room.

No one met her eyes. Every guest seemed absorbed in the party, but one of them had taken the time to write and deliver the note.

Marigold re-read the contents and shivered.

'Enjoy your freedom while it lasts. Soon you will pay for what you have done.'

CHAPTER TWENTY-NINE

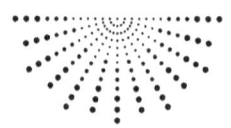

Marigold put the note back in its envelope and looked around the carriage.

Perry was playing an upbeat tune on the piano.

The Haigs were part of a group of people gathered around it singing.

Clara sat by the window with Osbert. They both looked bored as they sipped their cocktails.

Vivienne was holding court near the bar as a group of young men fought to get her attention. Aline stood to the side of her sister, looking as though she wished she was anywhere but there.

Dennis Cosette sat alone at a table nearby with a vodka bottle and glass on his table. Without his sisters by his side, he had a menacing air. He looked up, caught Marigold's eye and scowled.

She looked away hurriedly and heard someone call her name.

'Is everything alright?' Hermione said, looking at her with concern.

Marigold gave herself a mental shake. 'Yes, perfectly fine. I was just admiring the lovely gowns on display tonight, including yours, of course.'

Hermione looked pleased. She ran a hand down her beaded gown and patted her turban. 'How nice of you to say, but truly, your dress is the loveliest here.'

Marigold tried to stay focussed on Hermione, but her mind was still spinning. 'All credit for my gown goes to Miss Mueller. Left to my own devices, I'm just as likely to have turned up wearing knickerbockers.'

Hermione laughed, and her hand moved to her throat. She hooked a finger through the chain under the bodice of her dress. The ruby ring on her left hand glowed in the candlelight.

'You're funny.'

'I like to think so, but others would dispute it.' She glanced at Vivienne.

Hermione followed her gaze. 'I wouldn't worry if you don't have Vivienne Cosette's endorsement. She seems to have no sense of humour at all. I can't tell you what a disappointment it was to discover she was such a pill.'

Marigold raised her eyebrows. 'Really? What happened?'

Normally she wasn't one for gossip, but on this occasion, she justified it in hopes she might learn something to help Renée.

Hermione took a sip of her cocktail. 'I'm embarrassed to say it out loud, but she snubbed me when I tried to speak to her. I shouldn't have taken it personally, but I had admired her for such a long time.'

'How disappointing.'

'It really was, and I felt quite pathetic afterwards.'

She gave her a sympathetic nod. 'I'm sorry it happened to you.'

Hermione sighed. 'It's fine. I probably was a little over the top in my enthusiasm, but at least it made a good story for my letter to my friend.'

'The most embarrassing situations end up being best stories—once the sting has worn off.'

Hermione nodded. 'You're right, although I can't imagine you find yourself in those situations too often. You're so poised and composed.'

Marigold shook her head. 'Oh goodness, you're being very kind. I assure you it's not the case at all.' She put her a hand to her head as pain began to blossom over left eye.

'Are you alright?' Hermione said, looking at with concern.

'Yes, just a headache. I'm going back to my suite to get some powder for it, but before I go, I must write down your address.'

She opened her handbag, intending to take out her notepad and a pencil, but as she reached for it, someone bumped her from behind.

'My apologies,' Dennis Cosette said, but his tone and his expression suggested otherwise. He looked at the contents of her handbag, which were strewn all over the floor, and for a moment she thought he was going to collect them for her, but then he walked away.

'It seems rudeness runs in the family,' Hermione said bending to help her. She handed her a tube of lipstick.

'I find Aline to be quite personable, but otherwise, I agree with you.'

Hermione picked up the envelope containing the threatening note. An odd expression crossed her face. 'I think that's everything.'

'I received this note tonight during the party. It's unsigned. I wonder if you recognise the handwriting?' She held it up to show her the front of the envelope.

Hermione's eyes widened. 'No, I'm afraid I don't. Is it from an admirer?'

'Not quite.'

'How peculiar.'

'Yes, it is rather, but I'm afraid it's a puzzle I'll have to solve another day. For now, I must go and lie down.'

'Of course. I hope you feel better soon.'

Marigold continued her search for Elke, but she seemed to have disappeared.

Next, she looked for Bentley, but he too was nowhere to be seen.

Unsettled, she had a sudden urge to leave the party and would have done so, but Lady Haig was making her way toward her.

'Is everything alright my dear? You're rather pale.' Lady Haig's face was full of concern.

'Just a headache, I'm afraid. I'll take some headache power and lie down for half an hour. Hopefully, it will go away so I can return in time for cake.'

'You won't regret it if you do. Chef Dubois has outdone himself.'

'I'm sure he has. He's very talented.'

'If you don't return, I'll save you a slice.'

'That would be lovely.'

She said goodbye and made a detour to the powder room to splash water on her face. She wanted to make sure she was calm and composed before she returned to the suite.

Marigold frowned at her reflection. She pinched her cheeks to return some colour to them. There was no point scaring Sebastian and Florence, and she was sure she was overreacting. The note was probably someone's idea of a silly joke, not a real threat.

It felt like one, though.

But who would threaten her? Who thought she was the killer?

She was certain Loxley wasn't behind the note. He would have just come out and said it if that were the case. So who was it?

The list of suspects ran through her head, along with the uneasy sensation she might be in danger.

She left the powder room and turned left, intending to depart the carriage. But just as she stepped into the vestibule, a shiver ran up her spine.

The idea she was being watched came unbidden, but as soon as it did, she was convinced her instincts were right.

Marigold pushed open the door and hastened her steps as she crossed into the first sleeper carriage.

A quick check over her shoulder revealed she

wasn't being followed, but then she collided with something hard that smelled like pine cologne.

Her heart leapt to her throat, and she gave a cry of alarm. It snapped her out of her fear state. She refused to be intimidated or show weakness. Whatever or whoever came her way, she would meet them head on.

She forced herself to glance up and spotted a man glaring down at her. 'Mr Jorrisen. My apologies. I didn't see you.'

'What are you doing out here, Lady Marigold? Shouldn't you be at the party?' His voice held an edge and fine hairs on the back of her neck prickled.

'I have a headache, so am returning to my suite.' She took a step forward.

He moved sideways, blocking her path.

'You're alone?' His dark eyes bored into hers.

Marigold willed herself not to break eye contact. A surge of adrenaline flooded through her, as did her determination to hold her ground.

'Miss Müller will be along shortly. She forgot her shawl and returned to the lounge car to retrieve it.' She crossed her fingers behind her back and prayed she sounded convincing.

His scowl deepened.

'Perhaps you need to get some rest? With all

this detective work you've been doing; it's no wonder you're unwell. It must be exhausting?'

She frowned. 'I'm not sure what you mean? I haven't been doing detective work. Inspector Loxley only asked me to observe his interview with you.'

Marigold glanced around the corridor, hoping someone would pass by. Alas, it remained empty.

He licked his lips. 'I must have been misinformed. I had been told you have been asking questions about Mr Olivier's death.'

'Oh? By whom?'

He waved his hand dismissively. 'It matters not who, but why you continue to concern yourself with the matter.'

She dug her fingernails into her palms. 'Naturally, I'm curious about what happened to him. I was the one to discover his body, after all.'

'Yes, I imagine it must be quite perplexing, but you must exercise more caution. Until Inspector Loxley apprehends the killer, I suggest you don't walk alone, especially at night.'

There was nothing in his tone or his gaze to suggest he was anything other than genuinely concerned for her welfare, but still he didn't step aside to let her pass. She met his gaze, refusing to blink or avert her eyes.

If it was the last thing she did—and she hoped

it wasn't—she wasn't going to let him know she was rattled. After all, she'd been in far stickier situations than this. Of course, on those occasions, she had her gun for leverage. Silently, she cursed Loxley for confiscating the weapon.

Marigold suppressed a smile when he was the first to break eye contact. Apparently, she hadn't lost her touch.

'I only ask questions because there are so many of them unanswered.'

His jaw jutted forward. 'And I suppose you think I'm the culprit because of the fight you witnessed. But you know nothing. I didn't kill Mr Olivier.'

'Neither did I'

His eyebrows shot up. 'You?'

She shrugged. 'Yes. I'm as much a suspect as anyone on this train, and someone seems to think I might be the killer. I wonder if it's you?'

He rolled his eyes. 'I confess you and your dog have been challenging guests, mademoiselle, but unlike you, I have never tried to have you put behind bars.'

Marigold kept her eyes trained on his face. 'So, you didn't send me the note?'

Confusion flitted across his features. It appeared to be a genuine reaction. 'Note?'

She pulled the envelope out of her purse and

waved it in front of his face. 'Yes. Just now. Someone had a waiter give this to me. It contains a threat.'

'How distressing for you,' he said, not sounding regretful in the least.

Marigold took half a step towards him, but he held his ground, continuing to tower over her. Not for the first time, she cursed her small stature.

'As I said, I have a headache, and I'd like to return to my suite. Please let me pass.'

'What will you do if I don't? Scream? There is no one to hear you here,' he said, leering at her.

Her stomach flipped. Whatever happened now, she would need to get herself out of it.

'I'll tell you what you're going to do, Lady Marigold,' he sneered.

'Please, do enlighten me. It's rather chilly standing here in the corridor.' She was relieved her nerves weren't obvious in her voice. Despite her rising panic, her voice sounded strong and calm.

'You're going to go return to your suite and write me a cheque for one hundred pounds to cover the cost of my destroyed shoes.'

She nearly laughed with relief. The shoes! Was this what he was threatening her about?

'I'll, of course, be happy to reimburse you for the damage Pepper has done.'

'See to it you do,' he said, standing aside at last.

She wrapped her shawl around her shoulders and swept past him.

CHAPTER THIRTY

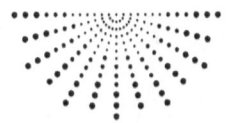

The lights flickered as Marigold made her way down the corridor.

She resisted the temptation to check over her shoulder to make sure Mr Jorrisen wasn't following her.

Instead, she relied on the reflections in the window, but she need not have worried. When she arrived outside the door to her suite, there was no sign of the deputy director.

She unlocked the door and rested against it once she was inside. The light and warmth of the room enveloped her, and she the stress of the evening slipped away as Sebastian and Florence's faces lit up.

Pepper, who had been racing around in a

circle in the centre of the bed, gave a yelp of delight and launched himself at her, clawing at the beads on her gown.

Marigold sank to the floor to greet him and to save the dress.

Elke was curled up in an armchair wearing her robe and eating Turkish delight as she read Lady Clues.

Marigold's heart rate settled back into a normal rhythm. 'Have you had a good evening?'

Sebastian's face glowed with happiness. 'The best, miss. We ate pasta and had chocolate cake for dessert.'

'And Pepper had a little cake made of minced meat,' Florence said, holding out her arms as the little dog abandoned Marigold and curled up in her lap.

There was a clap of thunder, and the lights flickered.

Sebastian's face paled, and Florence buried her face in Pepper's fur.

'It's alright. Just a storm. It'll pass soon.' She glanced out the window as the sky split apart by a bolt of lightning.

'I hope there will no further delay because of this storm,' Elke grumbled, not looking up from her book.

'When did you sneak out of the party? You could at least have said goodbye,' She kicked off her shoes.

Elke shrugged. 'But then you would have insisted I stay.'

'You're right, I would have. Well played.'

'Plus, when I departed, you were involved in a discussion with Inspector Loxley. I didn't want to interrupt.'

Marigold rolled her eyes. 'I would have welcomed the interruption. He was asking about my war service.'

Elke put the book down. 'What did you tell him?'

She sat at the dressing table and took off her earrings. 'I told him the truth. That I was a translator.'

'Technically, that's true.'

'He doesn't need to know anything else. My war service is irrelevant to his investigation. Hopefully, he knows now.'

Sebastian's eyes widened. 'Were you in the war, miss?'

She smiled at him. 'Not in the fighting, but I played my part.'

'I would have fought if the war hadn't ended.'

She ruffled his hair. 'Be glad you didn't have

to, Seb. War is dreadful. Don't believe anyone who tells you otherwise.'

Another clap of thunder made the window rattle, and the two children shrieked and ducked their heads under their arms.

She sat between them and put her arms around their shoulders. 'I take it the two of you aren't fond of storms?'

Florence shook her head. 'No miss. I know it's silly, but I've always hated them, and poor Seb is the same.'

She realised Florence was trembling.

There was a knock at the door, and she answered it to find Nico and a trolley containing a pot of hot chocolate, four mugs, and a chocolate cake.'

'I thought you and your young company might like a hot drink and a treat, my lady.'

She gave him a grateful smile. 'You're an angel, Nico. Thank you. Is there any news on this storm? I hope it won't delay us?'

'Monsieur Jorrisen is taking precautions in case it gets worse.'

As if on cue, the lights flickered again, and lightning flashed across the sky outside the window.

Sebastian and Florence cried out, and Pepper

let out a high-pitched whine and dove under a pillow on the bed.

'Nico, could I ask you to bring me some extra pillows and blankets? I shall have two overnight guests this evening.'

'Of course, my lady, I shall return momentarily with them.'

When he had departed, she turned to Sebastian and Florence.

'I wonder if I can ask another favour of you. As you can see, Poor Pepper is very frightened of storms. Can I ask you to stay here with him tonight? To help keep him company?'

Relief washed over Florence's face. 'Of course, miss, but where will we sleep?'

She smiled. 'Don't worry. We'll work it out.'

An hour later, with the wind whistling outside, rain beating against the window and thunder rumbling overhead, the two children and Pepper were settled in Marigold's bed.

'Where are you going to sleep?' Elke said.

Marigold pointed to the settee. 'Nico's coming back to make it up for me.'

'You're becoming very attached to these children.'

She sighed. 'I know. I feel very protective of them. I hated storms as a child, but I had to suffer through them alone. If I can help them avoid a little night-time terror, it's worth it.'

There was a tap on the door, and she opened it, expecting to see Nico, but it was Bentley.

'I wanted to check you were alright, my lady. You left the party early.'

Marigold put a hand to her left eye. 'I needed some headache pills, but I'm feeling better now.'

'I'm very glad to hear it, but what's going on here?' Bentley said, his voice heavy with disapproval as he looked around the chaos in the suite.

'An impromptu sleepover.' She gestured for him to sit. 'I'm glad you're here, Bentley. I need to show you something.'

She took the note off the dressing table and handed it to him.

'What's that?'

'I was about to tell you. While I was at the party, someone wrote me a threatening note.'

Bentley's eyes skimmed the note, and the line between his eyes became a crevice.

'Have you told the Inspector about this?'

'No, and I don't plan to.'

'Is that wise?' Bentley said with a sigh.

'Probably not, but I'd rather sort it out myself. I want to find out who this person is and what they have against me.'

'They could be dangerous and possibly the killer.'

'Even more reason to find out who they are as soon as possible.'

Marigold cut a slice of cake and offered it to Bentley. He refused, so she sat and took a bite. She savoured the richness of the chocolate and the sweetness of the frosting.

'How did you get this note?' Elke said as she examined it.

'Someone put it on the waiter's tray. He didn't see who it was.'

'Neat penmanship. It's unlikely to be a man.'

'That's not necessarily true. Inspector Loxley has neat handwriting.'

Elke raised her eyebrows. 'But I assume it was not sent by him?'

'No. He wouldn't bother with a note. He'd just come straight out and tell me I was a suspect. Oh, that's right, he already has.'

Bentley pulled a notepad and pencil out of his coat pocket and looked at her. 'If you won't tell Inspector Loxley, we must try to narrow down the suspects.'

'Good idea.' She thought back to the party. 'There was Sir Fredrick and Lady Haig, of course. Inspector Loxley, Clara and Osbert Yorke, Perry Bligh, Chef Dubois, Hermione Carey and the

Cosettes, Mr Jorrisen and many others. Too many to name.'

'Was anyone acting strangely?'

Marigold pictured the party in her mind, then shook her head. 'Not any more than usual on this train.'

'You didn't notice anyone glaring at you?'

'Only Clara and Vivienne, but by now I consider it normal behaviour.'

'Anything else out of the ordinary?' Bentley said.

She put her plate on the table. 'Only Mr Jorrisen. My goodness, I can't believe I haven't told you this yet, but he accosted me in the corridor.'

Bentley's eyes darkened. 'He what?'

Marigold stood and paced by the window. She glanced at the sleeping children in the bed and lowered her voice.

'Yes. It was the oddest thing. I left the party right after I got the note and perhaps I was being paranoid, but I felt I was being followed.'

'You should have returned to the party.'

She smiled at the reproach in his voice. 'Perhaps, but I was eager to return to the suite, so I kept walking and collided with Mr Jorrisen.'

'What was he doing there?'

Marigold watched lightning criss-cross the

sky. 'I don't know. It wasn't a social conversation. The man was quite threatening.'

'How dare he,' Bentley said, his chest expanding.

Marigold felt a rush of affection at his outrage. 'At first, I thought maybe he was the author of the note, but upon talking to him I realised it wasn't true. His only concern was to be reimbursed the destruction of his shoes by Pepper.'

'Mr Jorrisen is the deputy-director of the train. He shouldn't be intimidating guests, least of all a lady,' Bentley growled.

'I admit it wasn't a pleasant experience, but I think he's mostly bluff, Bentley.'

He crossed his arms over his chest. 'Let's hope we don't have to find out.'

'I promise to avoid him from here on in, so it shouldn't be a problem.'

'So, if it wasn't Jorrisen, who wrote the note?'

She sighed and took his pencil and the list from him. She scanned it and crossed off two names. 'Well, it wasn't Hermione or Mr Klassen. They aren't even suspects.'

'What about Clara?'

'She certainly hates me enough to write it, but we have a truce, of sorts, and if she wanted revenge on me for getting her expelled from school

—and I admit she probably does—she would have done it long before now.'

'And Chef Dubois?'

Marigold nibbled on her thumbnail. 'Surely not. He's always been pleasant to me.'

'The problem is, there is a killer on this train. Someone is not who we think they are,' Elke reminded her.

Bentley paced by the window. 'Miss Vivienne Cosette might have written the note to scare you. She's been under scrutiny from Inspector Loxley, and she hasn't made any effort to hide her dislike of you. Not that I understand it.'

Marigold sat at the dressing table and applied a lightly scented cream to her hands. 'Thank you, Bentley, and I agree, Vivienne makes the most sense. I find it hard to believe she would send a note though. It doesn't seem her style. It could have been Aline or Dennis. Now that I think of it, Dennis was more menacing than usual.'

Bentley stopped pacing. 'What did he do?'

'He didn't do anything, but it was clear I wasn't the only one who didn't want to be at the party. Aline has always been pleasant to me so we can discount her, but Dennis remains a possibility.'

'We need to check both their handwriting.'

'After Clara, Vivienne is the person who despises me the most on this train.'

'Vivienne may despise you, but she loves being adored,' Elke said, her eyes flickering to the two sleeping children.

'What are you suggesting?'

'I'm not suggesting, I'm proposing, and I'm sure your two young friends would be delighted to meet a famous prima ballerina in person.'

Marigold smiled. 'That's an excellent idea. We'll go to see her first thing in the morning.'

CHAPTER THIRTY-ONE

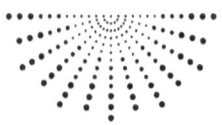

Marigold had drunk four cups of coffee by the time Aline arrived in the dining car the next morning. She had dark circles under her eyes and her shoulders were hunched. Her head was bowed as the attendant showed her to a table.

'Good morning, Mrs Martin.'

Aline lifted her head slightly and her mouth formed a smile, but it didn't reach her eyes. 'Good morning, Lady Marigold.'

'Would you like to join me?' She gestured to the spare seat opposite her.

'I don't want to interrupt your breakfast.'

'You wouldn't be. I was just about to order coffee.'

'If you don't mind, some company would be

welcome,' Aline said with a heavy sigh. She sat opposite her, unfolded her linen napkin, and glanced out the window.

'I'm afraid it's going to rain all the way to Paris and ruin our view of the countryside.'

Aline shrugged. 'I don't mind. I have taken this train many times I know the scenery as though it were a film projected in my brain.'

Marigold frowned. 'How many times have you travelled on the Lunar Express?'

Aline put a hand in front of her mouth to smother a yawn. 'Forgive me, I didn't sleep well last night, and I'm exaggerating. I have been on this train three times this year. I'm afraid the novelty wore off after the first two.'

'Your sister is fond of train travel, then?'

Aline's expression darkened. 'She was fond of Mr Olivier. She enjoyed his attention, but now he's gone, I imagine this will be our last journey on the train.'

'I wonder if I may ask a favour of you.'

Aline took a sip and closed her eyes. She appeared to be savouring the taste and smell. 'If it's something I can help with, I would be happy to.'

Marigold did her best to set her coffee cup on its saucer, but the effects of her morning excess had made her hand unsteady.

'I have made friends with two young people

on the train who are great admirers of Vivienne's. I was hoping I could bring them to meet her.'

'I'm sure Vivienne would be happy to receive them. She rarely says no to being admired,' Aline said with a wry smile.

'Thank you. They will be so excited. I didn't want to say anything to them before I asked you, as I know Vivienne isn't fond of me.'

Aline frowned. 'I wouldn't take it personally. Vivienne is hard on people she doesn't know well.'

'I think perhaps I got her off-side by asking too many questions about Mr Olivier—and also the unfortunate incident with her shoes.'

'The shoes were undamaged, but I must ask, why were you interested in Vivienne's relationship with Mr Olivier? Surely that's a matter for Inspector Loxley?'

Marigold nodded. 'You're right, of course, but I wanted to help Renée. I'm sure she's not guilty, and I thought Vivienne could help.'

Aline sighed. 'I felt bad for Renée, but I'm sure the Inspector will realise she isn't a killer.'

'I hope so too and I'm very glad to hear I can bring a little happiness to the children. What time might be convenient for a visit?'

Aline rubbed her eyes. 'Vivienne is not a morning person, but perhaps this afternoon? I'll check with her and send the conductor with a message to tell you the time.'

She sipped her coffee and tried not to fidget as the caffeine buzzed through her body. 'I'll look forward to it.'

~

'I CAN'T BELIEVE we're going to meet the Vivienne Cosette,' Florence said for the tenth time since she and Sebastian had knocked on the door of her suite.

'She's the one who is lucky to meet you.'

'We're going to meet a real prima ballerina star. Mama loved Vivienne's dancing and collected all the magazines with her on the cover. We had to leave them in Istanbul, though,' Sebastian said, his smile dipping.

A pang of sadness washed over her. She had been a similar age to Sebastian when she'd lost her parents. 'She'll be looking down on you and be very excited.'

She brushed aside her misgivings about the visit. She hoped Vivienne would behave herself. If not, she would ensure she lived to regret it.

After Florence had checked her hair for the final time in the mirror, they left the suite and walked to the end of the corridor, where Nico was busy answering calls.

'We're here to see Miss Cosette.'

Nico smiled and rapped on the door. 'She is waiting for you.'

The door opened, and Dennis glowered at Marigold.

'Show them in,' Vivienne called from inside the suite. Her voice was uncharacteristically high and bright.

Sebastian didn't need a second invitation, but Marigold had to nudge Florence in the back to propel her forward. The girl seemed starstruck.

She couldn't blame her. If she hadn't known the truth about Vivienne's personality, she too might have been dazzled by her beauty and glamour.

The prima ballerina was sitting on the sofa, posed as though it were a throne. She was wearing a fur trimmed, floral silk robe and matching turban. Diamonds sparkled on her fingers, wrists, and around her neck. Her face was made up as though she was about to take the stage. She batted her eyelashes at Florence and Sebastian and gestured for them to approach her like a queen to her subjects.

Vivienne held out a hand, and Sebastian grasped it so tightly she winced.

'Who do we have here?' Her voice dropped several octaves.

'I'm Sebastian Smith, Miss Cosette, and this is my sister Flo.'

'Florence,' his sister said, her voice croaky and barely above a whisper.

'I'm pleased to meet you,' Vivienne said, shaking hands.

'Do you know Lady Marigold?'

Vivienne's smile faltered. 'Yes. We're acquainted.' She gave Marigold a glare that could have frozen time.

She pointed to the sofa and gestured for the children to sit. Marigold declined and instead left the children to talk to Vivienne while she walked around the suite.

Dennis stood by the window with his hands clasped behind his back. When she passed by he said, 'Are you looking forward to arriving in Paris, Lady Marigold?'

She stared at him, taken aback at this unexpected invitation to conversation. What was that about?

'I am. It's one of my favourite cities, but I confess, I'm hoping this dreadful business with Mr Olivier will be resolved before we arrive.'

Dennis scowled. 'I can't say I liked the man, but it's shocking he was murdered.'

'I imagine it was also a shock for Renée to be detained?' She watched his face closely. The briefest hint of surprise appeared in the lines on his forehead, but otherwise his expression was impassive.

Dennis nodded stiffly. 'Of course. Her arrest was a shock to us all, but you don't always know people.'

Marigold frowned. 'Surely you don't think she killed Mr Olivier?'

'That's for Inspector Loxley to decide, but I know she was keeping secrets.'

'Yes, I imagine it was a shock to learn she was Mr Olivier's daughter.'

Dennis's jaw dropped. Either he had a hereto unknown talent for acting, or it was a genuine reaction. She leaned toward it being the latter.

'She was his daughter?' He smashed his fist on the desk. A lamp wobbled and crashed to the floor.

Vivienne looked up, clearly annoyed. 'Dennis, what are you doing?'

'My apologies sister, but Lady Marigold just shared some surprising news.'

Vivienne's eyebrows rose. 'And what was that?'

Dennis looked at Sebastian and Florence. 'I'll tell you once the children have gone.'

'I'm sure the children don't mind if you tell me now. You know how I hate to be kept in suspense,' Vivienne said. She narrowed her eyes, and her voice held a hint of menace.

Dennis's fingers found a packet of cigarettes on the desk. He clenched them in his fist and cleared his throat. 'Lady Marigold has just told me Renée was Mr. Olivier's daughter.'

Vivienne's face froze, but there was something in the flicker of her eyes made Marigold suspect she wasn't as shocked as her brother had been.

'Did you know she was his daughter?' asked Dennis

Vivienne put her nose in the air. 'What I knew or didn't know is no business of yours.'

Sebastian and Florence recoiled at the harshness in her tone. Vivienne plastered a smile on her face. 'Forgive me, my young friends. I didn't mean to snap. It's been a long and stressful journey.'

She resumed asking them about their favourite ballets, but she sensed both children had seen enough to tell them everything they needed to know. They had met their idol, and she had disappointed them.

Vivienne seemed to sense it too, and from the looks she was giving her, it was clear who she blamed.

Vivienne autographed two magazines with her face on the cover. Did she carry a supply with her for this purpose?

Marigold walked around the suite, deliberately passing close by Vivienne's writing desk table.

A feather topped pen and pile of letters were scattered across it. Some letters were open, some were sealed. One was written and waiting to be folded into an envelope. A man's fountain pen lay next to it, as though the author had laid down his pen upon signing his name.

She froze. Her eyes skimmed over the content of the letter. Her talent for languages didn't extend to the written word, but it wasn't the prose that caught her interest, it was the handwriting.

The author of the letter was Dennis, and there was no mistaking the handwriting. It was the same as the one on her note.

Sebastian clutched the magazine. His expression made her want to slap Vivienne, but she had to contain her emotions. This wasn't the time or the place to confront Dennis.

'Thank you for your time.'

Vivienne frowned at the politeness of her tone. 'I'm always happy to meet my admirers.'

'Goodbye Miss Cosette and thank you,' Florence said, but her eyes were on the floor.

'You're most welcome,' Vivienne said. She put the back of her right hand to her forehead and closed her eyes at the same time as she dismissed them with her left.

Marigold put a hand on Sebastian's back and steered him to the door.

'She was nice at first, but then she started acting strangely,' Florence said soon as the door closed behind them.

'Yes, she did, but sometimes you don't know a person until you take a closer look at them.'

She caught Nico's eye as he emerged from the suite next to Vivienne's. 'Would you mind escorting Sebastian and Florence to the dining car?'

'Of course, mademoiselle, I would be happy to.'

'Are you not coming, miss?'

She shook her head. 'I'll meet you there shortly, but first I need to have a chat with Inspector Loxley.'

CHAPTER THIRTY-TWO

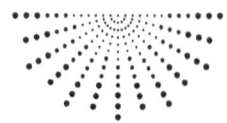

Elke looked up from her book as Marigold entered the compartment.

'Did she behave herself?'

Marigold paced around in a circle, avoiding Pepper, who seemed to think it was a game.

'Mostly, but it wasn't Vivienne who I was concerned about.'

Elke frowned. 'Did Aline write the note?'

'No, it was Dennis.'

Elke's jaw dropped. 'Dennis? I can't believe he had the nerve.'

'I think he's involved with Unity,' Marigold said as she sat in front of her dressing table.

Elke laughed. 'Surely not?'

Marigold opened her hand and showed Elke what she had picked up from the dressing table.

'Cufflinks?'

'Not just any cufflinks. Those belonged to Mr Olivier.'

'How can you be so sure?'

'Because he was wearing them the first night on the train. One of them fell off, and I picked it up. His initials were engraved in them.'

Elke squinted and held the cufflink up to the light. 'I see it, but perhaps Vivienne took them. That makes more sense.'

'It does, but combined with the note, Dennis and Unity killed Mr Olivier, and I'm going to take this to Loxley.'

Elke sat at the dressing table and drummed her fingertips on the polished mahogany. 'I don't think it's a good idea.'

'Why not?'

'Loxley isn't going to be able to arrest Dennis. There's still no evidence against him.'

'What do you call these?' Marigold pointed to the cufflinks.

Elks shrugged. 'A gift? A coincidence?'

'It's more than that. It all fits. Why are you so reluctant to see it?'

Elke waved her book in the air. 'Because there should be more proof.'

'Are you coming with me to talk to Loxley?'

Elke shook her head. 'No, and I do not think

you should go either. You need more evidence before you can make an accusation of murder.'

'There's no time. Renée is going to be carted off to a French jail first thing in the morning. If Dennis is the killer, he must be exposed now.'

'But what if he isn't the killer?'

'He is. I know he is.'

'Based on a cufflink?'

'Because of that and the note and my instincts.'

Elke shook her head. 'You want to help Renée, but making an allegation against Dennis you cannot prove will not help her or you.'

There was a knock at the door, and Marigold went to open it, grateful for the break in the conversation. She was struggling to hide her irritation.

She was relieved to see Bentley. 'Come in and help me make Elke see sense.'

Bentley frowned. 'About what?'

Elke scowled. 'She should not be accusing Dennis Cosette of Mr Olivier's murder without more evidence.'

Bentley's eyebrows shot up. 'Dennis Cosette?'

'I know it seems unlikely, but he was the one who wrote the note, Bentley, and he has a set of Mr Olivier's cufflinks. I suspect there is something between him and Unity. They conspired to kill her husband.'

Bentley was quiet for a long moment, then he tugged at his collar. 'I'm afraid I agree with Miss Müller. We need to investigate further before an accusation can be levelled.'

Marigold dropped onto the bed. 'But we don't have time.'

'Then we must hope Inspector Loxley finds the killer before we arrive in Paris.'

She rolled her eyes. 'Trust me, it's Dennis.'

'I'm sure your instincts are sound, my lady, but it's not wise to act on your suspicions just yet.'

'Fine, I can see I won't dissuade you, so I might as well get ready for dinner.'

Elke frowned. 'You are not dining in tonight?'

She shook her head. 'No, I promised Madam de La Baume I would dine with her.' Even though she enjoyed spending time with the French woman, the last thing she wanted to do was have dinner with her.

What she really wanted was to spend the night win her compartment figuring out a way to prove Dennis was the killer.

Reluctantly, she went to bathe and returned to the suite to find Elke had selected a bright green silk wrap dress with an outer layer of black chiffon. The bodice was covered in sequined flowers. Her accessories included jade teardrop earrings, an elaborate diamond and emerald necklace, and a matching bracelet. The finishing touch was a forest green feather boa and a pair of pointy toed silver t-strap heels.

'I never imagined a dress could be so beautiful,' She twirled in front of the mirror, admiring the way the glass beads on the skirt caught the light.

'I hope this means you will be willing to order a new wardrobe when we arrive in Paris?'

She ran a hand over the bodice of the dress. 'I still can't wait to get back into my ordinary clothes, but I confess, it would be lovely to see what's on offer in Paris.'

Elke clapped her hands together. 'I will make the arrangements as soon as we arrive.'

'I feel guilty talking about dresses when poor Renée remains locked up, unsure of her fate.'

Elke frowned. 'I hope you are not planning to do anything rash this evening?'

She scowled. 'Of course not. As you and Bentley have so clearly pointed out, I don't have enough evidence to make an accusation.'

'I'm glad to hear it.'

Her momentary good mood ebbed away as her anxious thoughts returned.

'I must go, or I'll be late.'

'Enjoy your evening.'

She left the compartment and quickened her step, reaching the dining car just as the clock chimed seven.

'Good evening, mademoiselle.'

'Good evening. I'm dining with Madam de La Baume.'

'She's waiting for you.'

She smiled, but inwardly rolled her eyes. She should have realised the French woman would arrive early.

'Ah, Marigold, you're late,' Madam de La Baume's lips pursed as she reached her table.

'My apologies. It took longer than I expected to get ready.'

'I can see why. Your dress is exquisite.'

'Thank you. As usual, I can take none of the credit for it. My assistant, Miss Müller, is a great lover of fashion.'

'She has an excellent eye. Be careful or you'll lose her. When word gets out of her talent, every lady in England will try to steal her away from you.'

She nodded as the waiter offered to fill her glass with champagne. 'Elke is a woman of many talents, and she's more friend than employee to me. I only want the best for her, but I doubt fashion is where her future lies. She's quite fond of solving mysteries.'

'Ah, is she a reader of Lady Clues?'

She nodded. 'She is, as am I.'

'It's a shame Lady Clues is not on the train. She would have found the killer by now.'

'I don't doubt it.' Her eyes were on the Cosette's as they entered the dining car. Dennis was rude to the waiter and demanded a table in the centre of the room, meaning Hermione Carey and Mr Klassen had to move. Marigold's blood boiled.

'Are you angry about something, my dear?'

She looked at her. 'No.'

'Then you may want to tell your face, because when Vivienne Cosette walked into the carriage, your face looked like thunder.'

She sighed. 'My apologies, but it's not Vivienne who has enraged me. It's her brother, Dennis.'

Madam de La Baume's eyebrows rose. 'Indeed. He's a most unpleasant young man. Dreadfully rude.'

'I agree, and between you and me, He may have played a role in Mr Olivier's murder.'

'You think Mr Cosette murdered Mr Olivier?'

She looked around the carriage, but no one appeared to be listening to them.

'I do, for a number of reasons, however Miss Müller and Mr Bentley are against me bringing my suspicions to Inspector Loxley until there is more evidence.'

Madam de La Baume narrowed her eyes. 'But you don't agree?'

She took a sip of champagne and nodded. 'I'm convinced it was him.'

'Then you should say something.'

She chewed her lip and watched Dennis smirk as he looked around the dining car. His eyes met hers, and she forced herself not to break eye contact. His icy gaze sent a shiver running down her spine

She forced herself to concentrate on Madam de La Baume as the waiter arrived to take their orders.

She ordered and agreed to a second glass of champagne.

'I never liked the man. He has the eyes of a killer.'

'If only I could prove he killed Mr Olivier.'

Suddenly, he got to his feet and walked towards them.

'Lady Marigold, why are you're looking at me in a hostile manner? Have I done something to offend you?'

'My apologies, Mr Cosette. I didn't mean to be rude.'

The dining car had fallen silent. Every eye was upon them.

'Do you have something to say to me?' Dennis said, slamming the heel of his hand on the edge of the table so the crockery rattled.

'How dare you? Leave at once.'

'I asked Lady Marigold a question.'

She drained her champagne and opened her mouth, fully intending to apologies once more, but her mouth didn't seem to have gotten the message and instead she heard herself say.

'Yes, I'm offended by your presence here tonight, Mr Cosette, because I don't enjoy dining in the presence of a killer.'

There was a collective gasp, then a ripple of voices. 'Did she just accuse him of being a killer?' she heard Hermione say.

Dennis leaned close to her face. 'What did you say to me?' A droplet of spit hit her glove.

Marigold's temper boiled over. 'I said I don't enjoy dining with a killer in the room.'

'How dare you accuse me.' He raised his hand, as if to strike her, but someone restrained him.

'What the devil is going on here?' Loxley said, his face tight with fury.

'This woman has just accused me of murder,' Dennis said, wrenching his hand away.

Loxley frowned. 'I'm sure you're mistaken.'

'I know what I heard,' Dennis said, glaring at Marigold.

'Then Lady Marigold clearly has made a mistake.'

Marigold shook her head. 'No, I haven't. He killed Mr Olivier.'

Loxley's left cheek began to twitch. 'That's enough, Lady Marigold. I think it's best you return to your suite.'

She got to her feet. 'It's not me who should leave; it's him. He killed Mr Olivier.' She pointed at Dennis.

His eyes bulged. 'What proof do you have? What evidence to make these claims?'

'You wrote the note threatening me. You knew Renée was Mr Olivier's daughter and you killed him when you learned he'd stolen Vivienne's money.'

To her surprise, Dennis burst out laughing. 'Do you hear the rantings of a madwoman? She's reading too much of her detective stories and now thinks herself one of them.'

'That's enough,' Loxley said, but Dennis was just getting started. He turned on her.

'I didn't write you a note. I don't know how to

write in English, and I have an alibi you will not be able to dispute.'

She narrowed her eyes. 'Who is it?'

Loxley cleared his throat. 'It's me. The night of the murder, I found Mr Cosette passed out in the lounge car and stayed with him all night.'

Her mouth went dry. After a long moment, she muttered, 'My apologies, Mr Cosette. I have made a terrible mistake.'

'Your apology is not accepted,' Dennis hissed as he returned to his table.

'I suggest you return to your suite,' Loxley said, not meeting her eyes.

'I think he's right, dear. You've made a bit of a mess of things,' Madam de La Baume said, shaking her head.

Marigold's throat and chest burned as acid rose from her stomach. She kept her eyes on the floor. 'My apologies again. I'll bid you goodnight.'

CHAPTER THIRTY-THREE

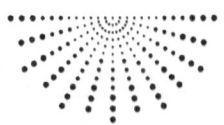

On the final day of the train's journey, Marigold woke to leaden skies and raindrops streaking down the window. Trees were swaying wildly in the fields, and the wind was howling around the train.

Her chest was heavy, and her head was pounding. She sat up and stared gloomily at Pepper as the memory of the previous night came rushing back.

Elke's bed was neatly made, but there was no sign of her. She'd said very little when Marigold had returned to the suite and confessed what she'd done. Was she so angry she couldn't bear the sight of her?

Much as she wanted to find Elke, she wasn't inclined to join her in the dining room. The memory of the judgemental stares from the previous night made her stomach churn.

'Disappointing Elke is bad enough, but there's still Renée to think about,' she told Pepper. 'I've made a real mess of things and there's no chance I can help her now. Why did I have to open my big mouth?'

Pepper climbed into her lap and nuzzled her cheek with his wet nose. She stroked his soft fur and sighed. 'Well, there's no point moping. I've brought it all on myself.'

She slid her arms into her robe, put on her slippers, and crossed the suite to the door. She opened it slowly and poked her head out, checking for any signs of life.

Fortunately, there were none. She hurried up the corridor to the bathroom and quickly washed.

She dressed in an all-black ensemble to match her mood. A sheer blouse worn over a floral-patterned camisole with high-waisted black silk faille pants with wide, flowing legs and large pockets. She finished the look with black lace-up t-strap heels and ruby earrings.

She looked at herself in the mirror and barely recognised the woman who had spent the night in an Istanbul police cell wearing knickerbockers and a khaki shirt.

In the elegant clothes Elke had bought for her, she looked like the poised and well-bred young lady her great-aunts had spent years trying to turn her into.

A sense of unease crept over her. Who was she now? Someone who accused an innocent man of murder? And yet, she'd been so sure she was right about Dennis.

Marigold sighed and closed the wardrobe door. Life certainly had been a lot simpler before she'd boarded the train. Still, she couldn't blame the clothes for her actions. The only way to put things right was to own what she'd done and apologise to Dennis again.

She was about to leave the suite in search of him when there was a knock at the door and Nico appeared with a trolley laden with silver dishes and a pot of coffee.

'Good morning, mademoiselle.'

'Good morning, Nico. I didn't order breakfast.'

Nico flushed. 'You usually dine early, my lady. I assumed you wanted to have breakfast here.'

She nodded. 'That was very considerate of you, and it's probably for the best if I stay away from the dining room. After what happened last night, I don't think I'll be too popular there.'

Nico looked solemn. 'As you wish.'

'I note you didn't argue with me, so I assume it's true. I'm a pariah.'

Nico shuffled his feet. 'It's true, some people are unhappy Mr Cosette was so publicly accused, but I, for one, don't blame you.'

A hint of hope rose within her. 'Really? That's very kind of you, Nico.'

'I too have had suspicions about Mr Cosette, and I should not say so, but he can be a difficult man to deal with. You on the other hand, have been nothing but kind and generous during the journey. I know you wouldn't have accused him unless you felt you were justified.'

She swallowed the lump in her throat. 'Thank you, Nico, but I fear you're being too kind to me. I made a terrible mistake. I should never have accused Mr Cosette the way I did. As a result, I've disappointed a lot of people I care about.'

'I'm sure it's nothing so bad you can't find a way through it.'

She gave him a smile. 'I refuse to feel sorry for myself. It's my own fault and if I could think of a way to make up for it, I would.'

'I hope you enjoy your breakfast.'

'Thank you again,' she said, staring at her reflection in the silver coffee pot.

Nico nodded and left the suite just as Bentley arrived.

Her fleeting moment of hope plummeted at the expression on the butler's face. She was reminded of the time he'd arrived at school to collect her after she and Clara had managed to get themselves expelled.

'Before you say anything, I'm so sorry I didn't listen to you. I didn't mean to accuse Mr Cosette the way I did. It just slipped out.'

Bentley frowned and hitched up his trousers at the knees as he took a seat in the armchair. 'It was a most unfortunate situation, but what's done is done. How do you plan to manage it?'

She sighed. 'I apologised to Mr Cosette last night, but I'll go to his compartment to do so again this morning. I'm sure he won't forgive me, but I must at least try.'

'Admitting you're wrong and sincerely apologising is the mark of a good person, my lady.'

Tears stung her eyes. She turned to glance out the window while she blinked them away. The weather seemed to be closing in again.

'Thank you, Bentley. I know I've made a real mess of things. It's kind of you not to remind me of it.'

'People make mistakes and errors of judgement all the time. It's how we deal with them distinguishes who we're.'

Marigold sniffed. 'I suppose you're right, but I

feel wretched about the whole thing. Much as I dislike Dennis Cosette, embarrassing him the way I did was quite dreadful.'

'Perhaps the person you don't wish to form a bad opinion of you, is not Mr Cosette?'

She frowned. 'Yes. I must also apologise to Madam de La Baume. She was expecting lively company for dinner and instead ended up dining alone.'

'I was speaking of Inspector Loxley.'

She frowned. 'Loxley? All I did last night was live up to his terrible first impression of me.'

'He holds you in higher esteem than you may be aware.'

Marigold stared at him, momentarily speechless. 'Well, on that, we must differ in our opinion,' she finally scoffed.

Bentley nodded and clasped his hands in his lap.

The door to the suite opened and Elke walked in. Marigold's heart sank at the disgruntled expression on her face.

'Although I don't agree with what you did last night, I cannot help but share your sentiment about Dennis Cosette. He's a very unpleasant young man.'

Marigold stared at her, relief making her voice shake. 'Really? I thought you admired him?'

Elke sniffed. 'Not anymore.'

'What's happened?'

Elke sat in the armchair near the window. 'He was at breakfast and not bothering to lower his voice as he discussed last night's events. His words were unkind at best, slanderous at worst.'

'About me?'

'I'm afraid so, but rest assured, I have managed the situation.'

Marigold raised her eyebrows. 'What did you do?'

'I may or may not have spilled tea in his lap.'

Despite herself, Marigold laughed. 'Oh dear, I can just imagine his face.'

Elke's smile had an edge of malice. 'I cannot lie, it was very satisfying.'

Bentley gave them both a disapproving look. 'Putting aside the unfortunate incident with Mr Cosette last night, only one day remains to prove you and Miss Seydoux are innocent.'

Marigold sighed. 'I don't see what I can do now, Bentley. No one will want to talk to me after what I did. I'm afraid I've failed Renée.'

'You may not be able to speak to anyone, but Miss Müller and I can.'

Marigold drummed her fingers on the dressing table. 'Perhaps, but I still think we're missing something.'

'We can speak with the conductors again. I have a feeling they still have more to tell us,' Elke said.

Marigold nodded. 'Very well, you do that while I go to check on my young friends.

She spent the day in the second-class carriage playing chess with Sebastian while Florence asked questions about Lady Clues. She was reading the book Marigold had given her.

The three of them had an early dinner, then made their way back to her suite so Florence and Sebastian could visit with Pepper.

To Marigold's relief, she didn't run into anyone from the first-class carriage, but as she approached her suite, she heard someone call her name.

She turned and her heart leapt as Renée hurried towards her.

'Lady Marigold, I have been released. The Inspector says I'm no longer a suspect,' Renée said, her eyes shining.

Marigold clapped her hands. 'Really? I'm so relieved.'

'So am I, my lady. I was beginning to fear I would be locked away forever.'

'Do you know why he released you?'

Renée shook her head. 'He just said he was

confident from the evidence he had collected it wasn't me.'

'That's wonderful news and I'm pleased for you.'

'Thank you, my lady. I'm not sure what I'll do now, but at least I'll be free.'

There was a scratching noise on the inside of Marigold's suite, followed by two high-pitched barks.

'Oh dear, poor Pepper. Do you have a moment to talk?' she asked Renée as she unlocked the door.

Sebastian and Florence rushed inside and began playing with a very excited Pepper. Elke, who had her nose in her Lady Clues book, looked up in alarm, then a smile broke across her face as Renée followed Marigold into the suite.

'Miss Seydoux, I'm so relieved to see you have been released.'

'So am I Miss Müller. I wanted to come and thank you and Lady Marigold for everything you've done for me.'

Marigold shook her head. 'I'm afraid we can't take the credit, especially me.'

'That is an understatement,' Elke said, and Marigold rolled her eyes.

Confusion clouded Renée's face. Marigold gestured for her to sit. 'I'm afraid I made an accusation of murder last night and it turned out to be incorrect. Miss Müller had counselled me against it. Of course, I feel terrible about it now.'

'I'm sure you meant well, my lady.'

'You're very kind, Renée, but can I ask you a question?'

'Of course. Anything you need to know, please ask.'

Marigold leaned forward. 'I was wondering if you heard your mistress and Mr Olivier arguing the night of the murder?'

Renée nodded. 'Yes, I told the Inspector, they had a dreadful row after dinner. She stayed in her compartment all night sulking about it.'

The back of Marigold's neck began to prickle. 'But surely Miss Cosette wasn't in her compartment all evening. She went out for some fresh air?'

Renée shook her head. 'No, my lady, I was stuck in there with her, so I know she didn't leave for a moment. She took some medication and fell asleep.'

Marigold bit the inside of her cheek. 'But Vivienne told Inspector Loxley she went for a walk and got into an argument with Mrs Olivier.'

Renée's eyes filled with tears. 'That is what she told me to say. She said is friends with a lady who employs my sister and said she would make sure we would both lose our positions. Our mother needs money for medicine, I had no choice but to lie for her.'

Marigold patted her arm. 'It will be alright, but if Vivienne and Unity lied about their alibis, then we'd better go and find Inspector Loxley.

CHAPTER THIRTY-FOUR

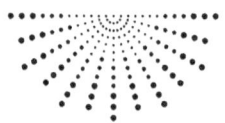

'The one time I want to find him, he's nowhere to be found,' Marigold fumed as she and Elke left Mr Olivier's empty office.

'Here comes Mr Bentley, perhaps he's seen the Inspector.' Elke waved her arms in a windmill fashion to get the butler's attention.

He approached them with a look of trepidation. 'Is everything alright, my lady?'

She nodded. 'Yes, but have you seen Inspector Loxley? We have something to tell him.'

Bentley frowned. 'The Inspector is in the lounge car. He has asked all guests to gather there. I was just coming to find you.'

'Do you think it's about the murder?'

'I can only assume,' Bentley said as they

crossed the vestibule and walked into the lounge car.

Loxley glanced up as they entered. 'Ah, Lady Marigold, Miss Müller. Nice of you to join us.'

Marigold scowled but said nothing as she scanned the lounge car. Unity was sitting with Madam de La Baume, Sir Fredrick, and Lady Haig. Mr Jorrisen was pacing by the window.

Clara, Osbert, and Perry were sitting at the bar. Chef Dubois was perched on the edge of a chair wearing a sauce-stained apron.

Vivienne, Aline, and Dennis Cosette were sitting on the velvet covered settee. All three wore sullen expressions that deepened into scowls when she walked by them. Marigold couldn't blame them.

She walked over to Loxley and said in a low voice. 'Have you found the killer?'

'I'll be providing more information once I begin the meeting.' He gestured for her to take a seat.

She held her ground. 'I have learned something important about Vivienne and Mrs Olivier. Are either of them suspects?'

He leaned towards her and lowered his voice 'I think we've all had quite enough of your meddling in this case.'

She blew a stray curl out of her eyes. 'I admit I

made a mistake last night. I shouldn't have accused Mr Cosette the way I did.'

Loxley's eyes narrowed. 'As I have repeatedly told you, this is a police investigation, and you need to stay out of it.'

'So, you're not interested in hearing about two suspects who lied about their alibis?'

Loxley looked at the ceiling and exhaled slowly. 'If I let you tell me, will you sit down?'

'Of course, but I can't tell you here. Can we go to Mr Olivier's office?'

He rubbed his forehead, then surveyed at the assembled group.

'Come along, Loxley, we don't have all day,' Sir Fredrick called.

'Ladies and gentlemen, please excuse me for a moment. I need to speak with Lady Marigold.'

Ignoring the rumble of unhappy words and muttered insults, he took her elbow and steered her out of the room and into Mr Olivier's office.

'Let's get this over with. Much as it pains me to ask, what have you learned?'

Marigold put her hands on her hips. 'Why? Don't you believe a woman who likes reading detective stories might be good at solving them?'

He drummed his fingernails on Mr Olivier's desk. 'Lady Marigold, do you have something to share or not?'

She took a deep breath and exhaled in a huff. 'Yes. I believe Unity Olivier and Vivienne Cosette joined forces to kill Mr Olivier.'

Loxley sighed. 'Please tell me this theory is based on actual evidence.'

She glared at him. 'Of course, it is. The two of them claimed they were each other's alibis, and who would doubt them—they hate each other so had no reason to lie, but I believe it was a rouse.'

He scowled. 'I'm still not hearing what this claim is based upon.'

'It's based on what Miss Seydoux just told me —on the night of the murder, Vivienne took some medication and passed out. She didn't leave her suite all night, so she couldn't have met with Unity.'

Loxley got to his feet and paced in front of the window. 'An interesting development, however, if she didn't leave the compartment, how can she be the killer?'

Marigold tapped her bottom lip with her index finger. 'Just because she wasn't there doesn't mean she wasn't an accomplice. Perhaps Unity paid Vivienne for her alibi on the promise of sharing a life insurance payout.'

'But why would Unity wait until Mr Olivier was on the train to kill him? She could have done it anywhere.'

She shrugged. 'She wanted to frame someone —in this case, me or Renee—for the crime.'

Loxley looked doubtful. 'That makes no sense. She'd never met either of you.'

A flicker of doubt tickled the edges of Marigold's mind. It made sense that Unity might have a grudge against her husband's love child, but why would she have tried to frame Marigold? And if she hadn't killed her husband, who had?'

'It feels like there's something more going on. Someone else on the train must have been wronged by Mr Olivier and concealed it,' Marigold said. A horrible thought popped into her head. It wasn't possible, and yet, suddenly, it seemed like the only logical explanation.

A rush of memories flashed through her mind.

Bentley telling her about her cousin Richard breaking off his engagement.

About the girl's father being conned out of his fortune.

A newspaper clipping.

A photograph with the name Dickie on the back.

Dickie? Short for…Richard?

And an '*unfortunately redheaded fiancé.*'

It couldn't be—and yet suddenly she was sure it was.

She slapped her forehead. 'Of course. How didn't I see it before?'

Loxley put his hands on his hips. 'See what?'

'Vivienne and Unity didn't kill Mr Olivier. They may have wanted to. They might have planned to. But in the end, someone else got to him first.'

'Much as it pains me to ask, who is it?'

Marigold turned and saw a figure in the doorway. Her blood ran cold as she jumped to her feet, lifted her arm, and pointed to the door.

'See for yourself.'

CHAPTER THIRTY-FIVE

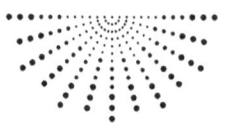

'Hermione Carey pointed a familiar pearl-handle gun at Marigold's heart.

'Put the gun down,' Loxley said, his voice sharp and ringing with authority.

Hermione ignored him and raised her left arm so she could hold the gun with both hands.

A buzzing sensation spread through Marigold's body. Adrenaline, she assumed. It made her fingers and toes prickle, and her arms and legs heavy as lead. Strangely, she experienced no fear. Just annoyance she hadn't realised Hermione was the killer and she was now in this position.

She glared at Loxley, who had moved beside her. 'Really? You left my gun just lying around for anyone to find?'

A muscle in his left cheek twitched, but he kept his eyes on Hermione. 'Miss Carey, you need to put the gun down, slowly.'

'Why would I do that?' Her voice was high and brittle.

'There's no need to make this any worse for yourself.'

Hermione snorted. 'In case you haven't noticed, I'm the one holding the gun.'

'That's my gun and shooting me with it really would serve no purpose,' Marigold said, trying to keep her tone light.

Hermione redoubled her grip and glared at her. 'Of course, it's yours. Who else would own something so ridiculous? And you're wrong, it will serve its purpose. It will get rid of you once and for all.'

Marigold raised her hands in surrender. 'To what end? You'll be arrested and spend the rest of your life in jail.'

Hermione smiled, but her eyes glittered with hatred. 'Not if I shoot the handsome Inspector first. I'll tell everyone you shot him after a lover's tiff and I wrestled the gun from you, sadly killing you.'

Loxley snorted. 'No one in their right mind will believe the first part of the story.'

'I'll try not to take it personally,' Marigold said

under her breath. 'And for your information, I'm an excellent shot.'

She continued to shuffle her feet and wriggled her fingers, trying to restore the feeling in them. Was this what it was like to go into shock? She'd seen it many times during the war, but never experienced it herself.

'Always with the fast talk and witty remarks. You do think rather a lot of yourself, Lady Marigold. The thing is, you're not half as smart as you believe you are,' Hermione said, her arms shaking with the effort of keeping them raised.

Loxley moved in front of Marigold and held up a hand. 'Miss Carey, I couldn't have said it better myself, but this situation can be resolved peacefully if you just put down the gun.'

Marigold stepped out from behind him. 'I admit, I'm annoyed at myself. It never occurred to me you might have killed Mr Olivier, but I see now I should have suspected you all along.'

'You're not helping this situation,' Loxley said, giving her a warning look.

Hermione rolled her eyes. 'She loves the sound of her own voice, does our Lady Marigold.'

'Why would Miss Carey have killed Mr Olivier?' Loxley asked Marigold. She suspected he was buying time while he formulated a plan.

'Hermione wanted Mr Olivier dead for the same reason she wanted to frame me for his murder. She blamed both of us for the loss of her fiancé.'

'How clever of you to have worked it out.' Hermione said with a sneer.

Loxley frowned. 'I'm afraid I don't understand. What fiancé?'

'My cousin Richard. He was engaged to Hermione, but he broke it off a few weeks ago. I assume it was around the same time my Uncle Thomas died?'

Hermione's face twisted into ugly lines. 'Yes. Your uncle left Richard his title, but you managed to convince him to leave you the house. That's why Richard had to end the engagement—because you stole the house from him.'

'I had nothing to do with Uncle Thomas' decision to leave me Mayfair Manor.'

Hermione's face turned red. 'That's Richard's house. We were to be married there. We were going to raise a family.'

'I didn't ask for the house. Trust me, I don't want it, but I'll honour Uncle Thomas' wishes and I suspect Richard will, too.'

'You robbed him of his inheritance,' Hermione said as sweat beaded on her forehead.

Marigold shook her head. 'I promise you; I had nothing to do with it.'

'Perhaps your fiancé broke things off for other reasons?' Loxley suggested.

Hermione thrust the gun at Marigold. 'No. Everything was fine until her uncle died. As soon as Richard realised he wasn't inheriting the house, he broke things off with me. It's all her fault.'

Loxley nodded. 'That must have been very hard for you and trust me, I understand how frustrating it can be to deal with Lady Marigold, but why did you kill Mr Olivier?'

Marigold snapped her fingers. 'Because he killed her father, didn't he? Bentley told me about the business deal that went wrong. A lot of people lost their livelihoods, and your father was ruined because he put his trust in a conman—Mr Olivier.'

'He took everything from me,' Hermione said, her voice a low growl.

'You planned to kill him, but make it look like I was responsible. That's why you transferred ten thousand pounds into his bank account under my name, but where did you get it?'

Hermione's mouth twisted. 'I had to sell my grandmother's jewels. That's another thing you've take from me, but it was worth it—as they say, two birds and one stone.'

'You knew Bentley was coming to tell me about Uncle Thomas's death and it wasn't Mr Olivier who booked my passage on the train, it was you. You wanted to make sure we would both be on the train.'

'Olivier had to pay for what he'd done to me and everyone else he'd taken money from, and who better to frame for his murder than you? With you out of the way, Richard can take the house, and we will be reunited.'

Marigold chewed her lip as she processed this information. It was all coming together. She could almost see the murder play out in her mind like a film.

'You said you were good at copying hand-writing as a child, and you still are. You wrote the note in Dennis Cosette's handwriting when you thought I was getting too close to the truth.'

She slapped her forehead with the palm of her hand.

'And you sent Mr Olivier a note and pre-tended to be Vivienne, then you waited in the kitchen and stabbed him.'

'He never saw it coming. I couldn't believe it was so easy,' Hermione said with a satisfied smile.

Loxley edged closer to her. 'It's not too late to talk about this.'

She gave him an incredulous glance. 'In case you haven't noticed, I'm the one holding the gun. I have the power.'

'We can resolve this in a peaceful manner.' He took another step.

'Your time is up,' Hermione said, swivelling her arms so the gun was pointed at him.

Marigold readied herself to act. She had no idea of Loxley had a plan, but if she could get Hermione's attention long enough, he might be able to grab the gun.

There was a clap of thunder. The train shook and lightning flashed outside the window.

'Put the gun down and let's talk about this,' Loxley said, his voice calm and reassuring.

Sweat ran down Hermione's face. 'You're wasting time. Get on your knees.' Her voice was croaky as she waved the gun at him.

Marigold cleared her throat. 'I hate to be the bearer of bad news, but did you know Richard is already married?'

Hermione's head whipped around to meet her eyes. 'What?' she hissed.

Loxley tackled Hermione to the ground and the gun flew out of her hand. She screamed and cursed as Loxley pinned her arms behind her back.

Marigold scooped up the gun, pointed it at Hermione's furious face and blew a stray curl out of her eyes.

'Inspector Loxley, I believe you have your killer.'

CHAPTER THIRTY-SIX

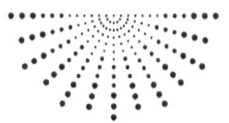

When Marigold arrived in the dining car the next morning, she found Unity sitting at a table, staring out the window. Marigold paused and cleared her throat. 'Good morning. Only a few hours until we're in Paris.'

Unity jumped in her seat and flushed. 'Lady Marigold, how kind of you to stop by. I'm surprised you're still speaking to me after what I have done.'

Once Hermione had been locked in the boiler room, Unity had broken down and confessed she planned to kill her husband. Vivienne, on the other hand had stubbornly refused to admit any involvement. Her collaboration of Unity's alibi was due to the aftereffects of her medication, she'd claimed. Without evidence to pursue the matter, Loxley had let both women go with a warning.

'May I sit down?' Marigold said, gesturing to the empty seat across the table.

When Unity nodded, she slipped into the plush covered bench seat.

Unity took a sip from her teacup. It rattled against her teeth, and she raised her left hand to steady it. Once the teacup was safely back on its saucer, she looked at Marigold with tears in her eyes. 'I'm mortified by what took place last night.'

Marigold reached for her hand. 'You've really no need to be. You did nothing wrong.'

'That's a matter of opinion,' We both know only a fortunate set of circumstances prevented me from being in the same position as Miss Carey this morning.'

'I think, when it came down to it, you would have made a different choice.'

Unity sighed. 'I appreciate your faith in me, but I'm so disappointed in myself I can hardly look in the mirror. I don't know what I was thinking.'

Marigold frowned at her. 'Your husband's death wasn't your fault. No matter what took place that night, whatever your intentions, you're innocent and free to live your life on your own terms now.'

'I can't imagine what that looks like. I was sixteen when I married Rueben. I've never been on my own,' she said, dabbing her eyes with a napkin.

Marigold squeezed her hand. 'You will find your way. Adventure awaits, trust me. There is nothing a modern young woman can't do now.'

Unity blew her nose. 'I'm certainly not young, but I take comfort in your words, Lady Marigold. I won't be alone though. I've engaged Renée to be my lady's maid.'

'That's wonderful news. I was considering offering her a position at Mayfair, but she'll be much better off working for you.'

Unity nodded, then her cheeks flushed. 'Oh dear, here comes Chef Dubois. Suddenly I don't know what to say to him.'

'He's been a good friend to you and will continue to be so.' She smiled as Chef Dubois approached their table.

'Madam Olivier, Lady Marigold, I was hoping to see you this morning.'

Marigold got to her feet. 'I'm afraid I need to pack, but I wanted to wish you all the best with Josephine and your restaurant, Chef Dubois.'

He beamed and winked at her. 'Thank you,

mademoiselle. She's preserved and ready to shine in the competition.'

A waiter arrived at the table and bowed. 'Lady Marigold, I have a message for you from Inspector Loxley. He wishes to see you in his office.'

Unity bit her lip. 'What on earth could he have left to talk to you about? Surely all the bad business is done with.'

Marigold shrugged and squeezed Unity's hand. 'I suppose I had better find out. Goodbye and I wish you both the very best for the future.'

She left the dining car and took the now well-worn path to Mr Olivier's office, where the door was open.

Loxley was standing by the window wearing a navy pinstriped suit. He glanced at his watch and turned at her knock.

'Inspector Loxley, you look like a busy man. Don't let me keep you.'

He rolled his eyes and gestured for her to take a seat. 'There are a few loose ends I need to tie up before you depart the train.'

Marigold smiled. 'I'll miss our little chats.'

'I can't say the same, but I'm sure it's not a surprise to you.'

Marigold took a seat and placed her handbag

on her lap. Loxley sat behind the desk and picked up a pen.

'What will happen to Hermione?' she asked, looking at the hole in the wall. It was the only sign of the previous night's struggle.

'She'll be taken from the train upon our arrival in Paris and charged with Mr Olivier's murder. What happens after that depends on the French justice system.'

'How lucky for you I was able to solve the mystery.' Marigold reached into the jar of boiled sweets on Mr Olivier's desk and popped one into her mouth.

Loxley raised his eyebrows. 'Luck is a more accurate description. However, you do seem to have a talent for seeking out trouble—be it someone else's or your own.'

She smiled. 'I'll take that as a compliment.'

He put down the pen and clasped his hands as he sat back in his chair. 'As you wish, but there remains a question about your presence in the police station in Istanbul. What were you arrested for?'

She chewed the sweet in her mouth and swallowed. 'I'm really not sure why you're so interested.'

'Scotland Yard is always interested in British citizens who are arrested in foreign countries.'

She smiled. 'Then I'm sure you can find out why I was arrested, so there is no need to ask me.'

Loxley sighed and examined the ceiling. She bit the inside of her cheek to stop from laughing.

'You could save me the paperwork and just tell me.'

Marigold pretended to think it over as she chose another sweet from the jar.

She tipped her head to the side and peered up at him. 'Will I be arrested if I don't? Is there some law about withholding information from the police when one is not on British soil?'

He set his jaw. 'There might be. I don't recommend you find out.'

She stood and brushed a non-existent crease from her dress. 'Then I think I'll take my chances.'

'I'm beginning to think you're incapable of providing a straight answer.'

She raised her eyebrows. 'Only beginning? Oh dear, you really don't know me at all, do you, Inspector?'

She reached into her handbag, withdrew an envelope, and held it out to him.

He frowned. 'What's this? A confession?'

'Goodness, do you think so little of me? No. It's a cheque for Mr Jorrisen. Could you give it to him for me, please? It's to cover the cost of the damage Pepper did to his shoes.'

'I'll see he gets it, but you should know he has confessed the plan you heard him arguing about with Mr Olivier was about finance for a film starring Miss Bligh. Sadly, it now won't be going ahead.'

'What a shame,' Marigold said, not bothering to hide her disdain. She took a step towards the door, then turned back to face him. Reaching into her handbag, she held out a book. 'Oh, and this is for you. It's a collection of Lady Clues' cases. I think you'll enjoy her work.'

He took the book with a shake of his head, but she was sure she saw the corners of his mouth twitch.

As she walked towards the door, he called after her. 'Stay out of trouble, Lady Marigold. In the nicest possible way, I hope we don't meet again.'

She thought of the skeleton waiting for her in the wardrobe at Mayfair Manor and hastened her exit in case her face raised his suspicions.

As she walked back to her suite, she passed the Cosette siblings. Dennis and Vivienne ignored her and continued walking, but Aline stopped to say goodbye.

'I'm glad to have met you, Lady Marigold.

Such an interesting time we have had on this train.'

'Indeed, but what will you do now, Aline? Will you continue to travel with your brother and sister?'

Aline shook her head and lowered her voice. 'No. I have decided to return to England and see if I can resume my university studies.'

Marigold squeezed her hand. 'I'm very pleased to hear it. I hope we'll meet again.'

'Come along Aline,' Vivienne called at the end of the corridor.

'Goodbye,' Aline said, and she hurried to join her sister.

Marigold heard someone call her name in the opposite direction. Perry Bligh strode towards her.

'How lucky to find you here.' He took her hand and dropped a kiss on her glove. She swatted him with her free hand.

'Really, Perry, you're incorrigible.'

He threw back his head and laughed. 'Never let it be said I backed down from a challenge, and you, my dear Lady Marigold, are most certainly that.'

She rolled her eyes. 'I'm really not Perry, and I'm far too old for you.'

He gave her a wink. 'As I said, I like a challenge.'

'Your sister might have something to say about it.' She pointed to Clara, who was walking towards them, her arm looped through Osbert's.

A mischievous glint appeared in Perry's eyes once his sister was in earshot. 'Isn't it marvellous this is only goodbye for now?'

Clara's eyes narrowed. 'What do you mean?'

'You two are practically neighbours, so you can count on plenty of visits from me, dear sister.'

'I'm sure Lady Marigold will be far too busy with her new home to do much socialising,' Clara snapped

Marigold nodded. 'For once, I must agree with you.'

Perry ran a hand through his hair. 'Well, I for one won't take no for an answer. I'm sure Lady Marigold can be persuaded to venture out when I arrive at her door in my new racer.'

Clara flinched. 'Don't be ridiculous, Perry. You're not getting another car.'

Perry's handsome face flushed, and not wanting to become a witness to a family argument, Marigold excused herself to say goodbye to the Haigs.

After accepting an envelope from Sir Fredrick and an offer to spend Christmas in

Scotland from Lady Haig, she made her way to the second-class compartment where Florence and Sebastian were packing their trunks.

'What will you do once we arrive in Paris?'

Florence's heart-shaped face grew serious. 'Don't worry about us miss. I have it all planned. We will travel by train to Calais and then to England by ferry.'

Marigold frowned. 'But what will you do when you reach London? Do you have an address for your English relations?'

Florence shook her head. 'We don't miss, but we'll find them.' Her voice was strong, but Marigold noted the break in her voice.

'But what if we don't find them?' Sebastian said quietly.

Florence's face fell, and Marigold decided it was time to take charge of the situation.

'I could help you find them. You could stay with me and Pepper until you do. I've just become the owner of a very large house in the country, so there's plenty of room and I know Pepper would be delighted.'

Sebastian's face lit up, but Florence frowned. 'We couldn't, miss.'

Marigold squeezed her hand. 'You could and I would really like you to. Plus, Bentley practically knows everyone in England. I'm sure he'll be able to find your relations in no time at all.'

Some of the tension left Florence's face. 'Well, if it wouldn't be too much trouble. That would be lovely.'

Sebastian let out a whoop and threw a handful of clothes into the air.

Marigold put an arm around Florence's shoulders and squeezed. 'Everything will be alright, but first, the two of you need to finish packing.'

'We will miss,' Sebastian said, and he hurriedly began tossing clothes into his trunk.

She caught Florence's eye and they laughed.

With relief, she entered her suite a few minutes later to find Elke and Bentley crawling around the floor.

'Whatever are you doing?' she asked, ruffling Pepper's top knot as she sat next to him on the bed.

'Miss Müller has lost her lucky coin,' Bentley said breathlessly.

'Here it is,' Elke said, sitting back on her haunches and holding up a silver dollar.

'Goodness, Bentley, you'll be glad to be back at Mayfair and away from such indignities,' Marigold said as he got awkwardly to his feet.

He brushed off his elbows and knees. 'I certainly will be, my lady. Travel doesn't suit me in the slightest. There truly is no place like home.'

Marigold nodded, but she wondered if it was true for her.

'So much for a quiet journey. We should make the most of what's left of it. Things are only going to get more complicated once we arrive in England,' Elke said as she pocketed the coin.

Marigold opened the envelope from Sir Fredrick. 'At least there's one less mystery to solve.' She handed the contents to Bentley. 'It turns out the ten thousand pounds you transferred was nothing to do with Mr Olivier. It was a loan for Sir Fredrick. He wanted to be sure you knew it had been repaid.'

Bentley cleared his throat. 'Your uncle was a kind and generous man. I'm sure he wouldn't have expected to be repaid, but Sir Fredrick is a man of honour.'

'He certainly is and I'm looking forward to visiting them in Scotland for Christmas," Marigold said. She gazed out the window, contemplating the future with a sense of excitement mixed with trepidation.

The events on the train had served as a distraction, but now she was days away from not only becoming mistress of Mayfair Manor but having to deal with the mystery of the skeleton in her uncle's wardrobe.

Where would she even start?

Perhaps Lady Clues would give her some inspiration.

She curled up by the window with Pepper on her lap and began to read *The Mystery of the Missing Letters*.

If you'd like to read *The Mystery of the Missing Letters*, click here.
Lady Marigold and friends will return in A High Society Murder available 30 April 2023.
To be notified when the next book in the Lady Marigold series is available, please join my mailing list by clicking here or visiting avanessauthor.com

ABOUT THE AUTHOR

Ava Ness writes 1920s cozy mysteries featuring smart, sassy sleuths, adorable dogs, found family, high society, fashion & will 'they or won't they', opposites attract romance.

Get news, updates and special offers when you sign up to her reader group at avaness.news

 facebook.com/avanessauthor